I0760757

Seven Deadly Sins

Book One

Monica Shantel

seven *deadly* sins

queens of orsadia
book one

monica shantel

Seven Deadly Sins

ISBN 978-1-960696-08-3 (Paperback) 978-1-960696-09-0 (Hardcover)

Book Cover by Monica Shantel

Illustrations by Monica Shantel

First Edition

For all those who had all the high expectations on their shoulders, when they had other dreams in mind.

3/9/24
Snow White

3/23/24
Luka

Monica
Symonds
10/6/20
Jerry

ORSADIA
Everinthian Castle
LUKA'S CAVE
KEENAIN RIVER
FOUNTAIN
Ash Forest
UNDERGROUND CAVE
GRAVEYARD
VILLAGE
Drecose Castle
Hypnotic Arythe

spotify

seven deadly sins playlist

monica shantel
don't save me.

ONE

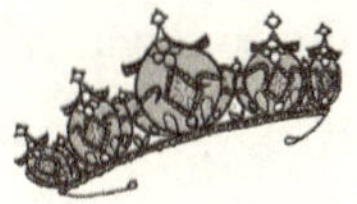

"Don't go out into the darkness or death will waste no opportunity to rip you from the world of the living."

Not those exact words, but he may as well have said it. He believed it like a proverb. However, I believed more in doing as I pleased than being made to fear the outside. Terror would only work in *her* favor, which I would never intentionally give.

A scream simmered deep within my throat until I let it go free while shoving open the doors of Drecose Castle. All I needed was a chance to recollect my sanity. From this distance, Ash Forest had never looked more inviting as summer slipped away while autumn slithered beneath the blue skies.

"Lana, where are you going?" my father yelled behind me.

Ignoring him, I crossed the long and unstable bridge, venturing into the forest. It called my name. Whispered sweet nothings. All I saw was red.

Crimson trees. Blood in my cheeks.

Everywhere. Dancing. On the prowl for another life to claim like a monster in hiding, just waiting for the perfect moment to strike.

As I disappeared amongst the vibrant leaves, the sun began to set.

I never understood the fear of the night. There was nothing to be afraid of out here. Everything that could hurt you in front of the moon could replicate the same action when the sun burned.

And when my blood boiled, it meant I had to flee the castle for the time being and find serenity in nature. It didn't rain flower petals.

Instead, everything was dull and withering away. I found comfort in the dying plants. Beauty gripped every stage of life, and that included growing old until nothing was left. I appreciated what others refused to touch.

Birds could not sing in Ash Forest and survive. The sound of a crow's caw indicated death—a death so brutal that not even the corpse could forget. There were no happy endings where I came from, and I vowed to change every law that controlled the land.

I made a promise to erase every sin plagued upon this kingdom by the one they called the *Evil Queen.*

As I walked through the forest, sorrow and pain kept a tight hold on every inch. Every bush. Every trunk. Every speck of dirt.

I came here to search for the answer to every question within my head.

To my right stood a rose bush. The roses bloomed in odd colors that most people could not find elsewhere. The minority of them were colored red but a few royal blue roses popped out among the mix.

They defied the natural order of death by exposing their bold petals to the thick, crisp air around us. Nothing could bring these flowers to rot away with the rest of the world. I'd been much like a rose—if my father could just see it that was.

They ignited a memory so buried beneath the surface that even the simple shade of blood could not remind me of everything I gave up. However, the glow of my skin painted a perfect picture. I could light up any darkness, and that was what I intended to do when I became the next queen.

My stroll through the trees did not stop at a bush. I pushed on until I was lost deep inside the dry woods. Over the bridge of Keenain River. I'd been so accustomed to oranges and browns after nearly an entire nightfall that when a black cave came into my view, I took notice of it right away. My curiosity got the better of me, and its depths I began to explore.

By now, it had been well past the middle of the night, but that hadn't frightened me a bit. After all, I glowed in the dark. I'd been my own light—and literally.

Every little sound I created echoed throughout. A scuffle of my boot. A kick of a pebble. An exhale.

An arrow flew past my ear and bounced off the rock to my right. I spun around and drew my sword, holding it in front to block my threat from reaching my most vital organs. "Who are you?"

There was no sign of a human in the branches above me, but I knew better. That arrow couldn't have shot itself.

"Are you a coward?" I took a few steps forward as my eyes narrowed, scanning the area. The culprit never revealed themself. Typical. Timorous.

I snickered and slid my sword back into my belt. I could wear a crown with class but that never took away from my skills with a weapon, and they acknowledged that. I wasn't sure if I should have been impressed with myself or pity them.

I trained endlessly to take down *one* person, and she would never see the light of day the next time I saw her face-to-face. She'd forever be a prisoner to what waited ahead. No more magic for her to play with.

"Stay hidden in the bushes and see if I care. Cowards get nowhere in life," I mumbled the last sentence.

I took a few steps backward until rock laid beneath my boots. Turning on my heels, I faced the darkness threatening to swallow me whole.

Something pushed behind a stone caught my attention. Reaching forward to pick it up, the lump in my throat grew with ease.

The rough, worn fur between my fingers was all too familiar, showing me the memories this stuffed bear held. I'd lost him when I was just a child and somehow, he ended up in a cave.

I was no longer that little girl. I had a duty to fill and that could not be squandered by silly toys. His black eyes begged for mercy which I could not give. Instead, I tossed him to the side and looked toward the end of the cave. There was nothing here for me to explore. The past was not something I ever wished to revisit.

Leaving the echoes of my childhood behind, I walked until trees were the only part of this forest that circled me. Ash Forest was my hiding place—my outlet. It would never judge me for what decisions I made.

Rotting leaves couldn't snicker at my anger. The death that spread through like butter on toast knew better than to punish me for my choices.

Leaves crunched under my feet as I made my way back towards the castle. I had to face my father someday. It wouldn't be long before I was Queen. He had no control over me.

I pulled my sword from my side and swung down on a thin branch. Yet another victim to my rage.

My father was not royalty. He lived in that castle because of me. If I'd never become a princess, he wouldn't eat as well as he did. He had to thank me for it when I had become the chosen heir.

The air attempted to suffocate me, but I sliced through with the long blade, my fingers tightly wrapped around the hilt. I shoved it into my sheath when I approached the large castle just an hour after sunrise.

It was dark gray in color, something not usually fit for a princess, but I was not one to complain. I had hair blacker than the walls that would encase me inside on rainy days. The castle sat on its own little piece of land, surrounded by the ocean. A wooden bridge connected me to the place I called home.

Orsadia.

I walked across and stopped in my tracks when the large, heavy doors opened to reveal Fallon. "Where's Father?" I asked him.

His eyes darted behind him before landing on me. "I told him to cool off before talking to you." As I started forward, he added, "you guys get so heated and I hate watching it."

"It'll end when he learns that I'm an adult and I make my own choices. He can't stop me. It is technically I who owns this castle. I'm royalty. *I'm* the princess." I passed him as I entered. The doors closed behind us.

"Snow, what about—"

I cut him off when I faced him and closed the space between us. "Don't you dare tell me to keep my mouth shut because I'm the daughter. There is no king on this land. There is only one queen and the throne chose me. It should be Father who bows down to *me*." I gripped the edge of my cloak and pulled it around me as I began walking forward once more. Everything I did was to protect him. Why couldn't he see that?

"Stop!" His words vibrated off the stone walls. When I obeyed his command, he continued, "we are not trying to control you or tell you to be silent. We are trying to prepare you to be a better queen than the one who sits on the throne as we speak. This kingdom deserves better than her."

"I cannot do this right now, Fallon," I whispered as a sigh escaped my lips.

As if on cue, his arms wrapped around my torso and he pulled me into his arms. "You may be older, but you are not entirely smarter." He released a little laugh. "Dad has fought so hard for your safety and your success. Don't forget *why* he's here."

"Father despises me. I've been chosen for this position and he treats me as if I stole his child. How could you not feel the same way?" I glanced up at him.

He let go of me, a shrug in his shoulders before lowering his gaze. "In his eyes, you did steal their child. You took Lana from us. I don't hate you, Snow, because you're still my big sister. You stood up for me when the assholes built up a group to fight against me."

"Bullies, Fallon. They're called bullies and they're terrible people who deserve to *rot* six feet under. You never did anything to them. Never let yourself forget that." I shook my head.

Something sinister flashed in his eyes, but I blamed that on my lack of sleep. My brother had always been the better one of us two. "What about you?" he asked.

I brushed a strand of hair from my face. "What about me?"

"You always help me out. It's my turn to help you."

"I don't need help. You're just a human. You won't understand the power I hold." I unclipped my cloak and folded it in half, draping it over my arm. "This is something I must do on my own. Please, respect that."

He opened his mouth to say something more but decided against it. He left me in silence until I was the only person standing in this room. Everything inside the castle was grand, much more than the outside.

The dark bricks outside were made to look dingy and dull, keeping the glamor inside a secret. Everything inside was made of white marble with black veins running inside, while gold trim added to the luxury of the castle. The walkway leading from the door and up the stairs was blanketed in red carpet as if we were the greatest people to live in this home.

All of these colors worked to ensure Drecose remained a reminder for all princesses who came through these halls to push forward for the crown.

They reminded me to train for the well-being—the safety—of our people.

I headed up the stairs to my room and laid my cloak on my bed. I called in my lady's maid to help me dress. "It's been a hectic day, Lynn."

She untied the lace of my dress and stepped back when I pulled it from my body. "How was your walk in the woods?" She gave me a warm smile that matched that of the pumpkin pies she'd made around this time of year.

I grabbed my nightgown from the closet and pulled it over my head. The sleeves hung off my shoulder, the cotton material thin and light to make it easy for me to breathe. "It was refreshing. Although, I ran across a little gutless wimp who refused to show their face. They shot an arrow in my direction but barely missed me."

"Miss Edmilla, are you sure it was not Luka you ran into?" She grabbed my dress and put it in a basket to take with her when she would do my laundry.

"Luka? Who is Luka? How have I never heard of him?" I pulled the pins from my head and brushed.

She grabbed my brush from me and ran it through the black sheet of hair. "He is the huntsman. He lives in Ash Forest and his face is rarely ever seen around here. The legend claims he works for the Evil Queen herself. Although, nobody has been able to confirm nor deny that tale." She paused. "As for why you've never heard of him, you're so focused on your own training to notice."

I turned my shoulder and looked up at her. "Huntsman? This

huntsman is said to work for the one woman who instills fear into every citizen in this town? He's a fool to think he could take me down. I have not been training for no reason. Are you sure Luka is the one?"

"Seems likely. He survives among the trees and uses his own arrows to fight off any threats. I know you can handle yourself, but I want you to stay safe." She put the hairbrush down on the table.

"I appreciate the kind words, but I am not going to fear the forest. Hiding in this castle until I'm queen will never prepare me to be the best there is. I would rather die fighting than live in the shadows." I pulled back the covers on my bed and slipped between them and the sheets.

"Understood, Miss Edmilla." Lynn took the basket of clothes and exited the room.

Aside from the disapproval from my father, I now had to watch my back in case of the huntsman they called Luka. I refused to let any man overpower me and make me feel weak. I rejected the Evil Queen's desire to stay in control. I was coming for her head, and she'd been waiting for me since her threat six years ago.

TWO

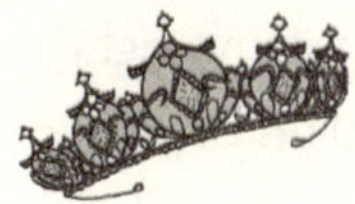

"Your father wishes to see you, Miss Edmilla."

I was never fond of those words. They smelled of foul remnants of the past. "Why?" I turned to face Lynn as she gave me a smile. I pinned my hair up as I patted down the skirt of my gown.

She replied, "He wishes to tell you a few important pieces of information to help you become queen."

Letting out a sigh, I dismissed the question. "I'll be down as soon as I can be. Thank you, Lynn."

She exited the room and left me to my own vices. I knew it was time to face him after our fight. We always had them and at the end of the day, until I moved into Everinthian Castle, I'd report to him purely for his protection.

I left the room and walked down the long corridors before finding my way to the Great Hall. Father sat at the end of the table on the opposite side of the room, waiting for my arrival. I came for the key to stopping the Queen and *just* that.

"What is it?" I asked.

"Lana, I'd like you to sit. I want to talk about more than just the

Evil Queen." He gestured towards the chair beside him.

"I'd like to stand if you don't mind." I folded my hands together in front of me.

He straightened his posture. As much as he wished to appear as the authoritative figure, he never would be. I'd been a grown woman for a while, and this castle had been provided by my luck. "Very well."

I lifted my chin. "You have no right to tell me what to do. The reason you live in this castle is because of me. I will go out when I damn well please. Is that understood?"

He stood from his chair. Unlike the stories, this one was no king. He didn't dress in the finest of fabrics embroidered in gold. He dressed in clothes most villagers wore, and every day he was reminded of the truth. He was not the owner of this castle. He wasn't even in line for the throne.

"I am your *father*. I raised you from birth. You have no right to talk to me like that," he said with a firm tone.

I let out a laugh. "We've been over this. I'm the next in line. I'm royalty. You are nothing to the castle. I could do this without you." I waved my hand. "That's enough of this subject. What is this about?" I kept my face void of all emotion.

The sooner we got this over with, the better. I'd been awaiting the Queen's message in what my quest was.

He approached me. "You only need me to know how to defeat the Queen, and I'm not naïve to that role. But I will not give you that information until you realize I am your *father*. What I do is to protect you from the darkness. I do it for your safety."

Information? How in the hell did he acquire the information that had solely been meant for my eyes?

"You don't think I'm ready?" I cocked both eyebrows as I gave him my sharpest look.

He pulled out a chair. "Sit."

Pressing my lips together, I took a seat down in the chair, reluctant.

Father walked to the other side of the table, facing me. "There are seven deadly sins in Orsadia you must search for, and you're required to *conquer* each one. That is the only way to defeat her. She keeps them out there to protect her position, but you have the power to take them down."

Leaning forward onto my hands, my eyes shifted to the collar of his shirt. "How did you get this information? She should have given it to me. It was my duty."

His demeanor changed. Shoulders sunk. Eyes lowered. A sigh passing his lips. "When you were younger, we sensed the darkness. Far before you ever did. What we feared came true, Lana, but it didn't stop me from trying to protect you. I placed a spell on you, and until you became the next heir, you'd be untouched by death itself. Until that crown is yours, the reaper cannot touch you." Reaper? Father believed in that kind of thing?

"You placed a spell on me?"

"Yes, and I don't regret it. She sent a bird with the message, but our friendly crow couldn't quite reach you. He got me instead."

I'd heard them caw. Seen things in the forest. Never had it dawned on me that I had a protection spell over me. But why did death follow me at all?

"And you won't let me go into the forest even if I'm safe?"

His nose scrunched up as his brows knitted together. "Why tempt death? Why the teasing? I did what I had to for my own daughter. Now it's up to you to conquer these seven deadly sins, Lana."

"Do you believe that?" I leaned back in my chair and folded my hands together. "Do you believe I can take the crown?"

He slammed his hands on the table. "Do you not believe in your own power? If you want to prove me wrong, *prove me wrong*. Do not let anyone stop you from being who you were always meant to be.

"But treating me like the enemy would only prove that you cannot put the people before your own needs. When I suggest that you stay inside, it's because I've heard the horror stories and I can't fathom the thought of my little girl ending up another body for the graveyard. All spells can be broken, even before they're carried out. Is that clear enough to understand?"

Ash Forest had been neutral territory. By Magic Law, the Queen could not enter Drecose Castle. I was safest here. In Ash Forest, she had full reign to do whatever she wished to me. Maybe others in the past had tested their luck or not, but I wouldn't allow her the satisfaction of my fear.

I shrugged off his frustration. "I must get going now if I am to prepare for the war ahead of me. The Queen isn't going to surrender her throne." I stood and left the Great Hall.

I made my way towards the tower. When I arrived, I neared the window and overlooked everything I needed to see from above. If I could locate these *sins* from here, I could make my job that much easier. However, I wasn't sure how I was meant to defeat these sins. Father said conquer but an inkling told me I was required to take drastic measures. And in what form did they appear?

"I heard Dad revealed the secret," Fallon said from behind me.

"You heard correct." I glanced back. "Did you know about the spell? Are you aware of what it means when he says the seven deadly sins must be conquered? He said they're scattered throughout Orsadia as a way to protect her."

"We knew." He came closer, stopping beside me. "Maybe the sins are inside you." He turned his head towards me.

I choked on a laugh. "I know I have my issues, but I don't think lust is one of them." Orsadia needed a new queen soon, and I'd be her.

The leaves rustled in the trees. The waves crashed against the bottom of the cliff that kept Orsadia from flooding. Everything from here appeared so small and yet so detailed. This was my home—the only home I wanted to ever know. I was responsible for its future and I was dedicated to my destiny. I was chosen for a reason.

Finding the cave I visited was a bit difficult. Lynn said that was home to Luka, the huntsman. If she was right about the rumors, he wanted my heart. The Evil Queen would stop at nothing to keep her place, including getting the huntsman to rip my heart from my chest. He was nothing but a coward. He hid in the brush to avoid confrontation. He couldn't take me on himself. An equal battle meant he would lose, and he knew that deep within his soul.

"Do you remember when we were kids?" Fallon asked. His gaze was locked on the decaying trees that littered Ash Forest.

A little laugh escaped me. "Kids? You still are a kid." I nudged him.

A smile shined brightly on his face as his eyes lit up. "I was referring to a time when we both were kids. We both would run through the forests. You always insisted on playing hide and seek."

"It was my favorite. I was the best; was I not?" I shot him a smirk.

He shook his head vigorously. "Snow, that was not fair play and you know it. You have better hearing than I do."

"You just had to hide better. Admit you were horrible, and I always came out on top. It's okay to admit it. I have to be better to hide from the Queen. Otherwise, Orsadia may never see light again." I looked out the window. "*Poison* has reigned over our land long enough."

A hand landed on my shoulder. "You'll be a great queen. I know so. I've watched you grow up."

I closed my eyes. "Mother." I turned to face her. "Father refuses to think so."

She pushed some loose hair back from my face. "You know he loves you. He's just worried. This is a big task to take on and our little girl is growing up. It's terrifying to see your child have to go to war with the Queen and risk a chance at losing her life." Uncertainty flashed in her eyes, and I thought I'd only imagined it.

"He has a funny way of showing his love." I pushed her hand away. "I have to prepare for my quest." I walked towards the stairwell.

"Snow White," my mother's voice boomed. "You will stop this instant."

I stopped, her voice bouncing along the tower walls. Lowering my head, I said, "What?"

She circled me until she stood between me and the stairwell. Mother lifted my chin. "Never let the darkness take away the love inside you." She placed a soft kiss against my temple.

"If I show the Queen my weakness, she knows what she can use against me," I whispered. If I pretended long enough, maybe I could save him.

Before I had noticed, my mother wiped the tear that strayed from my eye. "You would never want to die knowing your last days were spent pushing those you love most away from you. Don't be like *her.*"

Deep down, I knew she was right. Mother was always right. She fixed the tear in my heart by stitching it together before it could wreak havoc on my soul.

"Yes, Mother." I planted a kiss on her cheek. "I must go. Orsadia needs me."

She nodded and stepped out of the way. I descended, holding my gown on both sides so as not to trip and fall. A battered princess was no good for war.

I stopped by my room to grab my cloak before I left the castle. I headed towards the village to visit the citizens. Every now and then, I returned to my roots to remind them of their ally and myself of my humility.

People recognized me upon arrival. I gave them smiles in return.

Promises made and fulfilled.

"Snow White, eh?" a female asked behind me.

I spun around and pulled my hood from my head. "Who's asking?"

She threw an apple up, catching it a second later. "Zoe. Do you think you can really take on the Evil Queen?"

I reeled my shoulders back. "I've been training longer than you've been able to talk. Say, Zoe, where is your family?"

She pointed over at a mother and daughter. "Why do you think the Queen is evil?"

That was a question I couldn't answer. There'd been a day when the Queen was in my place, training to become the next in line. She had been good—pure of soul. Something changed the day she took the throne. Power changed people, and it certainly had blackened *her* heart.

Magic, however, couldn't change anyone. You were born with or without it. Magic was what decided on the next queen. I vowed to be the next queen who would not let power eat her alive and brown her to the core like an apple. I promised my family that much, and I was going to hold to that.

"I think sometimes that wickedness has a way of taking root in things and if you're not strong enough or willing to fight it, it controls every piece of you until who you are ceases to exist. I believe immorality kills what good is left inside. I promise to never let that happen," I said.

"I want to believe that." Her voice was sincere, eyes filled with so much hope. "But the Evil Queen promised the same thing. How do we know your words are true?"

I balled my hands into fists while my body began to glow. "They're true. Why do you doubt me? Are my words never enough? Who are you to *doubt* me?" I narrowed my eyes as red filled my vision.

Zoe shook her head, bowing. "I apologize, Princess. I didn't mean any harm with my words. I hope to see the day you rule Orsadia. We know it can't be easy to be the one who's chosen for the throne, but you've accepted your duty and we are forever grateful for your sacrifice." She curtsied—again—in her rags.

As much as I wanted to change the village for the better, it was not my place just yet. Until I defeated her, she owned this land. Those were rules we had to abide by. If I broke the law now, the consequences would be lethal, and the structure of our home could collapse beneath the faulty foundation. Every land needed laws to keep to, if we wished for the system to stay intact that was. My laws asked me to possibly kill seven sins. Whatever those entailed.

THREE

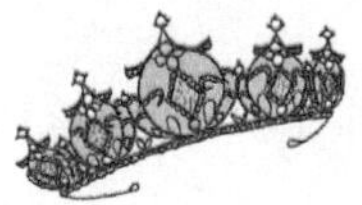

At my window, I stood, eyes focused on the horses that stopped just outside our castle. The men hopped off the horses and were welcomed inside by my father. I had no intention of meeting the prince he called to marry me.

A knock echoed on my door. "Miss Edmilla, your father asks for your presence." I welcomed Lynn but my father was a whole other battle.

Barely turning my head, I tilted my chin towards the floor. "Tell him I have no interest in marrying."

"Nobody has any intention to stop your journey to the throne," she said through the door.

I released a sigh and turned all the way before approaching, the clicks of my heels the only sound for seconds on end. I pulled open my door. "I'll be down in a moment."

Lynn bowed her head and left the corridor. I checked my mirror to make sure I looked my best when I told this prince to screw off. Everyone knew better than to arrange my marriage. I was in no mood to become some man's wife and be told what I could and couldn't do.

The corridor was long but the grand staircase that led down to the entrance was far longer. As I neared the bottom step, I folded my hands in front of me before pulling my shoulders back to straighten my posture.

A man dressed in fine, red cloth stepped forward and got down on one knee, bowing his head. "Princess Snow White Edmilla, it is an honor to meet you."

"Who are you?" I studied every detail of his body. He was the plainest man I'd set eyes on in a while. He appeared *too* perfect. That would pose a problem.

He got back on his feet. "*Forgive me.* My name is Prince Alexander."

A fitting name for a dull man.

“Prince?”

Had he traveled all the way here for me? Absurd.

Out of the corner of my eye, my father stood near the wall as he hoped this went well. "Why don't you two get to know each other?"

What was to know? A prince among these lands was rare, unheard of even. So, what exactly made Alexander the prince? Was he a sin? Merely a mirage from the queen?

I shot Alexander a smile. "Will you excuse me for a moment?" I twisted my head the other way. "Father, a word?"

The two of us headed towards the Great Hall. When the door echoed throughout the large room as we closed it behind us, I spun to face the man who aided in my creation. "How dare you bring that man into my castle?"

"He can help you rule when you take your place as Queen." He pointed his finger towards the door. “I believe an outside perspective would benefit this land.” As in, Alexander came from another land?

"Rule? As if I need a man to help me rule over Orsadia. I will do no such thing. Get him out of Drecose Castle or I will." I narrowed my eyes on my father.

He folded his hands behind his back and shrugged his shoulders. "I propose a deal."

"I don't make deals," I spat.

However, he didn't falter. "Spend the day with Alexander. If you do not like him by the end of the day, you will never have to see him again." His eyebrows shot up in surprise. "I will also stop bothering you altogether."

That was a deal worth considering. All I had to do was spend the day with a prince and he'd promise to never give me trouble again.

"Quite tempting, Father." I lessened the gap between us. "You have yourself a deal. I will spend one day with Prince Alexander and if I decide he's not fit for me, you cannot give me trouble for the way I choose to train for the throne, nor the way I choose to be a princess. Fair?"

He released a sigh. "Thank you for considering."

It was the proposal I had considered. Alexander's heart was not on my mind. I had no interest in him. Nothing about his dull demeanor stood out to me.

I exited the Great Hall and approached Alexander. "Allow me to grab my cloak before we head out."

He smiled. "Take your time, Princess."

His manners sent this morning's breakfast back up the way they came. He had no backbone. Some may have assumed I'd want that to complement my strong personality, but someone who could not defend those they loved was worthless. *If*—and that was a big if—I were to ever fall in love, it'd certainly not be someone who allowed me to boss them around.

I retrieved my cloak from my room and took my sword with me. Alexander had to know who he had chosen to marry. I was not the princess who stood back and watched my knight fight for me. In fact,

I was both the knight and the princess. I came as a package deal.

As I passed by Fallon, he stopped me to whisper, "If you don't marry him, I will."

With a smile, I said, "He's all yours after today."

Alexander and I left the castle. The walk to Ash Forest wasn't a long one. Maybe an hour or two at most. "Tell me about yourself," I told him.

He wore his story with pride. "I was born into royalty. I'm thankful I was never a commoner or peasant to anyone else. I'd never look good in that color." He fixed his jacket.

Lifting an eyebrow, I asked, "Color?"

"Dirt, of course." He nodded. "Say, shall we go down and see the ocean?"

I headed deeper into the forest. "I had different ideas in mind." I pulled out my sword and swung it against a bush.

"Should a lady be holding a sword?" he asked.

This prince was a piece of work. "Did you want to train and fight my battles for me? I didn't think so. A little boy like yourself is no match against the Queen. You've never fought a real battle in your life, have you?" I faced him. "Tell me, Alexander, have you ever had to protect your own life, or have your knights and guards always done it for you?"

He began to speak, "I've—"

"I'll have you know I was not born into royalty." I pointed my sword at his throat. "I was just a commoner before I was picked as the princess. I dressed in the color of *dirt*. I train every day. I practice to defend my own life and the life of those I love because that is what princesses do. We do not have time to hire guards and knights to do our dirty work for us." I walked closer, using the tip of my blade to hold his chin up. "I suggest you watch your words around a lady holding a sword."

He swallowed and stepped back. "I apologize for my offense."

I placed my sword back into my belt. "How do you expect to be my husband if you do not respect who I am? We both know it is not my father's decision who I marry. It is mine and I don't take kindly to princes who place themselves on pedestals. You, Prince Alexander, are no better than the peasant or commoner among *our* land. In fact, I dare say you fall below them. No prince is worth anything if he insults the people who look up to him."

He bowed his head. "You're right. I should never have said those words. I do believe Orsadia could be so much stronger if both of us united as one in marriage."

It was a tragic thing to see hope in the eyes of a man who couldn't get off his high horse long enough to see the beauty in the village and its citizens.

I had it in me to break his heart and remind him I was not here to find a husband. However, I chose not to. It would be much more fun to lead him on and break it off at the end of the day.

So we set forth. For hours upon hours, we walked in silence. The sun was beginning to set and Alexander was starting to appear uncomfortable in these parts. Fidgety hands. Uneven steps. Until the second I looked away, his aura changed. Confidence. Not an ounce of fear. Who was he?

And why had he put on an act of terror on my behalf?

"They talk about you all the time—the villagers. They talk about a woman whose eyes are as dark as her hair, skin as pale as snow, and cheeks as red as blood. However, your hair is blacker than any black I've witnessed. How do you get that color?" Alexander asked.

I pushed branches out of my way as I approached the same cave I had a few nights ago. "I sold my soul to a witch." I was met with silence, and so I sent a glance back at him. "It's a joke, Alexander." The color returned to his face as he took a deep breath. "I was born with this color. There is nothing I've done to attain it."

He stopped before the cave. "What is this place?"

An arrow landed in his right shoulder. He yelled out.

I spun towards the direction the arrow shot from and pulled my sword. "Head back to my castle. There, my medics can treat you for your wound. Do as I say!" I shouted at him.

He ran towards the direction of Drecose.

I searched every tree in the area but caught no sight of the coward. "Afraid to face me yourself? Afraid I'll win?"

I received no answer in return. Instead, I went on my way back.

Alexander certainly made it no quiet or easy trip. With all his complaining and whining, he had already made such a terrible impression on me.

When I arrived, he followed our medic. They'd removed the arrow and dressed the wound after it'd been cleaned. It wouldn't be long before my father questioned how I put Alexander in this mess.

Standing at his bedside, I admired the arrow. It's been carved from the finest of tools. Whoever made this—Luka, I was assuming—knew what he was doing.

"I'll fetch you soup to help your body heal." I left the room and headed towards the kitchen. I had the staff make soup for Prince Alexander. He may have been big-headed, but it was the least I could do for getting him shot.

The huntsman had a good aim and yet, he missed my head by a centimeter. Had he missed me on purpose? He appeared so afraid to face me and yet he sent me a warning shot.

If the rumors were true about him working for the Evil Queen, he would have had my head on a stick. However, maybe he wanted to play devil's advocate, too.

It was not possible to straddle the fence, though. One had to pick a side, and as far as I was aware, he chose her. He was going to regret his decision as soon as I took the crown. He could not hide forever, and I'd make sure he knew that.

Soon, my father found me and reminded me of who was being taken care of in our castle. We had a fair deal, and I spent a day with Alexander. I had decided *not* to marry him—although that came as no surprise to myself.

Alexander was no prince if he entered Ash Forest with no weapons at his disposal. How could he ask for my hand in marriage and expect to protect his loved ones without proper protection? I could never be with a man who did not believe his own children had a right to be defended from danger. If I could do it, who was he to say he could not?

"We should talk," my father said behind me.

I faced him. "If we are to talk, then you have agreed to hear my side of the story."

My side of the story was simple. I could not take a husband with no skills. I could never ask for a man who saw the citizens as lesser. The huntsman sent me my warning shot, missing me because I had the training to protect myself and Orsadia. His warning shot for Alexander was an arrow to the shoulder, reminding him of his place and how easy it could be for him to lose his position as a prince, whether he was an immigrant or not.

In his eyes, I needed a husband to help rule over Orsadia. In mine, a husband was no good if he did not care for the people he vowed to protect at all costs. It was better that I ruled alone than choose one who would hold me back from my true potential. Alexander was far too immature to be a king and Orsadia deserved better. My father would come to understand that one way or another.

FOUR

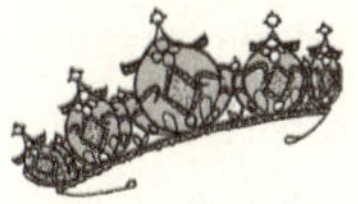

My rage boiled to the brim as I turned to face my father. "Why? Why would you do this?" He promised he wouldn't bother me and yet, he had already crushed it between his fingers.

"You must understand what this could do for our land. It would be good for you to marry Alexander. He's a prince!" His footsteps were slow and quiet as opposed to my quick steps, echoing throughout the large room.

My father never seemed to understand the seriousness of his words. How could he say he cared when he suggested what was the worst idea he had? "He's no good. He's an asshole and I do not apologize for saying such a thing. Whether or not I get married, I am still becoming the next queen."

"Don't do this," he yelled after me as I started walking out the door. "Lana, come back!"

As I left the castle, I yelled into the sky. I leaned over the brick railing that surrounded us, looking out over the ocean.

I hated that name. I *despised* the name Lana and yet he refused to call me Snow White.

The waves tossed, rolling onto the shore. They were begging for attention and inviting me to swim. Swimming was the last thing on my mind.

Ignoring the ocean's call, I walked across the bridge. My father's voice shouted from behind me, pushing me over the edge. "We made a deal, and you broke it!" I pulled my sword from my belt and lifted it above my head, swinging down on the rope of the bridge.

It hit me milliseconds too late as the bridge tilted to one side, dumping me off into the rash water. I hit it with a huge splash, the ocean engulfing me. The impact had knocked enough wind out of me to keep me weakened as the ocean filled my lungs—burning the tissue that lined inside.

My vision began to spot, reality warping no different from waking up after a nap. Fingers wrapped around my arms, pulling me down or up, whichever way I was going.

I was dragged up the shore and laid out onto the sand. Like that, the water inside me apologized as I coughed it up and ignored the roughness of my throat. "Next time, don't save me." I rose to my feet, leaving them on the beach without bothering to give them any of my time.

A male voice responded, "Right, because you were doing such a wonderful job saving yourself." He let out a low chuckle. "I wouldn't have saved you if I didn't have a morality that begged me to do so."

I spun around and pointed my finger at him, waving it in the air. "I don't need anyone. I'm fending for myself. I have to defend myself, and that water wouldn't dare fill my lungs. It knows who I am. I do not need a knight in shining armor, nor do I need a prince. Just because I'm a woman, does not mean I'm a damsel."

His hair had hung below his ears, a few waves hanging around. The windows to his soul were bright green, studying every inch of my own. He was well built and that meant he was highly active in his life.

This had to be the *huntsman* I heard about. And he appeared oddly familiar, like I'd seen him before. But where? Orsadia had been a small piece of land and every face had a name at one point or another.

A cunning smile rose on his face. "That's good news for us both. I'm neither of those things. You don't need them, and I won't be them. I'm not a prince. I'm no knight. That gives me room to stick around some more." He walked closer. "I don't bow down to women who insult me if that's what you were hoping for."

"Ah, yes, because you prefer to be controlled by the Evil Queen." I snickered and wrung out my skirt.

A laugh erupted from his mouth. "I do not work for the Evil Queen. I don't work for anyone."

"That is not what the legend says." I narrowed my eyes.

He folded his arms across his chest. "I guess that's why they call it a legend. It's not the entire truth." He put his hand out before grabbing mine and shaking it. "I don't believe we have properly met. I'm Luka, the huntsman." His name still rang no bells. He remained a mystery in my memories.

"I'm well aware of you." My eyes darted to the arrows on his back.

His eyebrows shot up. "Really? You could have fooled me by the surprised look when I aimed my arrow at you in the forest. It's very rude to enter someone's home without asking first."

I coughed up some more water and pounded against my chest to get it all out. "Are you not going to ask for my name?"

He dropped a look as if this question put a damper on his plans. "What is your name?"

I debated telling him who I was. If he knew I was the princess, he'd have more of an inclination to protect me and I wanted to steer away from that. "Lana. My name is Lana," I said.

"And what were you doing up on the bridge? That is the princess' castle." He pointed up at the large structure.

I shrugged my shoulders. "Maybe I have something against her. She angered me to my bones and so, I swung my weapon too hard on the bridge."

He let out a laugh. "Let me get this straight. Your anger was your karma? That's interesting, Lana. You should probably learn to control your anger so you don't cut the ropes of the bridge you're walking on." He fixed the position of his bow.

I walked up the sand, ignoring his remarks.

"It's not a bad thing, you know," he yelled out.

I halted and turned my head to face him. "What are you talking about?"

"Being a damsel. It's not a sin to accept help when you need it. You couldn't have pulled yourself from the water when you passed out from lack of oxygen. A simple thank you isn't going to stop you from being the queen." He followed me up towards the rock.

I pulled my cloak closed to hide my sword. "You know I'm Snow White? Why the hell would you ask who I was?"

He flashed me a smile. "I wanted to see if you would tell me the truth. It perceives me that you are nothing more than a liar, Snow."

Scowling, I shot a glance towards the trees. I knew without a doubt that I did not enjoy this man's company. I'd forgotten his face for a good reason. "I'm leaving."

He asked, "Where does Lana come from?"

"I made it up." I began walking up the beach.

I suspected he believed me because he dropped the subject.

Stopping in my tracks, I faced Luka. "Do not follow me. My quest is to defeat the Evil Queen and take her place. Is that understood?"

He bowed to mock me. "Understood, Princess." He passed by me and headed towards the trail that led up the side of the cliff. "Tell me about this quest you face. I suppose you need to keep yourself occupied until that bridge of yours is fixed. You can't enter your own castle unless you took up rock climbing in the past twenty-four hours."

Being around this man longer than I needed to be wasn't my idea of entertainment. "I'm not in the mood to talk. I would rather we both stay silent."

Luka followed my wishes right until we stood at the top of the cliff again. "I can roast some meat if you're hungry."

I pulled my hood over my head. "You live in Ash Forest *and* you're inviting me for dinner?"

"Whether or not you choose to take the offer is up to you."

"Up to me? It sounds more like you're attempting to kiss up to me given that I'm the next queen in line." I grabbed a leaf from the tree and crumbled it until it was nothing.

He bowed. "This is kissing up. Offering you dinner until you can return home is called being a gentleman."

A laugh erupted from my throat. "A gentleman? You shot an arrow at me and Prince Alexander. You are hardly a gentleman."

He shrugged as he turned on his heels to begin his walk back home. "I can eat dinner alone. I happen to enjoy my own company."

Narrowing my eyes, I jogged up behind him. "You had something in your cave, a stuffed bear. Care to explain why you own a toy?"

He paused and put his hand up to stop me as well. His head cocked to the side as he listened for danger. Grabbing the bow from his shoulder and tugging an arrow against the string, he let it fly until it hit a bird in the distance. Not danger—*food.*

Luka approached the dead bird and picked it up from the forest floor that now wept for a loss.

Then began the long walk back to his home, the sun long gone by the time we arrived.

"A toy?" He set the bird on a stone near the walls while he squatted in front of a circle formed by rocks.

His cave was no home to anyone but him, and if I'd been in his shoes, it wouldn't have been mine either.

He used a couple of rocks he gathered from the cave to strike one another, creating a spark that lit a small fire in the middle of the pit. The fire grew the longer it was exposed to the air around it.

It created a glow throughout the darkness, and as much as I wished to return home, that was not feasible. They'd have the bridge repaired soon and I would never have to see Luka for as long as I lived.

As the fire crackled, sending embers wandering, the fabric of my gown began its journey to dry and warm. And Luka plucked the feathers from the bird's lifeless form. He certainly lived up to all of the preconceived judgments I made of him.

My skin made like a fire and illuminated the dimness left around me. His eyes landed on mine, questioning the ability in itself but he never dared ask me about it. I would not have answered.

"My father wants me to marry Prince Alexander. That is what had my anger simmering a smidge above a safe temperature." I leaned back against the wall.

One of Luka's eyebrows had been lifted with curiosity. "I figured the man was part of some arranged deal. Not too many women come through Ash Forest, threatening a prince with their sword. Then again, I suppose not many princes exist in our land."

I lifted my chin. "He gave me no choice. Alexander is not the man he appears as. He insults the villagers and asks unwanted questions. That is no man fit to rule an entire land. Answer me this, Luka. Would you want to marry someone who doesn't believe you have a right to be who you are? Would you give up this lifestyle for a woman against hunting?"

He stabbed the bird and placed it over the fire to roast. "I never said a word of judgment. Who you choose to marry is not my business. If Alexander is not the prince you want, I have no opinion for or against it."

My eyes focused on the blazing flames that fueled my soul. "That's the problem my father sees in me. I do not wish to marry a prince. A prince serves me no purpose as a queen. Alexander is nothing more than a foolish boy and it pains me that my own father doesn't see what I see. Surely you have an opinion on that."

FIVE

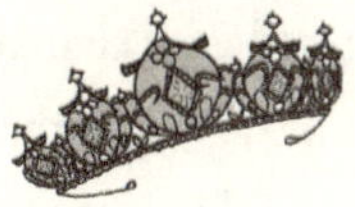

The library was located in the tower of Drecose to the back right corner. Books lined the seamless walls up to the ceiling and to access them, you had to stand on a ladder that stood taller than the grandest shelf itself. Anyone who wanted a book had to conquer their fear of heights. If I were to conquer these sins, I needed to do my research.

I placed the wooden ladder against the shelf and began climbing up to find some books on sins and the history of Orsadia. I found a few in my reach, laying the books out on the table in the middle of the room.

As I flipped through the pages, one of them caught my attention. I stopped to read between the lines and study what this world had been like before I came to be.

According to the book, Orsadia hadn't changed much. There had always been a queen since the beginning of our land. The first queen to rule had been given great power. Many said the power went to her head and evil grabbed a foothold. Others believed she had always been evil, but to this day, I questioned whether wickedness was born or made.

I followed the line of the queens who came after her, but everything stayed the same. Every queen who ruled here had been sour. Orsadia was begging for a queen of moral standing.

Every queen ruled for a total of three years. This gave her time to make the changes needed and get her home in order. However, nothing changed. Nothing had ever changed because all queens here were vermin, and oh, what a tragic tale that had been.

It could not come as a coincidence that they all held wickedness in their veins. Mother said that coincidences didn't exist, and everything happened for a reason. On a normal occasion, I would question things. However, the day I'd been chosen to be queen, I knew there was nothing to ask. Everything had a reason for coming to light.

My theory was that a curse plagued our land. A curse had a firm grasp on every queen, and if that were true, I would be the first who broke such a curse.

I skimmed the words in the book about sins and their representation. Most of these sins made sense. Murder couldn't be questioned because such a thing was vile. Taking a life was the perfect combination of shedding blood and stealing what didn't belong to you. It was two sins in one.

What had the gears in my head turning were the deadliest of all sins. Gluttony made sense. Deadly sins referred to the death of one's self, and gluttony was eating one's self until the body gave out.

However, the others were sins I could not decipher. Sloth couldn't be deadly if you were lazy. If it had mixed with gluttony, it could contribute to more health issues, but alone it did not kill a human being.

Envy was one that had my mind in puzzle pieces. Envying another could not be wrong. If it wasn't wrong, how could it kill the person involved in the act?

Greed and lust fell in the same boat. Wanting things that happened to be part of life did not kill a person. Nobody died from having too much sex, or too much gold. People died from not having *enough* gold. They starved and got illnesses. They couldn't afford the medicine that helped them fight it off—then gone. Like everything else in Orsadia. The land that'd been created on the manifestation of death.

Wrath—a sin many struggled with. I was aware that my fuse ran shorter than most, but it was not something that had gotten myself killed. *Except when I almost drowned.* However, my anger was justified. Breaking a deal was against all codes.

Pride was among the sins that made no sense. What made being proud so dangerous? If I struggled with any sin the most, pride would be the one. My pride still never grew beyond my ability to see others as valuable. I never chose to put myself above them the way Alexander had, and therefore I did not believe it was deadly. Just entirely ill-warranted with a hint of naivety.

As I closed the book, I released a sigh. This wasn't becoming any clearer as the sun rose higher in the sky. What were these sins I had to conquer? In what form did they appear?

I headed up to the top of the tower where I overlooked the entire forest. In one corner lived Luka, and yet that didn't come as a surprise. He was a huntsman, and he preferred his solitude.

Approaching the window that gave me a view of the village, I watched as a little boy stole bread from a stand. He ran as his life depended on it, and all I could see in my head was the word *thief.* He was indeed a thief but stealing to survive was not a crime in my eyes. He needed the food.

One could argue that the bread stolen was gold lost for the merchant, and while I agreed, I couldn't fault a boy for his actions by asking he be punished to death or worse.

I tilted my head to the side as I focused on another villager doing what they needed to survive. They appeared all over, and it was then that I had an idea in my mind. Could it be?

"You must have something important on your mind," Fallon said as he entered the tower.

I folded my hands in front of me as I studied the people of our land. "I believe I've come to a break in the mystery."

He stood beside me and followed my line of sight. "What do you think the sins are made of?"

"Flesh and blood."

"Pardon?"

"I believe these sins I must search for and conquer are humans that the Evil Queen forged somehow. Everyone struggles with sin and you've all decided on mine. What if the answer is not what form they come in, but *who*?" I glanced at my brother. The answer had been right in front of me all along.

I never wanted to believe they'd be human from the start. Never in history had any of the queens used other humans as obstacles for the up-and-coming heir. Of course the Evil Queen just wanted to make her own history.

But could I kill them?

Were they truly human?

He shrugged. "How will you find these humans?"

That was a question I had to answer. I had no idea how to figure out who these sins were. Would I be able to pick them out from the crowd? Who could I see the pride in? Alexander was proud of who he was, and it caused him to look down on those below him. Was I required to kill the prince? What would I tell people if I succeeded?

Gluttony could appear as anyone and yet it could also be the most obvious answer. The battle would be in discovering which direction was correct.

"I can't mask my identity. Everyone knows who I am. I must go on my journey alone to scope out these *sins.* I will get to know everyone in the village. I will search high and low before ensuring their timely end. If this is the fate of my future, so be it. Killing a few bad acorns has no bearing on what could happen if I replace the endless history of evil with good. Orsadia deserves her happy ending," I said. These sins were not real. Fabricated moreso described them. Made of the Evil Queen's own sins to slow me down.

However she'd been able to create them, I wasn't entirely sure. I was sure that she'd make them look real. To throw me off. To stop me from getting to her. Because if she lost the war, she'd lose her magic. She'd lose herself.

If she hadn't already...

But she couldn't form actual flesh and blood. Skin and bones. It'd been impossible to do. They could be hallucinations. Mirages. I just had to be able to spot them.

Twisting to look at me, his frown deepened. "Indeed, they do, but is it worth it if you lose your humanity in the process? Snow, ask yourself what the right answer is here. You're considering killing innocent bystanders to become queen. Is that the legacy you want to leave behind when it's your turn to step down? What good is a crown coated in the blood of its citizens?"

A shake of my head had Fallon running for the hills. "I refuse to believe they're living beings. What good is our land if an evil queen is destined to rule for eternity? I would rather die than consider a future where citizens suffer because they cannot afford medicine. It should be a right and not a privilege. Sacrifices must be made to make the needed changes required for a better future. You cannot win a war without some casualties. These just happened to be built by magic."

"Her ability is to see the future. In what world does that allow room for creating full, functioning creatures? I refuse to believe it. You're using it to justify what you're about to do. And if they are real people? What then?" He waved his hand and turned the other way. "I always looked up to you because you stood up for me. Maybe some people *deserve* to die, but being a pawn in this war of the queens? Hardly a reason."

I headed towards the door. "Then don't believe me. However, it is not your choice to make. It's mine and I must make it alone." I glanced back before exiting. I made my way through the castle before I found my room. The time to plan for the quest would be now and no later.

"Miss Edmilla, may I ask where you are off to?" Lynn asked, standing in the doorway.

I had my cloak laid out on my bed with a gown I could fight in. Gowns were practical when you didn't want your legs to be cut open. My dress would take the hit before I.

To say I enjoyed dresses was an understatement. I was a princess but wearing a gown was a jewel embedded in the hilt of a blade.

"If you must, I am going on my journey. I have discovered what it is that I must face and if I am to succeed, I will be leaving the castle for short trips at a time. Orsadia needs some hope for once." I approached her.

She gave me a small smile, but a tinge of sadness laced her lips. "Understood. Promise me you will do what is good for Orsadia and its people. We need you."

Had Fallon talked to her? Why was she saying such words that tasted of an argument? "I'm aware. I will need a few days to gather my things, but I'll be gone by then."

Everyone here was too interested in what I had to do that it worried me. They had no lives of their own. I understood why Lynn was curious about my plan but whether I was here or not, it didn't make a difference. One goal was on my mind—and that was to change this home for the better.

Some believed it was fate's way of telling women to let a man have a chance to control Orsadia, and that was why queens were filled with pure hatred. However, I begged to differ. Men and women could be just as evil alike. I would not let anything get in my way and tell me who I was and allow that to be set in stone.

I knew who I was, and nobody could choose that future for me.

"Lynn, if you could let my mother and father know of my quest, that would be appreciated. I have too much to account for before I leave, and I would not want to leave behind anything of importance."

She bowed her head. "As you wish, Miss Edmilla."

She turned on her heels, but I called out, "Lynn?"

"Yes, Miss Edmilla?"

"When I'm gone, promise me your beautiful soul will continue to bless this castle."

The desolation drained from her expression and left behind pure love. "I will forever keep that promise until the day I die." With that, she disappeared down the corridors.

I laid my sword that'd been hanging in my belt on the bed. Standing back, I admired the items. I needed nothing more than sturdy clothing and a well-made weapon to help guide me. They would never fail me as I would never fail them. It was a perfect match.

I gazed out my window, keeping my eyes fixed on the same ocean that had attempted to swallow me whole just days before. How angelic it appeared and yet how demonic it could become.

This body of water encasing the earth knew what title I could hold and yet it had almost taken my life. Had it not been for Luka, Orsadia would have lost any chance they had, and the Evil Queen currently on the throne would have had an extended term. That was the last thing we needed.

But I'd never admit to Luka these thoughts.

SIX

A horse's hooves clacked against the stone pathway leading up to the castle. My eyes landed on my father who stood near the guards, but I knew this was his doing.

Alexander pulled back on the reins and climbed down from the horse. "Come with me, Snow. Together we can ride into the sunset."

I glanced at my father again. "You made a promise."

The surprise on his face threw me for a small loop but I saw through his front. "I kept my promise."

Alexander furrowed his brows. "Is this a bad time?"

"Excuse me and my father." I led my father into the castle. "You said you would stop bothering me if I decided that I did not want to marry Alexander. I have not changed my mind."

He reached for my hands, but I stepped away from him. "Lana, you don't seem to understand what I am telling you. I did not call him here. I *kept* my promise. I think Prince Alexander wants to marry you on his own and this is his idea."

Swallowing my pride, I pulled my shoulders back. "Do you swear on Mother's life that you didn't call him here? I need you to mean it,

Father."

Father nodded his head. "I swear on your mother's life that I did not ask him to come here." He'd never speak such a dooming swear if he did not mean it. He may have wanted to control me at times, but he loved Mother dearly. And controlling her was not something he'd ever be able to do. I attained my fierce personality from her.

"Fair enough." I turned on my heel and faced the door before pausing. "I apologize for accusing you of something horrid. Excuse me while I go remind Alexander that I have no interest in him." With those words said, I exited the castle and approached the prince.

Alexander shot me a smile. "What is the verdict, Princess Snow White?"

"I will join you on a ride through the forest on one condition." I narrowed my eyes. "I wish you would stop calling me Princess." That title was too damning coming from his lips. It reminded me that if I married him, I would *never* be the queen I had been training to be for the past decade.

As soon as the princess became queen, she moved to a new castle and her previous castle became available. It wouldn't stay vacant for long. The next princess was chosen within the month and she spent her next three years learning to become queen.

He fixed his collar. "That sounds like something I can agree to. As you wish, Snow." He climbed up on the horse and held his hand out for me.

I grabbed it and pulled myself up over the horse. "Let's not waste time. The sunset stops for no one."

He grabbed the reins and gave them a little shake. So began our journey down to Ash Forest.

Alexander glanced back at me. "Enjoying this so far?"

"I enjoy it when you don't speak." A little smirk danced across my lips.

He swallowed. "Oh, dear." His reaction had me a bit puzzled, but it was only after a minute I realized what he thought I meant. He assumed I was inviting him to sleep with me. It was quite the opposite, in fact. I had invited him to sleep, but in a grave six feet under the thriving earth.

Above us, the sky had displayed a ray of pink and orange hues which left a blanket over the already vibrant array of foliage.

Alexander tugged the reins and climbed down. We'd come across a fountain that leaves had already claimed property of. The water was no longer sprouting from the bird's mouth and the water in the base had darkened from whatever algae grew within it.

As to why they built a bird, I could not answer. A bird didn't make sense as a fountain piece. Birds could not survive amongst the branches.

It probably symbolized Ash Forest and all it could offer if the *curse* didn't exist.

Growing up, father kept a close eye to ensure I didn't go into the forest. Whenever I'd succeeded, they came looking. Mother, Father, and Fallon. I could never get far without them perched on my shoulder.

When I took over Drecose, it became apparent that nobody could truly keep me locked away. But rather than explore, I trained. Endlessly. Blood, sweat, but no tears. I refused to give even an ounce of satisfaction to the Evil Queen and the demise that soaked in our earth.

I'd never gone far enough. I'd never known about this fountain, but now it had every drop of my attention.

Alexander grabbed my waist and helped me off the horse, and I wanted nothing more than to push him right into the disease-infested waters. He was enjoying this, but I'd been coerced. I certainly took no pleasure in his presence.

He walked over to the fountain, circling, hands clasped behind his back. "Its creator built this many years ago. It once served as a wishing fountain but when evil continued to drench this land, the fountain could not provide anymore. It had been drained of all its magic."

"What you're implying is that this had magic. Did this fountain grant true wishes?" I sat down on the edge of it, studying the green water and plant life dwelling within.

He admired the bird statue. "Indeed. It granted those wishes that made sense. It could not grant wishes that changed the fate of the queens who inherited the throne, but it had the power to bring the dead back. Of course, it had its limits. Corpses could only be revived to an extent. Zombies. Animated. No soul, for the soul had long ago left this realm."

Corpses? How...*charming.*

I leaned down and pulled a rotting leaf from the murkiness. "What happened to the magic?"

"The legend says the magic evaporated, but I am not sure if I believe it. Magic cannot evaporate. It had to go somewhere. Wherever it went, I pray it serves others better than it could for Orsadia." His eyes drifted towards the sky. He spoke of this Orsadia as if he'd been here his entire life and now I suspected he wasn't from another land. Who was he, and what exactly made him the prince?

Maybe I could search for the magic. If I located it and brought it back, maybe I could break this curse of poisonous fruit that plagued our land. However, this would be a secret only I knew of. Alexander could not be trusted. Something about him had been off, leaving my instincts to beg for help.

He sat down beside me. His aura had my stomach churning and yet, I couldn't tell him to get away. Every time I imagined a scenario in which I had to defend myself, I was flawless. Yet, every flaw here presented itself to me and I could not even so much as scoot the other direction.

"Maybe the magic could return if you are next in line," he said.

Maybe—just maybe—he was right. I could be the one who brought magic back and restored the beauty of Orsadia. That was my ultimate goal and Alexander had seen it from afar.

I smoothed out the skirt of my gown. "One can hope." I folded my hands in my lap and tuned my ears to focus on the sounds nature brought.

Squirrels jumped from branch to branch while leaves rustled under their little feet. Crickets communicated all that they could as the sun disappeared beyond the horizon.

Something soft yet firm pressed against my lips. As my eyes shot open, Alexander blocked my view of the forest while his lips pressed against mine.

I brought my hand up and shoved him away. He stumbled backward and fell onto the ground, but before he could get back up, my hand met his cheek with every bit of strength I had in me.

Leaning down, I grabbed him by the collar. "Do not ever assault me. I will have your heart ripped from your chest." I dropped him and walked towards his horse, then climbed on. "You get the honor of explaining to my father why I took your horse without you." I shook the reins while the stallion took me back to my castle.

Upon arriving home, I nodded towards the guards to keep an eye on the horse. I entered and put my hand up before my father spoke. "Alexander will explain himself." I retreated to my room where I locked the door behind me.

Tonight, I would reward myself with solitude for not harming him more than I had. It disgusted me that he had the audacity to kiss me without my consent. He had no respect for me, for any woman, or for anyone other than himself.

That was what had been wrong with this land. Too many had the wrong idea of consent. Nobody understood boundaries. It was not clear what was assault and what was not.

In my eyes, assault was obvious. It was my body, and I did not consent to what was happening with it. It came as an unfortunate realization that not everyone thought this way. They all had a right to say no to something that involved their body. If it made them uncomfortable, their voices mattered.

This would be my next goal when I became Queen. I could not fathom living in a world where one thought it was their right to own another. Married or not, every person had a right to their own body. I would make sure that became clear with no questions lingering.

A knock echoed on my door. "Come in," I said.

My back was turned toward the door and whoever came through it. Instead, my eyes were glued on the asshole who rode off into the dawn.

"Alexander told me what happened," Father's words came in quiet voice.

I knew what came next. It was always the same excuse. "Whatever version he told you is incorrect. I did not ask to be kissed. I did not *want* to be kissed. My rights were violated, and I don't want to see him again."

Silence ensued. Tension hung heavy in the air and I feared what could come next. If my father argued over this, I could never forgive him.

Relief and shock washed over me as a pair of arms pulled me in for a hug. Comfort stole my heart and gave it warmth. It'd been so long without his hug and this made it so much more difficult to push him away in fear of what was coming for him.

He whispered, "I would never wish harm on you. You are my daughter and you come before any outsider."

I peeled his arms from my torso and turned to face him. "Is this a joke?"

"Why would it be a joke? We don't always see eye to eye, but I am not going to dismiss your feelings when a man forces himself on you. Prince Alexander is banned from Drecose Castle. He may have an infatuation with you, but it does not overpower your wants." He grabbed both sides of my face. "When you were a little girl, the thought of you with a boy brought about nausea. I had to grow up to understand that you choose who you are with or not. Most importantly, I put myself in my past self's shoes. Would I have been okay with a boy kissing you against your will when you were younger? No. Why should it be any different now because you're an adult with an interest in men?"

Closing my eyes, I quietly said, "Thank you. Thank you for understanding it from my perspective."

He pulled me back in for another hug and this time, I didn't fight it. Regardless, our relationship was not mending itself. For his safety, it was best he kept a distance from me.

I mourned for others who did not have such a luxury—a father who stood by your side even when you didn't entirely stand by his. No feeling was worse than being alone with nobody by your side to support you. That was the kind of world I wanted to belong to. If I could locate the magic from the fountain, I could change so much more than just rules. I could restore what we had all lost.

Evil would be no more. Men like Alexander would cease to exist, or be far and few between.

Orsadia would become a place of peace. Everyone would smile and that was what I longed for. I wanted to be the kind of queen who left a legacy that didn't leave her citizens with dread in the pits of their stomachs.

It was because of people like Alexander having a higher status that I needed to kill these sins. I could not let Alexander continue to burn everything and everyone in his path. They needed to know that he, too, was capable of immorality the same way every princess was.

SEVEN

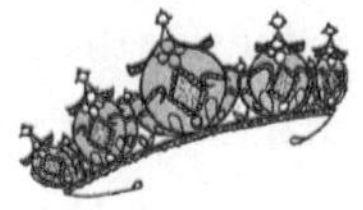

Leaves crunched while twigs snapped beneath his boots. "Have you ever considered archery?" a male asked behind me.

As I swung my sword in the air, I twisted my head towards him. Luka—the only one brave enough to venture into the woods. He also happened to live here, but that wasn't my initial point.

I spun around, facing the infamous huntsman. "Why would I do that? Do you think a sword is not fit for a woman?"

He let out a chuckle. "It has nothing to do with that. I was thinking about being able to attack your enemies from a distance."

"Bold of you to assume I'm not training in every possible way. I've been learning the art of throwing my sword." I glanced at the blade in my hand.

Luka lifted both eyebrows. "With bows, you can keep shooting them one after the other and your enemies never know where you are."

"Now why would I hide? I'm not afraid of a fight." I shook my head, recalling the first time he shot an arrow my way.

"It's useful when you are one person against many at once." He grabbed an arrow from his quiver and placed the end on either side of the string. "You can kill with one shot."

A laugh escaped me. "You can kill with a sword, too. Just separate the body from the head and you are golden. No more enemies."

He shrugged and put his arrow away. "How is life in the castle? Anything exciting?"

Nothing exciting happened inside the castle's walls. That was why I was in Ash Forest more than I was at home. "I've left it. Call it a short travel if you will. I'm determined to make my family proud." I couldn't ensure I'd live up to that, though. Their love came with conditions.

Fallon hadn't been too accepting of my idea, but it was never his choice to make. He had to let me go and it wasn't easy to do, but it was for my family and our homeland.

"Why do you have to leave for days at a time? Can you not do this from home?" Fallon asked as he stepped into my room.

Placing my sword in the sheath on the belt around my hips, I flashed my brother a smile. "If I want to get to know people, I must live the way they live. If I want to gain their trust and stop their hearts from beating, they must know I'm doing everything in my power to become the next queen this land needs to be."

Luka circled around the trunk of a tree. "What does this journey of yours involve?"

"If you must know, I'm here to get to know the people." I walked towards the tree he'd been intimidating.

He smiled while his eyes darted towards my attire. "How easy can it be to fight in a gown like that?"

I stopped inches away, narrowing my eyes. "And who is in charge of fighting attire? You, the almighty huntsman?" I laughed in his face.

He leaned closer. "Answer if you dare."

Stepping back, I picked up the skirt of my gown. "It has challenges, but I've trained in a gown since I held my first sword." I dropped my skirt. "I have no interest in pants. I think they are hideous. My fashion lies in gowns and I will make it work if I get to keep who I am. I should not have to give up my femininity to please others. Believe it or not and despite popular opinion, I enjoy showing the curves of my torso. I know it comes off as crazy that I, a woman and a fighter, would like to show my shape. I have breasts, Luka, and I am not ashamed. I want the world to know they exist. I want my enemies to know what I am when I defeat them with no mercy."

Luka lifted his hands up, palms looking me dead in the eye. "Apologies if I've offended you, Snow."

Some would have liked for women believe that breasts were a sin. If they were such a thing, we would never have been created with them. I had no reason to hide them from anyone. I appreciated the shape of my figure and I wanted to show it off. There was no harm in that.

A snicker came from behind me, but Luka stood *before* me. I twisted to face the source. "Don't apologize. Snow is nothing but a tease. She knows what she does, and she does it with venom on her tongue. Like a *snake*," Alexander said, enunciating the *S* in snake.

"Nothing I did implied I was interested in your dull personality. I never flirted, nor did I offer myself to you. You were the one competing for my hand in marriage and not the other way around." I pulled out my sword and pointed it his way.

He pushed my sword down. "You have everyone wrapped around your finger. I kissed you and you treat me as if I forced myself on you."

I swung my sword, slicing his sleeve. "You did. You kissed me. I never asked to be kissed, nor did I imply I was infatuated with you. My lips are on my body and you do not have a right to them."

Alexander's eyes narrowed into slits. "You're wicked, Princess

Snow. You're vile. You're *poisonous.*"

Luka put himself in front of me. "That's enough. She made it clear she does not have an interest in you. Let it go."

Alexander laughed. "Pardon? Is this your knight in shining armor?"

I stepped around Luka and pointed the tip of my blade at the base of his jaw. "I fight my own battles."

"Precisely." A cunning smile danced across his lips.

What had me scratching my head was why Alexander was so keen on marrying me. I had turned him down and I was not the kind of woman he was searching for and yet, he wasted his time to insult me.

Luka pulled back an arrow against the string of his bow, aiming for Alexander's heart. "Leave now or I won't miss your heart this time."

He stepped closer toward Luka. "You dare threaten a prince?"

Luka laughed but no amount of humor had been present. "Who I kill is my business."

Alexander backed away, his eyes shifting my direction. "This isn't the last you will see of me. I can promise that."

I sent him a fake smile. "Gives me a chance to kick your ass. I appreciate the offer." I lifted my sword to nick his chin. "If it is a curse that takes hold of Orsadia, I'm destined to be the next evil queen and I doubt you would wish to be on my list of enemies when *that* day comes."

Alexander shot me a glare before turning on his heel and blessing us with his absence.

Where that threat came from, I wasn't sure. The thought of being soulless haunted me and admitting my theory to Alexander terrified me while rattling my bones.

"Do you believe that?" Luka asked as he put his arrow away. "Do you believe a curse is what lives here?"

Swallowing my fear, I lifted my head. "No." A lie was better than the truth. As long as I could win, what harm could this lie bring? If my theory was correct and I fell under this curse, no one could stop what was coming aside from me. Telling people what I feared would have no use in the future.

I wouldn't create panic if I could help it.

I faced Luka and slid my sword into my belt. "I must go. I have training to get to and land to save."

He nodded. "Would it be wrong if I joined you? I'm a huntsman and this journey would be quite intriguing for a man like me."

I snickered with a roll of my eyes. "Why would you want to associate with a princess?"

The corner of his lips tugged upward. "Because it defies the stereotypes; does it not? People do not expect a princess to associate with a huntsman, and one rumored to work for the Evil Queen. With you, nobody knows what to expect. We are a surprise—an unpredictable duo. What else could Snow White ask for?"

"If I choose to take this quest with you, will people not assume I'm working with the Evil Queen?" I glanced at the trees behind me.

He shrugged. Must have been nice to live worry free. "They could, or they could also assume you have the ability to defeat the evil that resided within me. They may trust you more than they already do."

He had a point. This partnership could benefit everyone, and if I were trying to become a *good* queen, I had to put Orsadia's needs before my own. I had no interest in receiving help, but this was not about me. The people of this land mattered, and I had a duty to show them I valued their opinion.

"The seven deadly sins come in the form of humans—although not actual human beings—and I must kill them before I defeat the Queen." I was not a woman who would accept an offer without reminding them of the entire contract. A sinless heir did no such thing.

Luka's eyes smiled but his lips didn't budge from their current expression. "I'm a *huntsman.* I might surprise you with what morals I carry."

And so we formed our partnership and headed on our way towards town. As we approached the village, a woman screamed, making a break for the forest. I furrowed my brows and followed the line of sight of a man I perceived as her husband, my eyes ending upon a small lock of hair on their doorstep.

Their hut had been *cozy* and made of wood, leaves, and what mud they could muster together to keep the weather out. Many huts surrounded them, all fairly close together as I knew from experience that nobody's home gave them any true privacy. Any conflict would become everyone's business. This would be no different.

I walked over and lifted the soft locks, rubbing them between my fingers. "May I ask what happened?"

Her husband met my eyes. "She flipped her lid. She believes the superstition that a lock of hair tells you the next to die. This hair is from my wife."

If she feared death and its superstitions, why would she run towards the forest where most danger lurked? Maybe she had accepted her fate. Or she wanted to face it head on entirely and challenge it to a duel.

Luka leaned over my shoulder. "They're true," he whispered as soon as the husband left to find his wife. "I've seen the truth, Snow. That's what happened to my brother." My eyes darted to him for a second before returning to the man who disappeared among the brush.

I hadn't expected the huntsman to have a brother, but I didn't feel as if I had the right to pry into his personal life. Instead, I'd ask about this superstition. "How does this work? Who chooses who dies?"

"No one truly knows but there are a few theories running amok. Some believe the Evil Queen is the chooser of our fates, and others believe she does all of this to sacrifice us in place of something she gains. Only she knows the process behind it all—the one who lives behind the queen's walls." His eyes darted to the forest.

The queen's castle was located on the opposite edge of the forest, behind the graveyard, and away from all of Orsadia. I supposed it was for her own protection more than it was for ours. Few were willing to go beyond the forest line. However, I knew from experience that nothing fearful resided within the trees.

"How long has this superstition been around?"

"Twenty-one years."

"As long as I've been *alive*," I breathed.

Could there be a correlation?

"How do we stop her from dying?" I asked.

His face fell. "We don't. There's no force in this land but the Queen's that can stop the darkness from coming. I've tried and I wish I could offer hope but nothing good comes from this."

Those words rotted within my head. Hearing that no solution existed to save a woman from death was not something I wanted to hear, nor could accept. It wasn't in my blood to go with the flow and if anyone told me not to be the fighter I was, I would never be here on the final quest to become the next ruler. Failure was not something *I* would accept. I had to save her, even if it meant delaying my journey for however long it took.

EIGHT

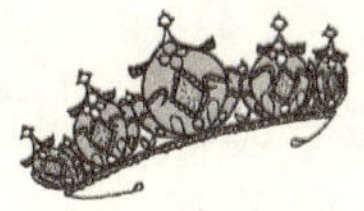

Luka's hand landed on my shoulder. "It wasn't your fault." He could say that until his face turned blue, but the fault *was* my own. It had been my duty to save her and I could not follow through.

Dropping my head, I rested my arms on my knees. The sun had set long ago, and darkness now engulfed our home. The moonlight was all we had to light the ground before it. As if on cue, my skin began to glow, surrounded by the black of the night.

"You really glow, huh?" Luka's surprise couldn't be hidden from me.

I lifted my head and glanced back at him. "It's not my choice."

He kneeled beside me. "Whose choice is it?"

"Every queen is born with an ability no one else has. We know we'll be chosen at some point but as long as we don't let anyone else know of our ability, our secret stays with us. Another young woman has an ability only she knows of, knowing she'll become the queen after my welcome has been overstayed. My ability serves no purpose but to provide a light in the dark. It's useless." I had never been fond of glowing in the dark. In fact, I was not sure how my ability worked. It happened at random and I had yet to learn to control it. What could I use it for? There was no reason to master it if it served me no real purpose.

Luka was careful not to say a word. Whatever he said couldn't offend me. I had built my skin to be thick if I was going to survive this world and whatever the queen was going to use against me on my quest.

I glanced over at him. "It's acceptable to say what's on your mind."

He chuckled a little. "Depends on what company you're with. I just think that maybe something out there...knows your future. Something or someone gave you your ability for a reason."

It hadn't occurred to me that Luka might have believed in a higher power. I believed in curses and magic but nothing beyond what I could see.

"Snow?" he asked.

Shivers ran up my spine. "My real name is Lana. That's the name I was given at birth. I renamed myself because Lana is associated with my past self and I'm not looking to go back to that era."

"We all have things we aren't proud of. But not everyone changes their name because of it."

"I do. I did." I stood up, flattening my skirt. "Nobody aside from my family remembers my real name and I'd appreciate it if it was kept that way."

He tipped his invisible hat. "Yes, ma'am."

We ventured off to visit the villagers, to check up on them and ensure what happened wouldn't happen again. If a sin were hiding somewhere, would it not be among the people?

I scanned the area for anyone who could not contain their wickedness. Nothing stood out of the ordinary. Everyone here took care of their own—whether it be their family or their home. Seeing the humanity in all of them gave me hope. The Evil Queen hadn't taken everything from them. If they could survive a bit longer, it wouldn't be long before this land saw a big change.

Luka walked beside the homes and headed down to the market. I followed him and paused upon seeing the man who had lost his wife. Guilt washed over me, and I wished to take away his pain. No one deserved to lose a loved one.

An apple was tossed my way and I caught it in midair. "I was curious if you were still paying attention." Luka smiled and grabbed himself another.

I swallowed as I glanced at the shine of the fruit's skin. "I hate apples."

He bit into his. "May I ask why?"

"You know too much about me already." I placed the apple back in the bin.

Apples did not have the taste other fruits did. Their skin was the worst part of the body and yet many enjoyed them. Nothing good came from them.

Somewhere nearby, I heard whispers. Her voice was calling out to me. I was convinced she was going to claim my life at any moment, but what she craved from me was much worse. She craved my suffering. Seeing me lose my sanity fueled her power.

Give up. Go home.

That would benefit her but no one else. I was not here to give her what she wanted.

"We should ask the villagers their thoughts. We could get some useful information from them," I said to Luka.

He nodded his head. "Lead the way."

Approaching a woman washing clothes, I kneeled in front of her bucket. "Excuse me, may I ask some questions?"

She recognized me right away and bowed her head. "Indeed, you may."

I gave her a smile. "I wanted to ask about the villagers here. Is there anyone in particular who gives off the wrong kind of impression?" I searched a few faces, locking them inside my mind.

The kind woman shook her head. "Not to my knowledge. Everyone in this town is friendly. There are a few thieves but stealing for food is not uncommon."

"Certainly not. Thank you for your time." I grabbed my skirt as I stood from the ground. I made my way over to Luka. "Either these sins are good at hiding or they're not in the village. Where else could they be?" Tracking down these mirages would be the victory of a lifetime. Nothing else could compare to such a win—being able to remove the queen's protection—her creations.

Luka's eyes fell upon the forest. "Could they be in the forest? If this is your key to victory, my guess is they won't be easy to find. The village would be too easy. If they represent the sins, their actions must be obvious. They must attract attention they want to avoid. We need to think like them." He tapped the side of his head. "Choose a sin."

I closed my eyes as I pictured the first one that came to mind. "Pride." Alexander was the one who reminded me of pride and if I had the chance to kill him, I *might* have taken it.

"If you were prideful, where would you go?"

"A castle. I'd go where I can be proud of everything. I'd be where I could look down on others." It was too easy to answer.

He cleared his throat. "Snow, I do understand that you dislike Alexander, and for good reason, but he would not be our sin. It would be too easy. Your quest is to kill these sins and if it's easy, why would it be yours to take? You're made to be challenged. Alexander is too easy of a target. He is certainly an imbecile but not capable of defending himself against you. He has no skills. I imagine these sins will have the ability to fight you."

He knew more about them than I did. Could Luka represent a sin?

Which sin would he even display? That was a question I could not answer.

I pictured the best thing that I could think of with pride. "I would want to go somewhere where I could not be bothered. I'd wallow in my pride. I might end up at a fountain I had built..." I hit Luka's arm and hurried past him before running into the forest.

Luka let out a groan from behind me. "It's not Alexander."

I didn't reply as I continued to my destination. Alexander may not have been pride but he represented it enough, and maybe he had led me to where I could find pride himself. Would a man not be filled with pride for building a fountain of magic?

Stopping at the fountain, I searched the area. No one had been here as far as I could see but I wasn't about to scrap my idea.

"What if he's here? Do not deny that I could be right. This fountain has to be connected to one of the sins and I won't give up on that. If you believe everything has a reason for happening, would you not believe Alexander had a reason to bring me here? This fountain means something to someone, and it's not Alexander. It must be someone proud of having built it." I brushed my hand across the stones.

He took a few steps closer. "You could be onto something. I'll give you credit for that."

I focused on something in the distance. It must have been an animal.

Luka could have his doubts and it wouldn't bother me. If I were right about this, that would make the satisfaction much more worth it. I wanted to be the one who told Luka: *I told you so.*

He had this energy to him that he knew best, and I was attempting to prove he was not the most knowledgeable at everything life had to offer.

"Alexander never mentioned who built this." I gazed into the gloomy water.

Luka shrugged. "If he had, he'd be one hell of an old man. This fountain must be old. Whoever built it must be dead."

There it was. He was trying to show me he knew better. Two were able to play this game.

"If this person represents a sin and magic exists, they could be immortal. We could be searching for humans who inhabit magic in a horrible manner. My quest could be about showing Orsadia that I am fit to protect them."

He gestured to the fountain. "Do tell, how is immortality a bad thing to have?"

I circled him until I had sight of the trees behind him. "Nobody should live forever. I would say I'm doing them a favor by ending their miserable curse." I turned my head just a bit to see him from my peripheral vision.

Luka laughed. "That should be for them to decide. Everyone handles their abilities in a different way. You tend to forget people are individuals."

"Did you agree to accompany me on my journey?"

"I did."

"Why are you questioning what I must do? If you don't wish to see me kill those who must sacrifice themselves for the greater good, do see yourself out. I won't make you stay." I spun around to face him.

To despite what I expected, he nodded in agreement. "You're right. I should be more understanding. I will do better." I couldn't tell if he was admitting the unthinkable or if he was using sarcasm to tell me to piss off.

I chose to ignore it. "If this person is to return to this fountain, we must wait." What I'd say next would come as a shock to Luka. "We will attempt to hide in trees like cowards until this person reveals themselves."

His lips curved upward. "You're offering to try my method of attack?"

"Don't push it." I flashed him a daring smile.

He walked over to a tree and patted the trunk. He climbed up and grabbed onto branches before perching himself onto one. "Coming, Princess?"

I shot him a glare as I grabbed the branches. He reached down and pulled me up until I squatted on a branch beside him. "Don't call me Princess."

I would become a queen at any cost and as soon as that day arrived, I would no longer hold the title of *Princess.*

"I can't make that promise." He winked at me.

He'd make it if he wanted to keep his heart. "What do we do now, Huntsman?" I asked him with a look of irritation plastered on my face.

He leaned forward and pulled out a bow, resting the string between the split ends. "Now, we wait."

Waiting—as I'd predicted—was useless. Nobody came into view for a few hours or so, and we were sitting birds at this point in our journey. I refused to be a sitting bird.

"Luka, I'm jumping down," I said.

He gave me a warning look as if I would be intimidated by his demeanor. Did he not know by now nothing could make me cower? "Don't, Snow. Not yet."

"Don't tell me what to do." Defying his order, I jumped down from the tree and froze in my tracks at the touch of something sharp against my neck. My blood boiled at the thought of Luka mentally telling me he'd been right all along.

But no, Alexander was no more than a bug buzzing in my face.

NINE

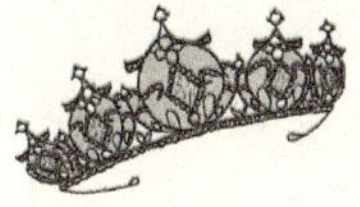

"Back so soon? Shame. I was just beginning to get used to the peace and quiet." I faced the very man whose ego was so big even God himself couldn't crush it, if I believed in one that was.

He stepped forward, one foot in front of the other but his movements were that of a robot. Stilted. Stiff. Was he such a thing? "Why don't we battle this out now?"

A laugh left my lips. "Battle? You? Have you ever held a weapon in your existence? I doubt so."

"I may surprise you," he said as he slipped the sword from its sheath.

I took my sword from position, tight grip around the hilt. "Give me your best shot."

He took a jab at my gut, but I threw myself back to avoid the injury. I fell against the trees behind me, but I quickly gained my posture before he had a chance to take another shot.

With my sword in my hand, I swung down on him, but he dodged it. Luka tried to help but whatever he did wasn't working. This fight had to be between me and Alexander. If I didn't stop his heart, this entire quest would be rendered worthless.

He could be my downfall. *Pride.*

He ducked again as I tried to slice open his abdomen, and he took this chance to stab his blade into the skirt of my gown and rip it open. As I spun around to avoid his attacks, I tripped over the fabric that now hung off my dress.

A liar. A cheat. That's all he was.

I grabbed one of the branches to keep my balance upright, but it was no use. He grabbed me by the hood of my cloak and pulled it back, choking me out. I spun around with my sword slicing through the air, knowing he would be in its path.

However, he jumped up to avoid the blade and I was left dumbfounded by his skills. Skills he pretended not to own. His hatred must have been much stronger. He had nobody to love, and nobody to remind him he was loved. Who could love a narcissist? He had strength that I would never possess, and I feared I wasn't going to win this battle.

"You underestimate my skills. Is it because I'm a good actor?" he mocked me.

How he knew things that others hardly knew was beyond me. He must have been spying on me, which meant there could be other sins who were following just as well. If that was the case, I desperately needed to get ahead in the game.

I ran towards the fountain and turned to face him with my sword in front of me. "A liar. I call you for what you are, and I never pretended to be into you."

With a smirk on his face, he swung his blade around my torso until he sliced through my gown and into my stomach, jumping towards me. I elbowed his wrist, forcing him to drop his blade. He fell to the floor and rolled across the ground, picking it up before he stood back on his feet.

I swung my sword at his head, but he ducked and grabbed my cloak, pulling me against him with his knife to my throat. "Tell me what you're so afraid of, Snow."

This wasn't a conversation I was willing to have. My privacy would be just that.

He nicked my skin. "What gets your blood boiling? What gets you screaming? You can't hide your feelings forever," he spat.

I lifted my sword, but he kneed my wrist, causing me to drop it. He pushed me against the bark of a tree, keeping me trapped with nowhere to go and no way out of this.

"Something makes you *mad.* What is it?" He narrowed his eyes as the flames burned within his iris'. His skin turned a shade of red. "Is it the way men touch you without your permission? The way people treat your little brother for being gay? Is it about your father, who never seems to accept your duties?"

Staying quiet wasn't easy.

He pulled a dagger from his other side, stabbing it into the tree beside my head. "You can't hide your fears forever. You know they'll eventually come out."

Luka attempted to pull him off of me, but it wasn't any use. Alexander yanked his dagger out and stabbed him in the leg, sending him a warning to back off.

He wrapped his fingers around my neck and squeezed, cutting off my air supply. Leaning in, he whispered, "Is it about Luka? Tell me now, or your boyfriend will bleed out and you'll forever be alone because nobody will ever love a poisonous queen."

I clawed at his arm as I struggled to get any bit of air into my lungs.

The prince loosened his grip, and I began gasping for some air. He laughed lowly and leaned into my ear. "It's such a shame that you'll end up just like her."

He let go and backed away as I collapsed and struggled to get myself back on my feet. He left the area before I had a chance to grab my sword.

Luka limped over to me. "Come on, we need medical attention."

I agreed and pulled myself off the floor with his help before leading us to my castle.

A snap of a twig, a crunch of a leaf.

Autumn was one season in which all the life in nature began to hide away or die off. How fitting for what I deemed to be the most beautiful time of the year. Delicate, and fleeting.

Chilling and burning all at once.

The air was crisp early in the mornings but muggy later on. Fresh of rain and mud. The lingering of hope and despair.

A taste of what was to come for everyone. Winter was just around the corner, and autumn was paving the journey. Like I was paving my way to the Evil Queen.

From the ocean a hint of salt sprinkled the air.

Birds hardly chirped at dawn, but crickets most certainly did it at dusk. Leaves would rustle at the whistle of the wind, bending to its whim. It'd be the same path taken every year, but the length of the quest always differed.

Everything would be cold—soaked with the pleas of the trees begging to stay just a little longer.

But despite all the hardships and the loss, autumn would remain perfect. She'd keep up her appearance to the best of her ability, fighting to show she was resilient and even if she lost, she'd go out with one last good memory.

Between the oranges, the reds, the yellows, and even some greens.

It was her way of leaving a lasting impression and nobody needed to argue that she held all the cards in her deck.

Most people in Orsadia favored this time of year due to crops. It was harvest season, and harvest season meant everyone got fed. Extra vegetables. Pumpkins. Corn. Watermelons. You could name it and it'd probably be ripe right when the temperatures dropped.

Winter in the mornings, summer in the afternoons, at least until the rain would begin to bless us with humidity—humidity we didn't entirely need as a land surrounded by the ocean. Even the center most area of our home got its fair share of hydration, and right where Keenain River flowed through.

Life thrived. As ironic as it sounded.

Summer offered too much heat and that never boded well for a woman training to kill a queen. A woman dressed in the finest of fabrics that laid heavy on the body, trapping and absorbing all the warmth. It made heat stroke a possibility and threatened my beating heart.

Therefore, I craved anything but the summer heat. Winter provided, but autumn gave more.

And on the perfect day, a day just right, it would be not too hot nor too cold. You could take a stroll in the woods unharmed. Despite rumors, the forest was not the enemy. Night was not a threat to our souls.

Nor autumn, for that matter. It became an ally, fruitful and plenty.

No.

The only enemy that plagued this land was the Evil Queen herself.

"Your doctor said it would take time to heal so I don't know how much use I can be with a wound," Luka said from behind.

"I don't need you to be useful," I replied. "Prince Alexander gave me the impression he had no idea how to wield a weapon and after today, he's proved to be stronger than I anticipated. We need to watch our backs. He's up to something and I've no doubt he was part of her plan to stop me from taking the throne."

"I agree."

Shooting a look of admiration at him, I stood. "You agree?"

He shrugged a little, his voice level as he said, "Yes, I agree. He's a threat. Do you believe he's a sin?"

I knitted my brows together. "I do. If he's a sin, we know who he is. The hardest part will be defeating him. Are you up for killing a prince?" It would certainly explain where Alexander appeared from, and I'd feel no guilt taking a mundane hallucination from its place.

"What makes him a prince, exactly? He's not your brother and as far as we all know, Mira has no one." *Mira.* The Evil Queen herself.

A tilt of my head and I whispered, "As far as we know..." We needed to expect anything. If we underestimated him, who else was there? I could not afford to fail. But if he were a sin—and I believed he was—that told us that he was a prince she created and that explained how he knew the history of Orsadia and the magic fountain. He didn't come from another land. He came to stop me from taking the crown but when romance didn't work, he showed his true colors. Contemptuous.

Eventually everything came to light. What hurt most was my father had been so quick to ask me to marry him with no questions asked. Judging me when I *did* ask questions. More contemptuous.

Why did he doubt me? I'd been right about Alexander, although it took me by surprise when he became stronger than I. Why did those closest to me leave a trail of breadcrumbs that I was left to pick up and turn into courage? I should not have had to do such things on my own accord.

I'd tell them to piss off. I'd shut out my father. I'd fight all Fallon's battles for him. I'd tell Luka just how little he provided on this journey we took just for a sliver of control. A fragment of sanity.

Because if I didn't, the poison inside me would no longer be just my own to bear. It'd become a burden to everyone in my path.

What began as a little irritation grew into something much worse.

"Are you prepared to be queen?"

Sizzling from the inside. Threatening to rear its ugly head. Desperate to claw its way out and put everyone in their place for the doubt they showed me.

"Excuse me?"

"Don't be coy, Firefly. Are you prepared? You become queen and this will be all you'll ever know. Do you ever wonder what else exists beyond Orsadia?" And like that, it fizzled out and left smoke in its wake as Luka closed a portion of the distance between us.

Firefly. Where the hell did that nickname stem from?

"I do not wonder. I do not experience onism as others might. This is my home, Luka, and I love every part of it. What else do I need to explore in this world? What else is there for me? My purpose is to become Queen and do right by the people. I was given magic for a reason. To stay, to rule and serve. Not to run like a coward."

"Oh, but don't you understand? Queens last three years on the throne. Another will take your place and you can retire. The world will become your oyster."

Three years? He believed I'd only last three years on the throne. Despicable.

Lifting my chin to meet his gaze, I squeezed the hilt of my sword for comfort. "Who says I want the world to be my oyster?"

"For a girl who fights so hard to run from her past, it's ironic that you'd rather stay in the same place the rest of your life. Where will you go when you're no longer queen?"

"The village. Where everyone goes."

He let out a chuckle with a shake of his head. "You do what you must. Someday I will leave Orsadia. I'm not needed here. I'm not useful. I have no purpose in this land."

A small crack tore through my heart. As irritating as he could be, he was still Orsadia's people. He was still part of the same land that I vowed to take care of, and by saying he was not useful to me, I had made him feel a different kind of worthlessness that nobody deserved.

"I apologize, Luka, for my words. You're not of no use."

A gleam settled in his eyes. "You did not offend me. I have thicker skin than that, Firefly, and how I wish you'd see the man I am. I accept your apology."

Bubbling in my blood. Heat in my cheeks. Numbness in my limbs.

Luka turned on his heel and started towards the door, a cunning game hanging over our heads. He dared to leave me humiliated.

"I take back my apology, Luka! I'm not sorry! You took advantage of my kindness, you bastard." I clenched my fists as I stomped over to him and circled him in a hurry to block his path.

He leaned forward into my space, those river green eyes boring into the very inner depths of my soul and picking apart every fear, desire, and need I could ever have. "Don't offer kindness if you're so hellbent on revoking it."

He stepped around me and left me to the voices in my head.

TEN

"Here," I said, waving Luka over.

Into the cave we descended.

The cave was a series of rooms—all connected. The room I entered had skulls the size of giants. There had been mention of giants in our past, but I had never witnessed evidence until now. It didn't come as a surprise, however. Anything about our world could surface at any given moment.

There was a faint glow from the light illuminating from the outside of the cave, but otherwise, darkness engulfed everything surrounding us. Luka nudged me with his bow, gesturing to my skin. I caught a glimpse of the glow that lit up our path, and it was all because of me. I knew inside Luka's head, he was telling me he was right all along. My power had a purpose—to find the sins and kill them.

We walked down two sets of stairs and came across another giant skull in the middle of the room. "What the hell is this?" I scanned the room for any clues, but nothing gave away where we had ventured into.

Luka ran his hand across the top of the skull. "This looks

like someone's lair. Maybe they were experimenting with giants or something else that was horrid, but this is not somewhere we should be for long. Let's find one, kill him, and get the hell out."

Nodding, I proceeded towards a door. When I walked through, I stopped before I walked off the edge of a broken stone bridge. Below was a glowing green river of water.

"Who are you?" a man asked from behind me, sword pointed into the soft of my neck.

A small smirk formed as I lifted my chin. "Do you not recognize your own princess? I suggest you drop your sword before you make it onto my hit list. I would hate to be in your shoes if I somehow turned cruel."

A moment of hesitation passed before he lowered his weapon. I turned my body to face him, studying his appearance before I lost him forever.

Something in his eyes shimmered and if I dared to guess what it was, I would say this man admired me. It was not every day that I, Snow White, saw admiration in a man's eyes.

"You've worked hard for what you have, have you not?" he asked, curiosity lacing his voice.

I wrapped my fingers around the handle of my sword underneath my cloak. I had to be prepared for the worst to come. "Indeed, I have. Now I must ask, who are you?"

He nodded his head. "My name is Matt. It's short for Matthias, but do not bother yourself with such a name. I ventured on my usual walk and heard some voices." His eyes lowered. "I must say, that is a fine cloak you wear. I have plenty hanging up in my closet, and every single one holds a special place in my heart."

"I'm sure they do. Are you a thief?" I did not hold back on my bluntness. What was the purpose of walking on eggshells for a short conversation? The direction of this topic begged the question if he was after my luxury.

He chuckled. "Nothing of that sort, I assure you."

"Why the interest in my cloak?" I was nothing if not straightforward.

With a shrug, Matt said, "It's a beautiful cloak and one should take pride in what they've earned."

What an interesting choice of words for a man like so.

I took a step forward. "And what do you take pride in, Matt?"

"Myself." His gaze never faltered. "I take pride in my luxuries. I take pride in all the giants I have slaughtered, and that is why their bones are trophies—reminders of what I've achieved. Is that a crime?"

"Answer me this. If a poor man was on the side of the road with no food or warmth, would you offer him your cloak?" How he answered would tell me if he was the man I was looking for.

Matt laughed at my question. "Don't be silly. My cloaks are too good for someone too weak to look for a job. He should get up and work for his earnings the way the rest of us do. I owe no man a damn thing."

I swallowed. Silence laid heavy in the air as I tightened my grip on my sword. I had a chance to take him off guard, and with one movement, I had my sword against his throat.

A playful smile danced in his eyes as he ducked to one side, sending his elbow forward and into my breast. The pain surged for a moment, long enough to hinder my strength. When I gathered myself once more, Luka shot an arrow from higher up in the cave, but Matt jumped out of the way.

He'd heard voices. He knew Luka was down here with me, as the cave echoed every hidden desire we held deep within our bones. It had been foolish of me to assume Luka was invisible to this asshole.

"You'll have to catch me if you wish to defeat that queen you're so sure you can take down." Matt laughed as he ran off into the woods.

Luka and I took off after him, but as we exited the cave, we caught no sign. He could have gone any direction.

What I didn't understand was if he represented pride, too, then what about Alexander? Two who represented pride?

And if I was *self-aware*, I technically made a third.

"Something is wrong, Luka. We should search his cave and see what he knows."

He nodded and we ventured back down. He tried his hardest to mask the seething pain in his leg, but I saw through his façade. I couldn't miss what I'd experienced my whole life.

As we descended further into the darkness where the rivers glowed green, I reached down to dip my fingers through the water, but Luka yanked me back. "Are you crazy? That could be acid or poison!"

"Acid would make a low frequency. Poison? Well, that needs to be ingested."

His eyes roamed every inch of the cave from what the light showed us. "So you know poison, and acid, but that doesn't mean I'm wrong for trying to protect you."

"Protect me? You're no knight, remember?"

Luka placed a hand against the stone wall. "And what is so wrong about a man trying to protect a woman? You can protect me all you wish, Firefly, and it won't hurt my ego a bit. You? You're so terrified of letting people in. That makes you a coward, and if you truly wish to take on the entire world without an ounce of support, then please, don't let me stop you."

I stood, spinning to face him and as I attempted, my heel missed the edge and I fell back. Green engulfed me.

Flailing my arms, I found the surface and gasped. "Damnit, Luka!"

With a shrug, he sent me a playful smile. "What did you want me to do? You don't want a knight in shining armor."

I scowled as I climbed out of the river, patting myself down to ensure my sword was right where I left it. As I wrung out my hair, I shot a glare at Luka. "Let's find his weakness. Kill him."

Luka headed towards one side, and I the other.

It was impossible to tell who pride could be at the point, but I wasn't going to take the risk and allow any to walk free. Nor did I have the time to interrogate either of them.

Sifting through femur bones, ribs, and skulls, I found hardly anything at all.

The air in this hole became muggy.

And without even trying, my skin began to glow.

"There's the firefly," Luka said with a sly smile.

I jabbed his gut with my elbow.

I whipped around with a gasp as the loud shifting of rocks and thumps echoed throughout the cave. "What was that?"

Luka followed me up to the entrance, but a boulder blocked our only way out. And as hard as we tried, our strength was no match.

"He trapped us," I spat.

"That much is obvious." Luka snorted as he headed back down to the bottom floor. "Let's find another way out."

"How can you be sure?"

"Because if Matt lives here, he'd have a back door in case of an emergency." He glanced back at an angle. "Everyone has another escape route."

Grumbling, I followed his lead and we searched for this other back door. My light was all we had to see in the darkness, aside from the river.

Something clanked and rattled in the distance.

"What is that?"

"We find out," he answered, pushing forward.

The sound bounced around, and with the entrance blocked, it never stopped bouncing. Repeating our lines back to us. Never allowing us to forget even a smidgen of determination—and stupidity.

Fingers wrapped around my ankle. A whisper drifted into my ear.

I screamed, drawing my sword and slicing through the air behind me. Was I beginning to lose my mind? No. Impossible. I believed in many things, such as: magic, ghosts, giants, and the undoing of the Evil Queen. What I didn't believe was that we were alone down here.

"Luka, find that back door. Now!"

We took off running full speed as I guided the way. I worked my way along the walls, feeling for doors or holes or any sign of life.

Life.

Ironic, given we were in a graveyard of giants.

We were the only life that blotted these caves like ink on paper.

"Here!" Luka grabbed my bicep, ripping me back before a hand swiped out and reached for my face. Much to our luck, we fell down yet another hole.

With a thump, I landed first. As I tried to sit up, Luka landed right on top of me, keeping careful not to crush me beneath his weight. "Apologies, Firefly. Not my proudest moment, but it was something."

"Then get off me." I seethed.

One flash of a white grin, and then he hurried to his feet, pulling me up from the ground with him. "It seems we've fallen further underground."

Gathering my skirts, I pushed past him. "Then let's not waste time."

We trudged onward, ignoring the rolling of a pebble, the brush of wind, and the eeriness of the silence suffocating us.

"Which way?" We approached a fork in the tunnel.

"Right."

I gave Luka a look. "Why is that?"

"Right is the right way. Left is where you get left behind. Let's move." He moved around me, leading the rest of our journey. I had to give him credit when we approached a door. "See? What did I tell you?" He pressed his shoulder against the door, palm flat, and shoved.

I didn't stand around like a useless statue, either. I helped him push the concrete door open, and before I could stumble forward, his arm wrapped around my waist and I dangled for a second before planting my feet again.

I twisted my body his way to scold him, but he wasn't even looking in my direction. "A mausoleum."

Taken back, I stepped out of his arm and faced the grave. As we walked further and exited the mausoleum, we stood in the center of the cemetery.

Alexander had bested me against my better judgment. Matt escaped our grasp. Here I was back at square one, on the hunt for the seven sins and not a single one to be slaughtered. How pitiful for the next heir to the throne—Queen Snow White.

"Welcome home," he said in a joking manner.

Home.

The graveyard where the dead slept.

And where I'd end up soon enough if I wasn't careful.

ELEVEN

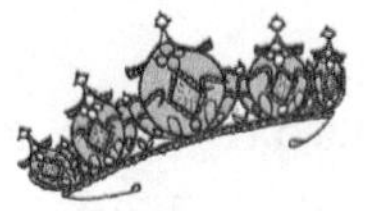

Luka stepped in front of me as I swung my sword around to relish in what would be the defeat of the Evil Queen. "You're brave to assume I won't stab you myself," I said to him.

A smile tugged on his lips as he pulled an arrow from his quiver and waved it in my face. "You should learn how to use a bow and arrow."

I snickered. "You're asking far too much of Snow White. She uses a sword as her weapon. You use a bow and arrow. That's your decision and I will not force you to choose otherwise. Fair?"

He shrugged and stepped forward. "I will be willing to learn how to use a sword if you want to use a bow and arrow."

Narrowing my eyes, I asked, "Why?"

His gaze wandered up towards the treetops as he leaned his arm against the trunk of one tree, crossing an ankle over the other. "It throws our enemies off their game if we are versatile with our skills. Say there's a point in which one of us loses our weapon but the other has it in reach. If you can pick up a bow and arrow and use it as well as you use a sword, nobody stands a chance against you. You'll be fit to be the new queen because you know your way around different weapons to protect your people. Not all villagers have swords, and if you visit them, they'll have just an arrow and a bow to hunt their food." He held out his arrow for me to take.

Inside, my blood was sizzling. I didn't take well to admitting Luka had a good point. Instead, I took the arrow and waved for him to give me his bow as well.

He stepped back as I pulled the arrow against the string. I let it fly but it hit the dirt. Luka had the audacity to laugh at me, and I wanted to put an arrow in his eye for it.

He swiped the arrow from the ground and straightened his posture. "You need to pose yourself. You're doing it all wrong." He grabbed the bow from me and got into position. His arrow hit a tree. "That is how you shoot. Your feet need to be about shoulder length apart, your body ninety degrees from the bow, and your arms exactly as you saw mine. Your front foot needs to be turned about forty-five degrees towards the target, and your chin over the bow arm. Posture straight, but don't lock it into place. Focus on your target, but don't aim directly at it. Aim slightly above because the trajectory or the arrow will curve down a little as it flies."

I growled as I grabbed the bow from him. "All right, let me try again." I did as he said and pretended to shoot an arrow.

Luka laughed at me—*again.* "You're not doing it right." He fixed my arm, then my shoulders and turned me so I was facing him. He squatted and placed my feet where they needed to be before giving me the bow again. "Try with a real arrow this time and remember to aim above your target. Think about the trajectory of the arrow." He handed it to me and took a step back.

As I grabbed it, I fixed my posture and pulled it back, following his directions. The arrow whipped through the air in one movement before slicing the side of the trunk of a tree. "Damn. I was so close."

He took his bow and gathered up his arrows. "You were but it'll take a lot of practice."

"Ready to learn how to use a sword?" I gave him my best smirk as I picked my sword up from the ground. "I doubt you know how to swing one."

He reached out. "Let me make you cry."

As I handed him the sword, a wail pierced the air. Both of us winced as it grew louder, cutting the air like glass. I dropped my blade and covered my ears. Luka used his fingers to plug his.

It stopped as suddenly as it began and we lowered our arms.

"What the hell was that?" I spun in every direction to figure out where it had come from.

Luka stiffened. "A wailing banshee."

I almost choked on my own saliva. "I thought they were a myth." Although, it wasn't the first time I'd heard that sound. I never put the puzzle pieces together.

"In Orsadia, most myths are true. Wailing banshees. Curses. Evil queens. Magic fountains..." He rubbed the bridge of his nose. "Wailing banshees... They're like locks of hair. Whoever hears them is meant to die next."

I furrowed my brows. I'd heard them for years and yet I was still alive. Was I going to die trying to defeat the Evil Queen? I refused to believe such nonsense.

Shaking my head, I said, "You heard it, too. There must be another reason. You're not going to die. I'm definitely not going to die."

The caw of a crow echoed in the trees. Crows followed me everywhere, and I never understood why that was. Not until now...

"Luka, it's me. I think it's me." Maybe my curse theory was true. Death was something that followed curses, and if I was cursed to become evil, I was responsible for breaking the curse. How could such a thing be done?

That had been why my father put a spell to protect me.

He let out another chuckle. His laugh was really beginning to irritate my insides, like bugs trying to burrow their way out of my body. "What? No."

"That's not the first time I've heard the banshee. Crows caw around me all the time. That lock of hair happened when I was around, and dare I tell you that they've been happening as long as I've been born. I don't know quite how else to explain this predicament, but I believe I'm the cause of this. I'm the *symbol of death*, at least until I defeat the Evil Queen and show Orsadia that I'm going to make this land a better place to live."

His smile fell. "You think you're a curse."

"Not a curse. *Cursed.* It's the only explanation that makes an ounce of sense. Have you ever considered why death follows me? I suppose nobody has, but I've wondered a few times. Most times, I wonder about this curse, and I'm the key to breaking it. However, many princesses before me have defeated the evil queens and they still turned evil, so something suspicious hangs in the balance. How do I break that curse?" I picked up my sword again and slid it into its sheath.

He shrugged. "If we are to answer that question, we must find what caused it."

I lifted my chin. "How do we find the root?"

His eyes darted back towards my home. "Does Drecose Castle have a library? Libraries have books and books have answers. Maybe it's time for a history lesson."

The wind whipped through the strands of my hair. "That would be a wonderful idea if I hadn't already checked my own library for answers. My best guess is the queen knows, or she has the books that explain everything. However, she's not willing to offer us any help to break whoever placed this curse upon us."

He grumbled as he turned to walk another direction. He was headed back to the castle.

"Luka, get your ass back here." I jogged to catch up, circling around and stopping in front of him. "You are not going to find answers there."

"What are you afraid of? Being wrong?" He lifted an eyebrow.

I released a groan. Why did he have to go there? I was afraid of nothing. "Let me lead the way." I spun on my heel and began walking us back.

Luka wasn't too fond of being in the back, so he strode up until we walked side by side. "I can't wait to actually meet your family when I'm not bleeding out. What are they like?"

"We're going to find answers. You're not meeting my family."

He snorted and used his fingers to brush through his dark, messy hair. "Whatever Snow White says."

The walk lasted what seemed like forever. With Luka, anything dragged on for an eternity.

As we approached Drecose, I halted and faced Luka. "I mean it, we are here for one reason."

"I got it." He put his hands up, but as soon as we started crossing the wooden bridge, he pointed at the water and said, "there's where I saved you. Have you gotten a handle on your anger issues yet?"

I squeezed until my knuckles turned white. When we entered the courtyard, I relaxed again. He was on my turf now. He had no leverage here.

The door slowly opened and my father stood at the entrance. "Lana, you're back. Who is this?" Luka never had a chance to meet my family when the medic was tending to his wound. I'd forbid them from it.

"Father, we have important business to attend to. We don't have time to get to know one another."

I walked past him, but Luka stopped to shake his hand. "It's an honor to meet you, sir. I'm Luka, the huntsman."

Father gave me a look as his lips curved up for him. "Are you helping Lana with her journey?"

Luka sent a smile in return. "I am."

Fallon came down the stairs and saw Luka. "Who is this?" It was no secret that Fallon thought my partner was far more attractive than Alexander, especially knowing what I knew about that damned prince. "Snow, who did you find in those woods?"

I brushed my hair from my face. "Nobody. He's nobody. We're going now."

Yet, Luka went over to Fallon to introduce himself all the same. "I didn't know that Snow had a little brother. She hardly tells me anything."

I stomped a foot. "Luka, get your ass to the library."

However, this journey was put on a longer delay as my mom came from the kitchen. "Oh, a new boy! How wonderful. Hello, I'm Snow's mother." She shook his hand.

"We have work to do! Does anyone hear me? Am I invisible?" I shouted, throwing my arms up.

Luka kissed my mother's hand. "It no longer plagues my mind as to where Snow got her looks from."

My mother giggled as if she were a young teen again who just discovered crushes for the first time. I knew they all thought maybe Luka was my suitor, but he wasn't. There was no room in this quest for me to date anyone and Luka was far from my type.

"Now we know why you didn't want Alexander," Fallon joked. "Luka is a real looker."

I grabbed Luka's hand and started to drag him up the stairs. "Goodbye!"

We had to walk a few stone bridges before we made it to the

tower where the library was. I locked the door to avoid any more interruptions for today.

Dropping into a chair, I sighed. "We have work to do, and we don't need more distractions."

Since Luka thought it was such a great idea to slow down our progress with introductions, he would get the honor of finding the books and climbing the ladder. It was the least he could do for ignoring my wishes.

He nodded while grabbing some books. "What's your brother's name?"

"Fallon. You can have a go at him when this is over, if that's your thing." I pulled a book from his hand and skimmed the pages.

"Have a go at him?" He sat. "Fallon is gay?"

I peered at him, placing the book in my lap and crossing my arms as I leaned back into my chair. "Yeah, everyone knows. Surprised you don't. The bullies tell everyone as if it's something to be ashamed of."

He seemed to know everything, but this was something he hadn't paid attention to. It was hard to ignore. The people of Orsadia were not always so accepting of Fallon. As kids, I had to protect him from the bullies who tried to humiliate him. Fallon came before anyone else in my life and he always would. He was my best friend, even if he didn't quite agree with my method of becoming queen.

He shrugged. "He's nice, but I'm not into men."

"You could've fooled me," I snickered, my snide comment hitting him in all the wrong places.

"Am I supposed to be offended that you assumed my sexuality? Like you said, Firefly, it's nothing to be ashamed of. Not worshipping you like Alexander did upon your first meeting does not a gay man make."

"Wasn't why I made the observation, but be my guest."

Silence fell over us for barely a minute before Luka decided to respond. Once I was queen, I'd never have to see him again. I had that to hold onto.

With a smile plastered to his lips, he leaned forward, his eyes glued to a book. "Between you and I, I'm secretly into princesses who refuse to be damsels."

TWELVE

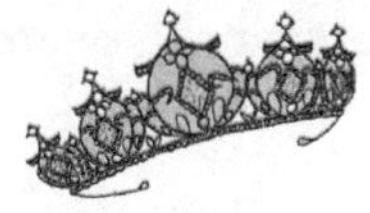

Running into the forest after spotting Matt, he spun around and held out his sword, eyes sending us warning shots. As if I'd listen.

"You won't live to see tomorrow," I threatened.

"Watch me." He jabbed his blade at us, but Luka spun around and let go of me before he could have a chance to get me in the gut.

Luka's cries were impossible to miss underground as his wound hindered him from fighting. I supposed that was why he needed the bow and arrows.

I hit the column and caught my balance. I knew deep down, I was angry at so many people. My blood rose at the thought of what bullies did to my brother, but in the end, I knew they'd never amount to anything. And my parents were still my parents. I knew more about myself than I ever had before. I didn't choose my history, but I did love the people in it.

Facing Matt, I pulled my sword from my belt. "You take pride in death. You can't feel anything else. You're using your insecurities to fuel your pride because someone has to be blamed, correct?" I swung and missed him. "But the reality is, you're nothing more than your ego. All you've done is shed blood and look down on those who've held you up on your pedestal. Nobody to actually be proud of you. I have real people who love me for who I am." I swung at him again, nicking his skin.

"Liar!" he screamed. He ducked and charged at me, tackling me to the ground. He pinned me down, his sword to my throat. "You have nobody."

I relaxed my muscles. "I used to think that. I thought nobody understood me or what I wanted, but I learned the truth. My parents are afraid of what this curse could make of me, and yet they still love me the same. My brother loves me despite knowing I'm out here getting myself killed by leaving for days at a time. That is unconditional love, and it can never be bought. I pity you for never getting to experience something so wonderful." I kneed him in the back. All lies I told to weaken my enemy. He knew, but I made such a convincing argument. Confidence was key.

He choked on some air as I knocked the blade from his hand and threw him to the dirt. I wrapped my fingers around the hilt of my sword and stood, pointing it at his neck.

"Do it. Kill me," he antagonized.

"I thank you, Matt, for teaching me that I myself am not pride. I have a chance at defeating this curse."

He laughed, coughing some more. "You have no idea what you're about to get yourself into." Before he could say more, I thrusted my sword forward, right into his jugular. Blood poured like milk from a bottle.

Blood.

No, that couldn't be right. They were hallucinations. Made up from the Evil Queen's magic. They shouldn't have been able to bleed.

What did that mean? What did that make me? A murderer? Would she require me to spill blood simply to acquire her throne? Possibly. To throw me off. To force me to surrender. Would I?

My shoulders slumped as the rest of me drained. Luka hurried over and wrapped his arms around my shoulders. "He's dead, Firefly. You killed him, and that makes you badass."

I lowered my arm, a sad smile forming. "I suppose." I leaned into his form. "But I need good sleep to recover from the fact that I'm no better than *her.*"

Luka leaned closer and pressed his lips against my hair. "Are you asking me to be your knight in shining armor?"

"Never. I would never ask such a thing." I glanced up at him, a smirk plastered on my lips as I sheathed my sword. "I just need to recharge from a battle."

"Nothing wrong with one soldier helping another recover."

"You thought it would be that easy?" Matt pressed his hand against his neck as blood wove between his fingers.

Luka and I stepped back, unsure of how he had survived. Nobody survived a loss in the jugular. Something was wrong.

A mirage.

If they could not die, or had multiple lives, then I could not be called a killer.

That removed the shaking from my breath and the numbness from my limbs. Everything was right with the world again. This time, I wouldn't doubt myself. I'd eliminate these sins with my head held high.

"Come get me, Snow White." His eyes screamed crazy but his form shouted military. Somehow, he'd managed to make my given name sound like a swear. So much for renaming myself.

I shot Luka a look and took off after Matt. He was fast and I'd be a liar to deny the truth in front of my eyes, but that didn't stop me from following him.

As I closed in on him, he slid down into the hole surrounded by rocks—his underground cave. We went right in without caution.

I twisted my sword a few times before gripping the handle and holding it in front of me for protection. "I know you're in here, Matt. You can't hide from me." Scanning the darkness, my skin began to light my path as if on cue.

I took a few steps forward before Luka tapped my shoulder and pointed towards a set of stairs that led further into the cave.

We both headed down, our weapons drawn and on the prowl. I reminded myself that Matt had his fists to protect him. He couldn't be a match against us. My training led me to this moment, and I was desperate to prove to everyone I could do this. If not, what else was I good for?

"Which way did he go?" Luka asked from behind.

I pointed at the water using my blade. "He couldn't have gotten across this unless he jumped in and climbed up the other side. He's in here somewhere and we'll find him."

Luka cleared his throat. "To avoid last week's obstacle, we may want to guard the entrance."

"We? You mean you, correct?" I faced him. "Good idea, Luka. You stand guard while I hunt this asshole. I warn you not to kill him. Capture him as you see fit but if his blood is on *your* hands, I've already lost against the Evil Queen and that is not a road I'm willing to walk. Understood?"

He flashed me a playful smile. "Yes, My Queen." He left the cave before I had a chance to scold him for mocking me.

I backed up and spun in a circle, holding my sword out in case it caught on something. "You can't hide forever. I will find you. I will kill you. The longer you hide, the worse your punishment will be, and the longer your death will be prolonged."

A laugh echoed but I couldn't pinpoint the direction from which it came. He thought I couldn't take him out. I *lived* for proving people wrong.

Something flashed by in a hurry as if Matt had run from point A to point B. I followed the direction he went, turning the corner and running up the stairs. He stopped at the top and faced me, a smirk on his lips. "It is a shame you made the mistake of following me up the stairs."

He pulled a bottle from his jacket and poured it down the steps. I attempted to walk up but the liquid was slick, and I tumbled all the way down. I had no way of getting to him unless I found another way out of this cave.

I wanted that throne enough to get my clothes wet.

I headed back to the doorway and stopped before the pool of green water. "This is your way out, Snow. Do it," I told myself.

Taking the plunge, I jumped into the water and hit the bottom, pushing myself back up to the surface. I swam over to the rocks and gripped, pulling my weight. Within five minutes, I was on my feet, walking through the other doorway.

My wet clothes weighed heavy on my muscles, but I wasn't about to let this asshole walk free. The Evil Queen thought she could stop me. Surely it was pathetic to see the attempts.

As my eyes darted to my right, I noticed the table of blood. Matt thought giants were worthy, or he thought they were an abomination to our world.

I headed up the stairs to my left and came upon two pillars. Nothing about them was special. They guarded the middle of the room to attract onlookers. They imitated what people thought a princess was for—to look *pretty*.

I passed between them and ended up in a cave of rocks with a skull at the end. What caught my attention was the light that shined down on me from the sky. Matt was foolish to believe I didn't have a plan, and now he would pay the ultimate price for such a grave mistake.

With one foot on a rock, I grabbed another and began hoisting myself up the rock side of the cave. The sun grew closer and the floor shrunk as I made my way to the top. I peeked above the ground to see Luka standing at the cave entrance with Matt in hand.

We both knew it had been smart to have him keep watch.

I clawed the dirt and used all of my strength to drag myself up onto it. Once standing, I stalked towards Matt like a predator to its prey and pulled my sword from its sheath.

"My apologies, Matt, but your death will be quick." One swing, and his head was rolling down into the cave opening once again. Luka dropped his body to the floor and stepped back. Blood splatter stained both of our faces, and we'd need to wash it off before finding our next victim. "To the fountain."

We both headed there, only spending about an hour and a half walking. When we arrived, I sat on the edge, scooping water up to my face. Luka had done the same and eventually all the blood washed away as if our sins were no more. I'd certainly attain a clean slate once I defeated the queen and removed this curse upon Orsadia. I looked forward to the day when I made the history books for an entirely different reason.

"Where to next?" I glanced at Luka for answers.

He leaned back and closed his eyes for a moment. "We haven't tried many places. We could go to the cemetery, or the tower. Someone in the village must be one."

"Someone..." I narrowed my eyes to focus my gaze on the trees. What about Zoe? She seemed a bit suspicious and I wanted to get to the root of her problem with me.

When I jumped up from the fountain's edge, I'd moved just a bit too quickly.

Vertigo.

Luka rushed over in mere seconds, steadying me with his grip on my shoulders. "You all right? You don't look so hot, Firefly. We should maybe turn in for the night and begin fresh tomorrow, once your energy is replenished."

"I'm fine," I forced out as my legs gave way.

Why had fatigue taken hold of me so suddenly?

Luka lifted me in his arms, carrying me on the long journey back to his cave. A breeze brushed by, reminding me that winter would be on its way. It could hit in days, or it could hit in weeks. It was never an exact science amongst our land.

"Tomorrow we may try the cemetery," he said in a low voice. "Seeing as our underground cave leads there. Matt shouldn't have been able to survive a hit to the throat and yet he did, his blood not fazing him in the slightest. Even his body had not been fazed. Do you believe that?"

"I believe a lot in this world, Luka, so yes I do indeed believe that." My head rolled against his shoulder. "Death follows me, so why not follow it instead? I think the cemetery is a great idea." Zoe would have to wait her turn.

"The cemetery it is, then." He continued his walk, not once complaining about the weight or the wound in his leg.

My eyelids grew heavier with every inhale of his breath. My light had only just now begun to dim despite us being out under the sunlight. If I hadn't been so hellbent on taking the throne, I might have had a chance to explore more about it. But for now, that mission would have to take the back burner.

As I closed my eyes and drifted from this land, I heard his voice heavy as he brought his lips close to my temple, "Sweet dreams, My Queen."

THIRTEEN

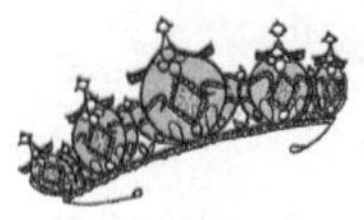

Luka was passed out in his cave which gave me a chance to sneak away. The first place I stopped at was Drecose Castle. I took a shower to cleanse myself before grabbing some products to help control the bleeding that seemed to grace me every month.

I didn't head back to Luka's cave when I finished. Instead, I ventured out on my own and headed towards the cemetery. I carried a lantern with me since darkness engulfed our land and fog hung thick in the air.

It seemed like a long shot but if death was following me, I needed to visit where death was most prominent. We'd searched those books for answers and yet we found nothing. I'd been right all along but Luka was afraid to admit that.

As I approached the cemetery, I gave it a second thought. Maybe this wasn't the right idea, and I could turn back now. However, I needed to cross off all possibilities of breaking this curse before I found the real one.

I stepped inside the gates and closed them behind me. There weren't many tombs in the cemetery. When people began dying, not everyone could afford a plot. Eventually, all the plots filled up and people had to bury their loved ones outside of these gates. There were many tombstones a little bit to the left of the graveyard.

I'd stumbled upon a skeleton decaying in the earth as vines smothered the bones and flowers bloomed from crevices. A lovely grave if one asked me. A fitting way to give back to the environment even when they'd long passed.

I uttered a few words in respect to the body as I moved on.

Walking through, I stopped near one that had a skull resting against the stone. I scanned the rest of the cemetery, but this was the only one with a cracked skull missing its jaw, and I knew I had to do something that wasn't ethical by any means.

I walked over to the corner of the fence and grabbed the shovel. I headed back to the tombstone and stabbed the dirt, picked up a pile, and threw it to the side. I repeated this until I hit something hard, and by the time I got there, I dropped the shovel and squatted over the coffin. "Who is inside this grave?"

It wasn't respectful of me to dig up a corpse but if it helped people in the future, was it not worth it?

I grabbed the edge of the lid and pulled it until it came loose. I lifted it to see inside and as I leaned over the coffin with my lantern in hand, a gust of cold air rushed towards my face.

The coffin was empty.

"No, an empty coffin, that isn't right," I whispered. "This should have bones."

I lifted my eyes until the name of the tombstone stared me dead in the face.

Aalia Drecose.

She was the original queen. The first. The one with whom the curse began. Drecose Castle was named after her. She'd been the first chosen queen which is why her legend was the most powerful. The end to this curse must have had something to do with her, and yet, her bones were missing.

Wind whipped through my hair as I stood to my feet and turned the other way. Someone stole her bones, or Aalia Drecose wasn't really dead. Those were my theories.

If I went with theory one, why would someone take her bones? Maybe the magic in them could be used to reverse a curse. I had to find them if that were true.

If theory two was correct, I had to find Aalia and use her help to lift this curse. However, the hardest part would be proving which theory was the right one. Who else knew Aalia in person? Nobody here. It'd been over a hundred years since she lived. Nobody in Orsadia was immortal, including those with magic.

Maybe she was...

Maybe this curse gave her immortality.

I turned on my heel to leave but the gates slammed shut. Metal clinked together and echoed into the sky as the squeak of the rusty metal pierced my ears.

"Who's there?" I asked.

No response.

Fingers brushed through my hair and I spun around, the lantern jerking to my right. Nobody was there. "No, ghosts are not real, Snow. You know that." However, everything in Orsadia seemed to be coming true lately.

"Find me..." a female whispered.

I grabbed my sword, before reminding myself I couldn't use a sword against someone who wasn't actually there in solid form. "Who? Find who? Are you Aalia Drecose?"

The voice was gone now, and the wind came to a sudden stop. Everything went still—an eerie silence draping over the gravestones. However, the fog didn't lift.

"Who are you?" I yelled.

I got no response again. Whoever had been here was refusing to talk, or they were already gone.

After I put my sword away, I tightened my fingers around my lantern. I took a few steps backwards, but something else illuminated. *I* glowed.

Even in the darkest of nights, I could light up a home full of corpses. Chills ran down my spine, goosebumps rising along my skin as my hair shot up.

"Whoever you are, you are more than welcome to stay here. I'll be leaving and unless you tell me who you are, I can't find you." I walked towards the gates but stopped when the same skull by the tombstone now sat at the base of the gates.

I assumed if this skull could move itself, whoever it belonged to wanted me to touch it. Blood was pouring from between my legs at this moment—thanks to the *lovely* gift that came with a woman's reproduction—so the thought of holding a skull didn't bother me all that much.

Bending down, I clutched it. "I will find you. I will destroy this curse that plagues our land."

With those words drifting between every resting place, I left without looking back.

It wasn't usual to be carrying a skull with me, but I needed it to find whoever it belonged to, and I was assuming it belonged to Aalia. It had been at her tombstone and the rest of her bones were missing. If this was hers, she wasn't alive. However, she was still connected to the curse. She was the first victim of it and finding her was the key to breaking it for good.

"I'm not making this up, Luka. A curse plagues Orsadia. Every queen is destined to be evil, including me. If I don't find the rest of Aalia's bones, we will never see a brighter future." I gestured to the skull in my arms.

Luka put his hands up, taking a step back. "Do what helps you, Snow, but I will not be touching any skulls, *or* burning bones. I came for one quest. I came to help you become queen. If you are so adamant on this curse, how can you prove it's real?"

I pushed my chest out and lifted my chin higher. "Every queen is evil. I fear I could be next. I don't want to gain pleasure from taking a life. I want to do what's best for the people of Orsadia and not just what's best for me."

"You will. Look at you; you're already doing good. You're putting people first. You're trying to eradicate a curse for our home. How is that not enough to become queen?"

I swallowed all my remarks. "A curse doesn't care what I want. A curse will poison me from the inside out. I will become victim to the poison dwelling within and eventually, I will be shedding blood for sport. That is not a future I accept."

Luka left the cave to get fresh air or food. I glanced at the skull, but something in the pit of my stomach didn't sit right. Nausea washed over me. Maybe Luka had a point, and I was looking too far into this. Maybe this was the Evil Queen's ploy to throw me off my game. I was going to defeat her, and no curse could stop me. If this curse was real, it had to come second. My top priority was my quest to become queen.

"Luka, wait," I said as I followed him out. "Luka." I rushed over to him, but he stood at the edge of the cliff, looking over the entire ocean as waves crashed against the base. "What is it?"

"Do you ever wonder if there's anyone else out there?"

"Excuse me?"

He looked at me. "Out there. Beyond the ocean. Do you think maybe there are other lands and we're not the only people here?" He pointed to the horizon.

I shrugged. "What does it matter? They're of no importance to us. Our focus should be Orsadia and our people. They're what matter most and what kind of queen would I be if I was worried about other people I don't know? I'm a firm believer in fixing your home first before you fix others. I won't leave these people behind."

Luka tilted his head. "Maybe one day, Snow, when Orsadia is a beautiful place, we can build a ship and sail to find others. Do you think they have magic?"

"Why is your mind filled with so many questions about other lands? What is your fascination with such things?"

He faced me. "I may spend my days hunting for food and surviving but unlike you, Snow, I haven't spent my life training to defeat an evil queen. I have time on my hands—time I spend wondering about things that interest me. Believe it or not, I'm not just a huntsman who thinks about killing animals for food. I have thoughts up here. Do you have any of your own that don't come from the Evil Queen and her reign?"

I gritted my teeth. "If I am to become a queen, I must think like one. These childish thoughts do not faze me." I waved him off with my hand before walking back into the cave.

I sat beside the skull and leaned against the wall. Luka could insult me all he wanted but if he wanted an *upstanding* queen, he would be thankful that all I thought about was what I needed to do to get there. A woman didn't become a good queen by hoping for the best.

She had to work for it, as hard and tired as it may have been. Someday very soon, I would make it and when the day came, it couldn't be about me or my childish thoughts. It had to be about our people. I was only preparing myself for what was coming, and Luka was foolish to think I wasn't serious about upholding such a title.

Someday I was going to die, and I wanted people to still be talking about my rulership long after I was gone. I wished to hear that I was the one who did not succumb to the darkness. I was going to be the change I wished to see.

As I closed my eyes, my muscles relaxed. I'd been up all night trying to find the source of the curse. I made progress, but now I needed to finish my sleep if I was going to recharge. Luka could eat breakfast by himself this morning.

I slipped away from reality into a void. Slowly, the void filled with color and my dream formed a new reality while I was away. In this world, everything seemed so simple.

There was no such thing as a curse. I was already queen, and I wasn't filled with wickedness. Orsadia was a happy place to live and I could sleep well knowing that was what my future *could* be. Orsadia finally deserved a queen that was going to put them first.

Wherever Aalia Drecose was, she would have to wait. I would eventually find her and restore what once was, but I first needed to take down the Evil Queen. Orsadia needed me and I didn't train most of my life to set aside my quest for a curse. I trained to defeat her, and I was going to see to it I did just that.

"Wake up, Snow," the voice started. "We have to go into the village today, and I will not let your silly side journeys get in the way. If you want victory, sleep will not get you there." They kicked my foot just enough to get my body into motion.

I jolted awake, heart pounding and sweat glistening against my skin.

One last look at the skull with a missing jaw.

I feared maybe the skull itself was what haunted me in nightmares and during my waking hours.

As I looked up, expecting to see Luka, I swallowed all fear chilling my bones. Nobody was in the cave, and now I was losing my sanity for the sake of what was supposed to be just a ridiculous burden that loomed over my head.

FOURTEEN

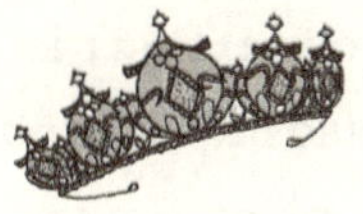

He gestured to the skull in my arms. "I can't believe you brought someone's skull with us," Luka said as he shook his head.

"Not someone's skull, but Aalia's," I corrected.

We approached the village, and people greeted us. However, when they saw the skull, they stepped away. I knew that look. They feared I was turning wicked, but I'd show them otherwise.

We approached a little stand and I pulled out some of my coins. "How much for a bag of pears?" I asked the clerk.

Luka leaned over. "And a bag of apples."

Rolling my eyes, I put the coins on the counter. "Yes, a bag of apples and a bag of pears."

The clerk smiled and gave me my bags, taking the coins. "Thank you, Princess."

We turned and took our fruits. When I dropped my skull, I leaned down to pick it up, but a pair of hands got to it first. I glanced at Luka, but he just gave me a weird look. I followed the arms to their owner. A man handed it back to me.

"An odd thing for a princess to be carrying, don't you think?" he asked.

I cleared my throat. "And who are you to be questioning what I do?"

He stepped closer. "Samael. My name is Samael."

Luka bit into an apple. "Great name, but we should get going. We have business to attend to."

Samael chuckled. "Of course. Don't let me intrude. Although, if you want to stay a bit, I could help." He pointed to the skull. "I know that is Aalia's. I saw you sneaking into the cemetery last night. If you didn't yell, it wouldn't have caught my attention."

Luka put his hand out. "Thanks, but we don't need help."

"Hold on now, yes we do." I gave Luka a look. "I do. If he has any information on Aalia, I need to hear it. You can go..." I scanned the village and saw Zoe. "Flirt with her. Samael and I will be chatting about the first queen." I nodded and walked with Samael. "Well, what is it that you know?"

He shrugged. "I know she *was* magic. Aalia was said to be one of the best queens, and she wasn't always evil. However, she struggled with...control."

"How so?"

He smirked. "She loved sex. Could you blame the woman? She was stunning. She could get any man, so why wouldn't she take advantage of it?"

I looked down at the missing jaw, scenarios running through my mind as to how it went missing in the first place. "How do you know she wasn't always evil?"

He leaned in and whispered, "It's knowledge every queen has of those before them. But you have to be close with the queen to know."

I backed away and swallowed. "You know the Evil Queen. What do you want with me?"

He shook his head. "No, it is nothing like that. I do not work for her. I once did, before I changed. She tried to kill me, but I've been on the run. She can never find me. Once you're queen, I won't need to worry anymore about a reward for my head."

I pressed my lips into a thin line. "I suppose not. However, I don't know if I can trust you. We just met. You could be here to stop me from defeating her."

He smiled but it never quite reached his eyes. Uncanny valley, almost. Like a doll. "I could be...but I'm not." He pointed to the skull. "Aalia was once pure of heart. Well, as pure as one could get having slept with every man. I'm surely not one to judge, though. I've had my fair share of women. Aalia was kind. She wanted to change things around Orsadia. One day, she became wicked. She became venom from the fang of a serpent. Nobody is certain of why she did, but we know that she wasn't always that way."

"How did she die?"

Samael looked at the people. "When Aalia was defeated by the second princess, she became a commoner. The villagers felt betrayed by her. She was hanged for her crimes against Orsadia, but it didn't stop there. Every queen since has been tainted by sin, and now the villagers blame her for everything. We all wish queens didn't exist, but since you still hold power over us, we're afraid to treat you wrong. They know if you become queen and remember how we insulted you, you'll use that as leverage to destroy our lives."

A frown disgraced my expression. "Never. I would never hurt or threaten you. You're just trying to survive, and I want to be a good queen."

He let out a sigh. "That's what *every* princess says."

"I'm offended that you would think such a thing of me." I turned to walk away.

"Just answer me this. What makes you so different from the others before you?" He folded his arms across his chest.

I gulped down my pride, but I didn't know how to answer. What *did* make me any different? Maybe every princess before me had promised they would never put themselves first, and yet that was exactly what they did. Aalia needed me to find her for a reason, right?

"Samael, I can't do this right now. I have to find the other six sins and defeat her. If I don't, something worse could happen."

"Worse? Has any princess ever lost? No. How do we know for sure that something worse could happen than becoming an evil queen? This is a genuine question." He closed the gap between us. "Why do you have this skull?"

I tightened my grip on it, feeling it *belonged* to me now. "Last night, Aalia was there. She was telling me to find her and the rest of her bones were missing. I have to believe that I can be a better queen because if I don't, why fight?"

"Exactly. Don't win. Let yourself be just a princess. Being queen is not all that exciting."

Narrowing my eyes, I growled. "You work for her. You're trying to stop me from victory. I see through your game."

"No, Snow, I swear I'm not trying to play a game. I'm being serious. I'm not allowed to say why, but defeating the Evil Queen is not the best idea. You will turn rotten to the core like an apple."

Luka heard the commotion and approached with no caution. "What's going on?"

I slapped Samael and started walking away. Luka followed but this time, Samael didn't. Nobody got away with telling me I was going to fail the curse like every other before me.

"Snow, what happened?" Luka asked, trying to keep up with me.

"He's an asshole and nothing more."

Luka glanced back at Samael. "What if he's...one of them? A sin?"

"Doubt it. If he was, we'd know by now."

He shook his head, clinging to his theory. "He could be. He seems to know about Aalia and maybe there's a reason. Maybe he's working for the Evil Queen and he's a sin but he's hiding it because he truly doesn't want you to win. Matt didn't want you to win because he took pride in being the best. But Samael... He could be one of them, too."

I stopped in my tracks. "And what, Luka? Go back and tell him we think he's one of our sins and we have to kill him?"

He laughed. "Damn, Firefly. No, I'm suggesting we spy on him. If we stick around these parts, we can find out if he's really a sin or not."

I sighed with the shake of my head, glancing at the village people who struggled to survive. "He's not. I talked to him. Matt is dead so pride is off the table. He isn't fat so it's not gluttony. He can't be sloth because he's not lazy. Lazy people get killed and he claims to be on the run. Greed? Maybe, but doubt it. Envy? He could envy being one of us. Maybe he wants our magic or our title. He's not wrath. He has a better handle on his anger than I do. Lust? Well, he did mention he's slept with many women."

Luka's eyes darted to Samael. "We'll know for sure by spying on him. If he really is a sin and we walk away, you'll hate yourself for it. It's not worth the risk, is it?"

I knew he was right. There had to be a reason Samael was in my life, and maybe this was it. "We spy on him for a day. If he doesn't prove to be one of them, we leave."

"And if he does prove he's a sin?"

"Then we do what we did to Matt. We slice his head from his body. We move on to the next part of our journey and hope more of these sins just walk into our lives." I nodded.

Luka agreed to my plan. The two of us followed closely behind Samael. He had ventured off into the forest, and it wasn't as easy to keep quiet with crunching leaves beneath our feet.

Samael stopped, and so did we. Then he continued on.

Hours passed. Dusk fell. Dawn arrived.

We walked through Ash Forest and over the bridge of the river, and at one point, the trees had changed from orange and yellow to pink and red. When we passed through the last of the trees, we came upon a tall stone tower that had been abandoned.

"I don't suppose a girl is locked up there," I whispered to Luka.

As for why Samael was here, we couldn't say.

He walked to the edge of the cliff and watched the waves the way Luka and I had yesterday. Nothing seemed out of the ordinary for this guy, and this was beginning to look a lot like a waste of a trip.

"You really shouldn't follow people," Samael said.

Luka emerged from the trees. "And what's the reason for that? It seems suspicious the way you told Snow not to become queen—to give up her crown."

Samael shrugged. "I did it for her safety and she didn't want to listen. That's not on me."

I rushed out of the trees, hand in front of me. "Hold on now, you are the one insulting me. Has anyone taught you how to talk to a woman? You do not tell a woman she'll become the villain and she's no exception. Not a single woman wants to hear such things."

He turned to face us. "And yet I get many women in bed with me. I don't think you have a right to tell me how to talk to a woman when you've proven time and time again that you're offended by men helping you. If you are going to criminalize a man for being a decent human being, I am allowed to ask you why you think you're the exception to this curse you speak of."

A humorless laugh erupted from the hollow of my stomach. "Answer me this. Are you one of the seven sins I must kill or not?"

He stepped forward and kept a straight face. "I just happen to be a man who once worked for the Evil Queen as I told you before. Is that a good enough answer for you, Princess?"

Somewhere inside my soul, I knew he called me that to piss me off. He was lying, and I could see right through his little game. He wasn't going to throw me off track. I had to find out if he really was one of the seven sins, and I would do so by tempting him in six different ways.

"This is more than a game, Samael. This is about life or death and I will not be another blood stain on the queen's gown. So, I ask you one more time, and don't be afraid to answer this correctly. Are you one of the seven sins or not?" I walked forward, my fingers wrapped around the handle of my sword.

In four simple words, he replied, "You've caught me, Princess."

It was a mistake on his part. The lies, deceit, and now the truth. It was up to me to tempt him and he was going to reveal which he was one way or another. His blood would have to quench the thirst of Orsadia.

FIFTEEN

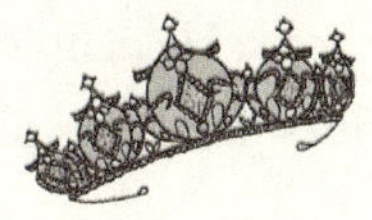

I circled Samael, eyeing him from head to toe. "We all know Matt is dead, so pride is out of the question. Are you envy, greed, or lust?"

He shrugged, never fully meeting my gaze. A tell, they called them. A lie. "I'm Samael."

I sniffed the air. "I smell bullshit." I pulled some gold coins from the pocket inside my cloak. "These are beautiful, are they not?"

Samael cleared his throat. "They are. But they're just coins, Snow. They're gold coins used for currency and that is all their value holds." He leaned against the side of the tower, his posture loose and his face unbothered.

The coins didn't interest him, so greed couldn't be his sin. I dropped them into my pocket and snapped it shut again. "All right, so you don't like gold. That leaves me two options. Envy or lust."

As for how I could tempt him with envy, I couldn't answer that. However, lust was as easy as they came.

Grabbing the bottom of my bodice, I pulled it down. I fixed the neckline and pushed my breasts up. Luka swallowed and tried to look anywhere else, but Samael didn't do the same. It was a known fact that men just happened to love what women offered.

I placed my hands on my waist and lifted my chin. "Well? What is it, Samael?"

It wasn't long before his eyes met mine. "Piss poor attempt." But not a lie when he gave me his full attention.

Every last breath left my body. He hadn't been affected, and maybe I had lost enough of my sanity that I was playing a game that had no players.

"You've made your point Samael." I faced Luka. "We're leaving."

Samael didn't say a word, but Luka did, "He's lying."

"No, he isn't. He proved that I'm crazy. I wish to leave before this escalates into something it's not. Please, let's go." I swung my arm for him to walk in front of me.

He grumbled and dropped it. We walked back to his cave for the night. I lost my appetite when I found out I was wrong about Samael. I despised being wrong. Luka had no issue devouring the juicy bird and squirrel he caught, but it made me nauseous—the smell alone causing last night's dinner to travel back up.

"Rest up. It'll be a long day tomorrow," he said once he finished. He laid back on the ground. When Luka slept, he rested an arm over his eyes, while the other stayed under his head as a pillow. He always fell asleep on his back, however.

I took note of that, placing it right behind my sly smile.

I pulled my cloak off and made a thin cushion on the ground. As soon as my head hit the hood, I was out.

Something was touching my arm. A dog? No, Luka didn't have a dog.

A feather? Nobody was using a feather here, and I knew that was a moronic suggestion.

A finger. It had to be a finger. Luka wouldn't do that to me, would he?

I opened my eyes but as soon as I saw his face, he grabbed my jaw. "You should never tempt a man like that, Snow."

I elbowed him in the side and rolled over until my back was against the wall. "Stay away from me. You get no right to touch me."

Samael frowned, his entire expression morphing as if he were made of no more than rags sewn into the shape of a human filled with sand. "Why not? You certainly wanted me to when you pulled your dress down."

Forcing down my anger, I grabbed my sword and pointed the tip of the blade at his throat. "No, I did not. You made it clear you didn't want me. You have no right to come back and touch me as you please."

He clicked his tongue to the roof of his mouth repeatedly in disappointment. "Why the invitation?"

I narrowed my eyes. "You think showing my cleavage is an invitation? You assume you have control over my body but that is far from the truth. Nobody has any control over me and my choices but me. I am a grown woman. It is disgusting of you to assume you could get more from that." I stood, pushing the blade in, drawing a bit of blood. “People have the right to withdraw consent at any time they please if they are uncomfortable.”

Samael chuckled. "If you don't want someone touching you, don't show them what you have to offer them."

I pulled my sword back and grabbed the handle with both of my hands. I brought the sword down into his chest, twisting the blade. "It wasn't an offer, Samael, and never assume it is." I pulled my sword out and his body dropped to the floor.

My heart ached for all the women he caused pain. Catching a glimpse at his horrid, impure thoughts gave me the realization that many of the women he claimed to have slept with did not consent.

The sun was beginning to rise over the horizon of the ocean as I left the cave. I had to clean my blade, so I ventured through Ash Forest until the river came into view.

Within a second, the water was mixed with his demise, and like I had predicted, Samael now became another stain on Orsadia.

It became a journey of several hours, to and from.

When I arrived back at the cave, Luka had dumped Samael's body into the ocean. "I'm not sorry I killed him."

Luka shrugged as he started a fire so he could cook our breakfast. The rest of our hour was silent between us both, and when we finished our food, we set out on another walk through the woods.

"I know what you're thinking," I said.

"What am I thinking?"

"There's something wrong with me if I keep attracting these types of men. Maybe I am asking for it." Chills slithered up my arms.

Luka furrowed his brows and stopped, blocking me from walking further. "Snow, you're the princess. It's no secret. Everyone knows who you are. You are the next queen and that is a big step up. A lot of people wish for that kind of power. The douchebags you attract are nothing more than that. You attract these men because you're going to be the most powerful woman of Orsadia, and we have some assholes here who do not want that. They want to control you because they want your power. You were not asking for anything except the truth." He straightened his posture, shoulders reeled back. "You're cleaning up the scum. You're exposing these men for who they are."

"I spend so much of my time hating anyone and everyone. I judge people before I know them, and I assume all men are the same, Luka.

Men like Samael and Alexander come along, and they prove me right. Why can't I come across some men who understand consent and respect me as a woman? Is that too much to ask for?" I folded my arms across my chest.

He ran his fingers through his wavy hair to move it from his face. "It's not too much to ask for. However, I didn't realize I was a man like Samael." He shook his head as I opened my mouth to respond. "Who's currently on the throne? The Evil Queen. Orsadia needs you to save it. Men like Alexander get away with it because the Evil Queen sits on the throne. Any woman who has a title as such can excuse horrible behavior. When you take over, you have a chance to change things. You can teach all women they have a right to their body at all times. You will teach men they have to respect that or there will be consequences. These men are bred from terrible leadership. They come after you because they know you'll use your boot to squander them into the dirt where they belong. They believe if they can get under your skirt, they can control you and the power you hold, and then they don't have to be afraid." He released a deep breath. "They're afraid of you, and that's why they target you."

I glanced back towards the cave. "These sins I'm after are afraid of me taking the throne from their current queen. They know what I stand for and they don't approve." I fluffed my cloak. "You make a good argument. I'll give you that." Pulling my hood over my head, I walked away from him.

Luka followed. "Where are we headed to?"

"We're searching for the next sin. We've gotten rid of two. Samael represented lust, correct?" I glanced at Luka.

He nodded, eyes dancing along the leaves in the trees. "He did."

"So how did you know that he was lying?"

Luka nudged me. "Because I know the way men think. To you, Samael saw your breasts and thought nothing of them. However, the bulge in his pants said otherwise. He got a boner at the bare sight of breasts. He was very lustful. He just wasn't ready to die. He was hoping for an opportunity to get in your..."

I lifted my eyebrows. "Get in my what? Pants? So, you can pick up on this lust and it appears you do it easily. Are you hiding something from me?"

Laughter bellowed from his abdomen. "Let's clear the air, Firefly. You're an incredibly attractive woman and I'd be lying to myself if I didn't admit I wouldn't say no to doing many sexual things with you. I'm also a man of dignity and I can control myself. Like any human in this world, we were given self-control because we are *not* animals. We need to use that gift well. Men like Samael and Alexander just choose not to. Self-gratification comes before respect"—he paused—"and I'm a visual creature so I am quick to notice beauty. The first thing I notice is appearance. It's the first thought that enters my mind. However, I'm also a human with a brain, and I know better than to do something cruel. This quest to become Queen means something to you and I want to help you get the throne. So, while a small part of me may want to have sex—the bigger, more human part of me says I have a duty to help you with your tasks. I want the best for Orsadia because I live here, too."

I stared at him as he gazed back, not a muscle on his expression dare giving him away. I would have assumed Luka had no interest in me the way he looked away from my cleavage, but he just happened to respect me more than most did. He had to have hope that I would be a better queen because if I wasn't, why was he still here when he desired to explore other lands?

"Firefly?"

"Yes, Luka?"

"Why are you looking at me like that?"

I pulled my cloak on my shoulders some more. "You're an

interesting man. Don't change who you are." I turned on my heel and ventured back to the village. "We've rid this land of two evils. We should keep our eyes peeled for more. The sooner we kill them, the sooner I become queen." Oh, how desperately I wanted to take the throne.

Luka scanned the area. "What am I looking for? Someone stuffing their face, someone punching someone, or someone stealing money?"

"It's ignorant to assume these sins would openly expose themselves to me. They must know by now that I'm searching for them. Look for people who refuse to make eye contact, or people who can't stop staring. They are hiding here. It's survival of the fittest." I pulled out my sword.

He eyed my blade. "I don't believe that's what that term is used for."

"That is exactly what it's used for. You should socialize more." I sent him a smirk before using my sword to draw in the dirt. "We are here. There are very few places where they could be, and with five more on the run or in hiding, there are bound to be a few in the village. There can't be any at Drecose Castle or Everinthian Castle. There could be one hiding in the tower where Samael led us to. There's a reason he went there in the first place. There may be a few hiding on this tiny island over here, so we could check at some point. However, these seem to be the only places they could hide. That leaves us three locations to scope out." I put my sword back in my belt.

Luka pointed to the island. "When are we going over there?"

"When we've ruled out the village."

He gave me a look. "Easier said than done."

"I didn't ask for easy." I brushed his shoulder as I pushed past him.

SIXTEEN

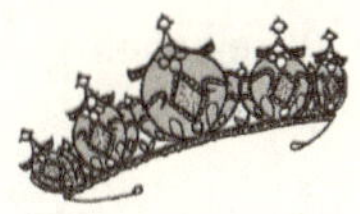

Cold was the tip of my index finger. Every now and again it would happen, and it was always just the one finger over the rest. The others kept their warmth, or at the very least agreed to share the same temperature. But this one has a mind of its own.

Was it possibly a sign of what was to come? A warning?

I gathered my skirts as I tracked my way back to the fountain where Luka played with the petals as a little girl would. I intended that the way I said it, too.

The gown I wore was one I didn't wear often enough. It was one of the first gowns Lynn crafted for me when I took residency in Drecose Castle. The fine fabrics—all so soft as not to irritate my pale skin. My complexion came at a price for which I paid in sensitivity.

Lynn was the woman who knew exactly what would fit me. The dark gray, electric blue, blood red, and of course white and black. This gown was a rich brown that brought out my eyes but hid most dirt stains.

When she had sewn it, she used a few layers of skirts to give it the shape as well as stability. The intricate detail work. The care for her stitching pattern. Not a single step had been skipped or skimped on. It was a gown that I could pass down even after I'd long moved from the castle.

The beauty of being chosen as an heir meant all the gowns made for me were mine to keep. They had been tailored to my measurements. Unfortunately, the reality for most queens after their term came with poverty. Eventually, they'd all sell their gowns off for whatever they could.

Queens were forgotten after their term came to an end. Orsadia focused solely on the current and the next heir. They never gave a bit of their thought for the ones who once were.

But that wouldn't be me.

No.

If I broke this curse, I could change the future of Orsadia for eternity and then I'd never become just another forgotten queen. I'd have a purpose and I'd be remembered. I'd be a *legend.*

Because what was there to fear besides the idea that I could be just another name nobody could recall?

And if I couldn't take my magic with me, at the very least I could leave a legacy in my wake.

For every queen, our magic faded out. After our term ended, we'd be nothing of importance. Another commoner. That had been why queens fought so hard to keep the throne, using whatever weaknesses they could muster against the next heir.

No queen could enter Drecose, as per Magic Law. Same as princesses entering Everinthian Castle. It had been a protective measure, possibly from the curse itself. It kept princesses from trying to end the queen's term early, and most queens never ventured far outside Everinthian for their own protection anyway.

"Which one of us is more of a nemophilist?" Luka asked while sitting on a rock as I approached.

Glancing at the trees and their comfort, I paused to consider my answer. Certainly Luka, given he lived here and he hardly left Ash Forest for its own good.

However, had I been given a choice and not been made to take the throne, I might have taken that cave from under his grasp. The forest had never been a fear of mine, even long before I glowed in the dark.

But the longer I contemplated his question, the more I thought of the cemetery and Matt's cave. Places where I felt more at peace. It was impossible to explain such tranquility and yet, I'd have to try somehow. Maybe someday. After the throne was mine.

"Maybe you're the nemophilist and I'm simply just your ghost," I said in a quiet tone.

Luka stood in one swift movement, inches away from me. "You? My ghost? I'd certainly say that's a humble response, Firefly, but I'm more your ghost than you are mine."

I pushed my shoulders back. "I haunt the haunter of the woods."

He reached forward, pulling a leaf from my hair. "I think maybe we should find you a place to bathe. Both of us, even."

Scanning the roots to the tops of the trees, I cocked an eyebrow in his direction. "The ocean? Salt will dehydrate us. The fountain is too small, and it's stagnant water. Full of diseases. I am not bringing you back to my castle again, either."

"You've never heard of the river." He turned on his heel, and I glared daggers at his back before following him.

I grabbed his shoulder to force him to stop and face me. "Are you referring to the river I fell into in the cave? That doesn't count."

A cocky smile. Eyes lightened. "Nonsense. Trust me."

We walked in the direction of his cave and the tower, but we never quite made it. Instead, we ventured a little further east.

Surely he couldn't be referring to Keenain River. It'd been wide. Deep. Far too dangerous, no? I supposed no more dangerous than the ocean I'd fallen into.

Rushing water entered my ears and the air noticeably cooled. I'd be damned—I was right.

Luka removed his shirt, then his boots, dropping them off to the side. "You coming?"

"Get naked with you? I'd rather pass."

He shrugged his broad shoulders, removing his pants with his socks. I'd gone from distracted by the muscles of his back to the firm ass. And before he caught me, I looked in another direction.

When his voice drifted further, his body wading through the current, I met his gaze. "You expect me to freeze to death? Not likely."

"It's warm enough that you won't freeze." He stopped to ponder for a moment. "At what point do you think I'm trying to end your life?" He locked eyes with me to ensure I wouldn't fib.

"I'm still wary, Luka. I can't put my trust in anyone." I removed my cloak before unlacing my boots. "You are high on that list." I paused to shoot him a look.

"I'm honored." He patted right where his heart laid.

"Honored to be on a suspect list?"

He shot a subtle wink. "You think about me. I'm on your mind. You can't help it."

I gagged as I finished discarding my attire, leaving only my chemise. "Avert your eyes." I waded my way into the river, gasping at the icy temperature. How Luka could withstand it was beyond me.

I supposed it was due to him only ever bathing in the river. I was the one who had hot water readily available at home.

Luka's eyes moved around the area.

I removed my chemise once the water hit my waist, turning my back towards him. "They say cold water is the best to wash yourself in. I disagree. Cold water only steals my will to live."

"You eventually get used to it and once you do, you find yourself preferring it. You acclimate to the temperature." He poured water over himself as I snuck a peek at him. "Like what you see, Firefly?"

With a scoff, I started to wet my hair. "What's there to see? A man with an ego? Not my type."

However, I kept to myself that he'd been very much what women called eye candy. Defined muscles all over his chest. Pecs. Abs. Biceps. You name it; he had it. A little cliche to say he was sculpted by a god of the finest but that was indeed what he was. The soaked waves in his hair didn't help anymore than his green eyes did.

The sun spied from under three clouds, and when they hit his eyes, they sparkled.

Yeah, I thought I was imagining it, too, but I swore by it that they did. How did that make it any more fair for me? As much as men had their issues, Luka was not one of them. And I had very much been lured in by subtle looks, shimmering eyes, and a man bathing in a river.

But I would never tell him that.

"Have you ever fallen into your tub?"

I furrowed my brows at his question. "No. What kind of question is that?" I slowly lowered myself into the water, fighting for breath from the grips of the icy touch. I turned my body as I gave him my sharpest look.

"I've always been curious. I hear the tub at Drecose is in the ground and if that's true, then would you not stumble into your own tub in the middle of the night when you get up to piss?" He shook water from his hair and I silently thanked myself for lowering my body for if I hadn't, my knees would have buckled.

"It's not inground. You might be speaking of Everinthian Castle. Although, if it were, I would not stumble into it. I've lived at Drecose almost three years and over the three years I have grown accustomed to the layout. Even in the dark I can feel around the bathroom. Spatial awareness. One does not just stumble into a tub.

"Tubs are on the opposite end of the bathroom. I don't walk in that direction. I have been able to decipher between a tub and a toilet and I don't use them interchangeably. That would be no different from going into my room to sleep and ending up on my desk in the opposite corner of my bed."

Chuckling, he leaned back into the little waves. "Fair point. No sunken tub."

"Certainly no stupidity, either." I began to comb my fingers through my hair. My body stilled as he moved closer. "What are you doing?"

"Studying your skin. It's bluish, probably because you're so cold. I knew you were pale, but now you appear deadly." He lowered himself until we were eye to eye. "Is that what you're going for?"

"Maybe," I said in a quieter tone.

He invaded my bubble, his body heat managing to radiate even through chilly ripples. For a small moment, the girl deep down imagined what it would be like to get a small taste of his kiss. Small indeed, and then I squandered the idea.

I had priorities and getting tangled up in a romance was not part of that. Huntsman or not. Innocent or not. I could not throw away my dreams for a man, no matter how tempting he could be.

He was hardly helpful, although he'd beg to differ.

"We should get a move on." I swam towards the edge. "The sins won't kill themselves." Would be helpful if they would but a woman couldn't have everything, could she?

"Yes, a move on." I hadn't realized just how close he followed until I heard his voice inches from my ear.

I hurried out of the river and grabbed my chemise, throwing it on first. After pulling up my drawers, I grabbed my corset, glancing back at Luka, the humiliation immeasurable. "Would you help me with this? Taking them off is much easier than putting them on."

He lifted his head as he finished pulling up his pants. "Thought you weren't a damsel."

"I hardly call lacing a corset a duty for a knight." I pulled it around my torso and turned my back towards him as he gathered it to begin tightening.

He leaned in, his chuckle deeper than previous times. "I thought we established I'm not a knight."

"Only if you know I'm not a damsel." I sucked in a breath as he tightened around my chest. Corsets were not always my favorite but they certainly helped with posture, and Father knew I needed that the most.

Despite that I almost bulged with his lacing, he hadn't been as rough as Lynn. Lynn—oh, I loved her dearly—was always trying to ensure I kept my shape. I didn't care too much for the tiny waist and puffed breasts, but I never argued against corsets for my own reasons.

He finished tying it off and handed me my gown. He waited while I pulled my gown on and gave him a chance to fasten the back where I could not reach. When he called done, I got the rest of my attire in order and we headed out for the tower.

"Has anyone ever lived in the tower that you are aware of?" I asked.

He confirmed that he had never seen anyone take residency there but that didn't mean people weren't sneaking in during the night for a roof over their head.

Did I blame them? Not at all.

But it became likely they could be who I was looking for and needed to kill.

SEVENTEEN

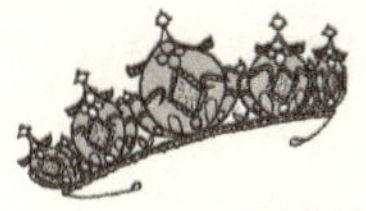

We came to a stop in front of the tower that stood at about forty feet. It was no taller than Drecose or Everinthian Castle but still, it was tall enough to be seen for miles.

Brick was crumbling over time, displaying much wear on the structure itself. Many of its bricks were missing or piled at the base. Albeit the roof stayed intact and the tower stood proudly. Ironic given who was here.

Why had he come here in the first place?

We were about to find out.

We entered through a hole in the side before ascending the spiral stairs to the top. Once we made it, I took a moment to gaze upon Orsadia and all its glory—or what it could be if a queen had been fit to rule.

Over the treetops, I could spot home. It was almost a dot compared to what I could see. The Evil Queen's castle was far more obvious to the naked eye.

The ruler in me was hellbent on finding any sign of life hidden in the forest. Just a rustle of a branch. Maybe a snap of a twig. It was never that easy, however, and so I never did find what I wanted.

My best bet was to search this tower low and high. Or in our case—high. At the base of the stairs, there hadn't been much to explore. A little brick, and some steps that led up here. Up here was an entire room with a small bathroom and even a little kitchen to match the empty bed. Nothing more.

We inspected the cabinetry as well as every nook and cranny surrounding the kitchen, but there still laid no clue. As far as it appeared, this tower was empty. Nobody lived here, and for whatever reason he came, I couldn't find.

As I approached the window again, I gripped the sill and narrowed my focus on Everinthian Castle. She had to be there as we spoke. What she was up to, I was certain it had to do with me and my defeat. Still, watching her from this tower had been tempting. It wasn't easy to spot her from her windows, given the view had been distant. But knowing I could still keep an eye on her somehow settled my bones.

"Do you think the Queen can see us?"

Luka stopped beside me. "I doubt she can see as well as a hawk."

"I was asking about other means. Maybe birds, or the sins, or some kind of...life. She could send them out to relay to her what they find. We are being watched and I believe that much. My question is do you think the same?" I cocked an eyebrow.

Reeling his shoulders, he folded his arms across his chest. "I don't. I've explored every inch of Ash Forest, seeing as it is my home. I've perched in every tree waiting for my dinner. You know what I've found? The queen is less nosy than people want to think. She's less involved. The entire island wants to see her as someone in control, but I don't wholly believe she is. Much less that she's watching every move. She wants to distance herself, and all she truly cares about is you and ensuring the future of Orsadia."

With a squint, I said, "You make it sound as if she has a heart."

"Everyone has a heart, Firefly. Villains are not born." He stepped around to my other side, pointing out towards her castle. "They're created."

His words began to sink in and a small part of me agreed. If there was a curse, and I believed there was, then she had a heart and she wanted the same thing I did. Maybe.

That didn't mean we agreed on the same methods to achieve what we wanted. She still sent these seven sins to stop me. I couldn't forget that.

He turned and headed back for the stairs, but his toe caught on a rock, lifting it from its place in the grout.

My eyes lingered on the stone as I strode over and bent down, pulling it up. "Luka, you've got to see this."

On cue, he kneeled to my level and peeked into the crevice. What we suspected was finally coming to light and I'd be a little foolish not to admit it sparked excitement to be right. Also, to get just a step closer to the throne.

As I rubbed the scarf between my fingers, I glanced at what Luka sifted through. A blanket. A can of food. A toothbrush. We both suspected it, and we hadn't been entirely wrong.

"They hid this beneath the stones. Why do you think that is? Are they embarrassed to be squatting?" I worded my question as not to pass judgment. Luka had a similar situation in his cave, and I by no means had any right to judge a soul for how they fought to survive.

His eyes darkened a tad as he lowered his head a bit. "I don't think someone wants us to know they exist."

EIGHTEEN

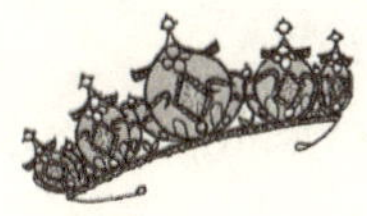

I bit into my pear and swallowed when I chewed enough. "No, Luka, I'm telling you right now that this is how it has to be. You cannot wear purple. It looks horrific on you. Stick with green, and you'll never draw unwanted attention to yourself."

He frowned. "You of all people are telling me which colors I should and shouldn't wear?"

I lifted an eyebrow. "This is for your own safety. If people see you wearing purple, they assume you're royalty and then what?"

"And then I am no longer just the huntsman who works for the Evil Queen. Sometimes it isn't greener on the other side. Sometimes the grass is not getting the water and sunshine it needs. I do not accept being the butt of everyone's legend. People fear me."

A laugh erupted. "Isn't that a good thing? You get to be left alone. Nobody wants to marry you and trust me when I say that's a good thing. All I hear about are men who want to be my husband. Did I ask for a husband? No. I asked for peace and quiet to train for a crown hiding behind a war. There is no husband in that equation."

Luka shrugged off my worries. "Sorry, I can't help you. People will continue to assume you need a husband while they assume I'm the enemy." He turned and walked in the other direction.

Narrowing my eyes, I took a step to follow him, but someone tapped my shoulder.

Must be the owner of this tower.

I turned and came face to face with a girl. She wore the purple I warned Luka never to wear. "Yes?"

"I wanted to introduce myself, your majesty. Your highness?" She curtsied.

"Either is fine. I'll be queen soon enough." I cleared my throat. "I'm Snow White, and you are?"

Her smile could light up a room, or three. "Kaliana, but please call me Kali. It is such an honor to meet your acquaintance."

This girl seemed to worry about her words more than any other. What was she hiding? She was a sin and I needed to kill her. Or maybe she wasn't and she was an innocent girl like Luka, needing a place to sleep.

"I'm honored to meet yours." I glanced back at Luka, but he was long out of sight. "Kali, did you want to join me on a walk?"

"I would love to!" She almost squealed but she caught herself. "Yes, I would."

I waved for her to walk with me and we both headed towards Ash Forest. "Have you heard about my quest?"

She shook her head. "I have not. Although, I have heard that you are already on your way to defeating the Evil Queen. Not all of us believe you will be a good one, which is why so many are afraid of you. However, I have hope. I know you will save us. Orsadia needs saving. May I ask what your plans are when you become Queen?"

"What plans are you referring to?"

She patted her skirt. "Well, I suppose it's no secret that the village is starving. I had to run and take refuge in the tower. We struggle to survive. I suppose my question is, how do you plan to help us and our market?"

I had never thought about that but now was as good a time as ever. "Well, I could always share my food. I could offer a hand in helping with the crops. I believe if a queen and her land is to thrive, she must be part of her village. To leave my people to fend for themselves is no village at all. I have a duty to make the changes I wish to see." Pause. "I was once a common villager. I was poor. I would attempt to make currency to get food for me and my family, and I know what it's like to be struggling to survive. I want to fix that for everyone. I want Orsadia to be a wonderful home to all. Rulership led by evil is destroying not just your home, but mine as well. Why would I wish to destroy my own home? Orsadia is all of ours, and to not care about it is the same as not taking care of myself. Every queen before me was or is wicked, and what is a prominent trait of sin? Being selfish. So, in reality, if an evil queen were truly selfish, she would better Orsadia just to better her own home as well. It's as if every queen is trying to let Orsadia wipe itself out and take them along with it, as if every sinful queen can't stop the curse from poisoning her...but she can stop the curse from existing by letting our home die with her legacy."

When I looked at Kali, she appeared to be confused by every word I uttered. "That is quite the theory, I must say."

Maybe I'd had this all wrong. The Evil Queen was not truly evil. She just had no other way to end this curse and so she was trying to let everyone die off so Orsadia would no longer be plagued by such a thing.

"Kali, where did you get such a beautiful dress?" I asked.

She smiled brightly again, twirling with the skirt in her hands. "Do you like it? It's the prettiest thing I own. I figured if I was going to meet you, I would wear my best gown."

She avoided my question, and now I was suspecting something was up. Why had Kali been so eager to meet me? Could she *possibly* be a sin?

"It's a stunning gown." I nodded and gave her a smile.

For hours upon hours, we strolled in silence. It had been the kind of silence that comforted and offered a cozy evening by the fire with a book. I'd give anything to be there if I could.

After the setting of the sun, we stopped at the fountain and she sat on the edge. "I was told this was once magical. Is that true?" She lifted her eyes to meet mine.

"I can't say for sure, but I believe it once was. I believe in magic because I have magic. As for how the magic disappeared, I cannot say." I admired the bird statue on top.

Kali tilted her head. "May I ask a personal question?"

I sat next to her. "Certainly."

"If your brother likes boys, do you like girls?"

I had not expected that kind of question, but before I assumed the worst of her, I had to see where this was going. "That isn't quite how it works. Fallon does like boys, yes, but I do, too. Well, not so much that I want to marry a man. I may see a man as attractive but I'm not in any state to pursue a relationship."

She nodded along with my reasoning. "That's fair. Does anyone know why he likes boys?"

It was easy to give her the side eye for that question. Maybe she was curious, but her tone said she was ready to judge Fallon. "It's the same reason you and I like boys, Kali. Boys are attractive. They have a structure to them that women don't, and Fallon prefers that over the feminine figure."

Kali swallowed. "Oh, of course. I wasn't trying to be rude about it. I just always wondered."

I'd seen two instances where people became curious about sexuality. In one instance, they were curious because they wanted to hear the other side before they began their judgment. In the other instance, they were trying to understand more about themselves.

Maybe Kali hadn't come to terms with parts of herself, but I wasn't about to question her personal business.

"I should get back to the tower. Luka is probably crying because I left him alone. Dare I say he's become attached." I chuckled at my own fib.

She got off the stone and brushed dirt from her gown. "I'll walk with you. The tower is my home, too."

If Kali was a sin, killing her would prove to be difficult. How could a sin act this sweet? Was it all a show or was she sincere? I was beginning to believe maybe she wasn't a sin at all.

The two of us headed back to the tower, and there I saw Luka waiting. "Oh, you stopped crying. I'm so proud of you."

"Crying—what?" he mumbled.

"Well, Kali, it was nice meeting you." I turned to face her, and she curtsied one more time. That would get tiring quickly.

Kali said her goodbye as she headed into the tower. Who here wore a purple dress? Nobody. That's why she stood out so well. Purple was a sign of royalty and she was anything but. Could she be the next queen after me? No. But why was she eager to meet me? She asked about a magical fountain. If she wasn't a sin, she had to be the next queen.

"Who was that?" Luka asked.

"Nobody important." I faced him. "Are we ready to head back to your cave?"

"I thought you'd never ask." He extended his arm out to his side. "Lead the way." He curtsied to mock the way Kali had treated me.

After rolling my eyes, we began our journey back to the cave. The walk was silent, and I wasn't complaining. However, I did need some food about now, something to get me through the night. Perhaps a squirrel would suffice.

"Give me your bow." I faced Luka. "I am going to do the hunting tonight."

He laughed. "Does your sword not work anymore?"

I cleared my throat. "Do you want me to drop you like a sack of flour? I do not need you for this quest. I let you tag along to boost your ego."

Luka's laugh faded and he forked over his bow and arrows. "Remember to grab all the arrows you shoot."

I wiggled his bow. "Of course, your highness." I left my cloak and sword with him while I searched for a squirrel. They were the one animal on this island that came out year-round. Most of the others would hibernate as winter approached. I also did not need a whole deer for dinner.

After hunting for a squirrel and coming up short, I sat at a tree and rubbed my face. They were hiding from me. Clever.

My body began to glow in the dark of the night, giving off the light for anyone to find me. If I had an off switch, I would have used it. However, I wasn't as easy to control as a light bulb.

Minutes later, something came crawling down the tree, landing on my shoulder. I looked over to see a squirrel just staring me in the eye. "Where did you come from?"

The squirrel didn't reply. He just sat there, munching on his acorn. He'd come to me willingly, and how could I just snap his neck?

I opened the palm of my hands and cupped them together. He crawled down my arm and sat in my palms while I took him back to the cave. "Look who came to say hi to me."

Luka squinted his eyes, but he didn't seem happy with what he saw. "We can catch a better dinner than a squirrel."

"Excuse me, we are not eating this guy at all." I moved my palms away from Luka. "His name will be...Jerry. You will not touch him, either." I placed a small kiss on Jerry's head. "Just look at him. He's the cutest squirrel you've ever seen. You can't eat this little guy."

"I could if you'd let me."

"Luka, I am warning you." I pulled Jerry against my chest. "Do not touch him."

He rolled his eyes. "Yeah, I won't touch him."

I sat down with Jerry in my lap. "Go to sleep right here. Nobody will harm a little fur on your head."

Jerry took my advice and curled up, falling asleep. It was by far the most precious thing I'd ever witnessed. Why was he so attached to me? What about me caught his attention?

"Goodnight, Jerry," I whispered.

Luka was giving me the stink eye for bringing back a pet instead of food. That was his fault for sending me out to do the hunting in the first place. I never hunted my food before. I just ate the meat.

Besides, could he blame me? Jerry wanted to keep us company and I would be a horrible queen if I denied such a little creature his wishes.

NINETEEN

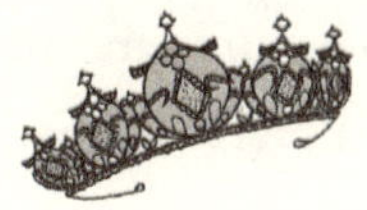

As Luka and I entered the village, people gathered around a man. We walked over to see what the commotion was about, and people moved as soon as they recognized me.

The man in the middle of the gathering was down on his knees with tears pouring from his eyes. "I did it. I am so sorry, and I do not deserve to live, but I did it. I killed Kaliana."

I widened my eyes. "No..."

No matter which way the cookie crumbled, that was by far the worst news of the day.

Luka knew by the look in my eyes, this was not in our favor.

He gestured for the man to get on his feet. "Come, let's go."

People scattered as Luka and I led the murderer back to a more private area. All I could think about was if I'd been so off with my theory, or what would happen if the queen who took my place was dead? How could Orsadia go on?

"How did you kill her?" I asked.

His chest heaved as he attempted to catch his breath. "I had a blade in my hand... I walked up behind her when she wasn't expecting it, and I stabbed her in the back. She fell and she choked but...then she went silent."

Luka put his arm out in front of me before I lost my head and went after the murderer. "How dare you? How dare you hurt an innocent girl?" I yelled at him.

"I am so sorry!" His sobs continued much louder.

I turned on my heel in a hurry and rushed away from the man before I did something I'd regret. He was a vile human being for committing such a horrible act.

"Where is she? Where is Kali?" I asked people, but nobody could answer.

I stopped dead in my tracks when a familiar voice asked from behind, "Where is who?"

Facing her, I swallowed my anger. "You're alive. That man said he killed you." I pointed in the direction of where he stood sobbing. "He said he stabbed you in the back."

She knit her eyebrows together. "That's not true. I'm perfectly fine."

Luka had the man by the arm as he dragged him to me. "What should we do with him?"

"Let him go."

"What?"

"I said let him go. He didn't kill anyone." I looked Kali dead in the eyes.

Luka glanced at her and released the man. "Why would he make up a lie that would ruin his life?"

"I can't say." I suspected someone had something to do with it. Why would an innocent man make up a lie like so? He was hiding something.

"Kali, may I ask how old you are?"

She nodded. "Twenty-one, why?"

Maybe Kali was my enemy. For the first time in Orsadia, Kali could have been chosen and she was the one I had to defeat to become queen. I'd never heard of the rose revealing two princesses but why else was Kali so eager to meet me?

I twisted my body until I was facing Luka. "We should get breakfast. Nutrition would help our strength."

We left Kali behind as we got ourselves some bread for breakfast. In no world could I kill another chosen princess who had done nothing wrong but end up the butt of someone's lie.

"I think Kali set us up," he said.

I dismissed his accusation. "What? No, that is absurd. She's a chosen queen, too, and I think we're supposed to kill each other but I don't think I can do that."

He shot me a crazed look. "I think Kali represents a sin and she tried to play dead to throw you off."

"How does that make more sense than what I said?"

"Kali represents greed. She wants to get on your good side, so you won't kill her. She wants nice things because she's greedy and she thinks if she can play dead, she can throw you off track and take your place as the princess. Then, she can have the throne. It's not enough for her to be under your ruling. She wants everything, including *your* crown," he said. "Maybe even your magic."

I had to give him credit for coming up with that. "Doubtful. The girl lives in a tower with no electricity or reliable resources. It's slim, but unlikely that a woman from her upbringing desires all my riches. One of us is right, and one of us is wrong. However, we both need to agree that Kali stays with us."

He pointed at me. "She stays with *you*. I want no part of this façade you've created."

"Then I have to keep an eye on her. However, you keep your little theory to yourself." Jerry poked his head out of my cloak. "Jerry agrees with me."

Luka shook his head, forcing a smile. "Well, this Jerry settles it. Let's befriend Kali." Maybe he was willing to put his differences aside to follow my lead. I did appreciate the respect. He treated me as if I was his queen.

We walked back to Kali, and I was the first—and only—to hug her. "I'm thankful you're not really dead." I pulled away. "I was so angry with him." Angry was an understatement, only I had been good at hiding it.

Luka nodded. "She had to walk away before she did something awful to the man."

Kali smiled at my distress. "I'm not dead, and I am so flattered you were upset by my death. You are the princess, and I can hardly believe that you of all people would be so affected by it. Thank you. It means everything to me." My heart ached as I realized she had nobody else to miss her if she did die.

"I'm not wicked. I care." I closed my cloak some more to keep Jerry from making himself known. I didn't want Kali to know about him. A small part of me decided he could be only a friend Luka and I were aware of. I wouldn't put it past anyone that a princess might have the magical ability to communicate with animals.

As far as everyone knew about the Evil Queen, she could see the future but only through mirrors. Every power had its own purpose, and yet mine seemed so useless.

Luka cleared his throat. "Shall we go get more bread?"

I nodded a little, glancing at his boots. "That sounds like a good idea. I know I'm still hungry and I imagine Kali must be starving."

Kali agreed and we took her to get more bread. I ate at a normal pace while Luka took more time, focusing on Kali's every move. If he spent more time watching her than he did being her friend, she would suspect something was up, so I kicked his boot and reminded him to quit staring.

It worked.

"What do you two usually do?" Kali asked us.

I answered, "We've been on a quest, so we try to visit as many places as possible. Next, we will probably search the forest for more clues."

Another smile graced her lips. "Can I join you? I promise I won't get in your way."

That wasn't something we wanted to do—take her with us. It was far too dangerous. I'd rather we bring her food every now and then to keep her healthy. However, if she was a second princess, we would have to let her tag along.

"If you promise not to get yourself hurt. We can't be your babysitters," I warned.

She swiftly shook her head. "No, of course not. I will be responsible and smart. I promise."

That was how it began. We took Kali with us on our quest for the day, and she asked many questions. I wished she would be quiet, but alas, this was not what I wanted. It was cruel to wish horrid things simply because she was curious.

"This is you." I looked up at the towering structure that had once been so pure and untouched. Now, it was exposed and vulnerable to the whole land. "I wonder if this has to do with the curse," I whispered to myself, yet loud enough for Kali to hear.

If my theory were correct, then she could help me greatly. Maybe all Orsadia needed was an anomaly like this to break the curse.

Kali frowned. "You mention this curse quite a bit. What is this curse you speak of?"

I glanced back at her and shook my head as I diverted my eyes towards the ground. "Luka hardly believes in it."

Yet, Luka read my mind and went against my wishes. "She always speaks of this curse. She thinks the queens are cursed to be evil, and

Snow fears she'll become just like the rest of them."

I let out a groan. "You don't go around telling that to strangers."

"What's the difference? You told me, and we barely met a few weeks ago." He gestured to Kali. "Eventually she's going to find out if she's joining us on this quest."

To ease my anger, I said, "Piss off." He had no right to tell others that I had a fear, or that I'd turn just like the Evil Queen herself.

Luka shrugged. "You know I'm right, Firefly. You know I'm right."

I turned my head and muttered under my breath. When I faced Kali, I swallowed and changed the subject. "Back to the tower. Grab anything you might need before we head out. Quickly."

"Are you expecting someone?" Kali asked as she lifted her head to look up at her temporary home.

With a snicker, I said, "It's not just any someone. Who I hope for shall lead me further to my victory." One of the five sins left had to be in this forest and I could not waste my time longer than I had. If they were, and I killed them, Kali could fear me and start a war here and now. However, she could also fear me and keep quiet about her plans once she knew I was a warrior, too.

Luka knocked against the stone. "The entrance is gone. How do we get inside this tower now? I don't suppose a woman will throw her hair out for us to climb," he joked.

Kali and I gave Luka a strange look.

He shook his head. "Right, I'm working with people who don't understand references. Carry on."

Kali approached the stones. "May I?"

"Please do." He stepped out of her way.

She lifted one from the ground and hit it against a brick and a stone came loose. She walked over to grab it from its socket, but Luka grabbed her shoulder before she could. "Careful. Slowly. The last thing we want is for this tower to come crumbling down on top of us."

"Appreciate it, but I was the one who blocked it to keep more people from getting in like you did." She nodded as she pulled a stone out, taking her time not to piss off the tower. She repeated this process until enough had been removed to create a hole big enough for us to get inside.

We all climbed in, one after another of course. Once inside, we spotted the stairs that spiraled up the inside of the tower. Moss grew in nearly every nook and cranny while more stones laid on the floor after having fallen.

I knew from the looks of it, the journey to the top would be long. I was debating if Luka and I should stay down here this time. Kali had to be wonderful at cardio to walk these stairs every day.

"Let's hope it's not an unconscious woman waiting up there," I said with a snort.

Luka furrowed his brows.

I smirked based on the look on his face. "Now who isn't understanding references?"

It was enough to lighten the mood, despite the dread that lingered. There'd been no light inside this tower except from the hole we had just made to get in, but the darkness wasn't what I feared.

"Who's going first?" Luka asked.

I lifted my chin and gripped the handle of my sword, giving Jerry a few pets to comfort him. "I will. A future queen must be willing to lead the way for her people by example." With those words now hanging in the air, I placed my boot on the first step. If there were a third princess locked away at the top, I would not be the one who kissed her to remove her curse.

TWENTY

We heard a scream from Kali as one of the steps faltered. Luka reached back and grabbed her arm to keep her from falling.

"Thank you," she whispered.

She could have fallen and splattered across the stones below, but that'd be horrific and I made a promise.

We made it to the top of the tower, and a huge hole had been taken out of one side of it. Nobody lived here anymore—not even Kali. The only objects in this room were stones that crumbled as the tower wore down.

Kitchen, gone.

Bathroom, taken out.

This tower had been targeted and now that confirmed what I knew. Kali was one of us and I'd protect her until my dying breath.

"There's nobody up here, but my home has been destroyed." Her eyes widened and glassed over. She had truly lost everything and she hadn't even had much to start with.

I looked out over Orsadia through the gaping hole that had once been a window. "No, there isn't. Our journey goes on, however. We don't give up just because we didn't find anyone." I faced her.

She nodded as she wiped her tear-stained cheeks. "No, right, of course. I understand. It's important to never give up on the light at the end of the tunnel."

I could only hope a light did illuminate the end of this tunnel. "You can see Everinthian Castle from here." I pointed.

Kali came over to look at it. "You can. It's a massive structure. Beautiful, nevertheless." As she turned, her gaze locked on mine. "I can't continue this journey. I must fix my only home. I understand the risks of staying here but if I don't, where will I go? I'm not saying I don't believe in you, Snow, but if you don't win, I'll have nothing. This tower, as damaged as it is, is all I have. Please, let me be."

I turned to look at Luka, rage building. He grabbed my sword from me after I pulled it from its sheath. "Sit. Take a moment to breathe."

"I don't need to breathe." I swiped my sword back and headed towards the stairs. There was nothing to talk about. Kali wanted to stay. It was the bottom line.

Luka sighed and followed me down the stairs. "I can feel the anger radiating off of you."

I stopped and spun on my heel, but the speed of my movement caused the edge of the step to crumble and the world tilted backward as gravity won the battle.

The world spun so fast that I could barely grasp where I was. Everything blurred, and even Luka's yells weren't clear.

Everything came to a sudden stop as I hit the floor of the tower. My front side slapped the stones and I laid there, processing the aches in my side. My cloak and gown had protected me to an extent but there'd be damage.

"Snow!" Luka stopped and kneeled beside me. "Can you hear me?"

"You're just as annoying as always." I groaned as I flipped onto my backside.

He examined my body. "Yeah, you're definitely okay. Mentally, anyway. No brain damage. As for physically, I have to examine you."

I narrowed my eyes. "You're not getting my clothes off."

I tried to sit up but that was a terrible idea. Luka glared daggers. "I need to see where the damage is. I don't need you naked to see where wounds are. There could be internal bleeding."

"And what if there is? Are you a doctor?"

He chuckled. "Someone has to be your doctor and if you want that throne, you'll accept help."

He leaned over me as I gave him a look. "Let me do it."

"Examine yourself?"

"Take off my own clothes."

He shrugged and moved back, sitting on the bottom step. "Go ahead. Do it yourself."

I undid the clip of my cloak. I yelled out as I sat up. Something was bruised or broken—or both. I stood on my own two feet and wobbled but grabbed the wall for support. "I need help."

"Oh, do you now?" He gasped.

"Shut your damn mouth." I leaned against the wall. "Just help me get my dress off. Lynn usually does it but she's not exactly here."

With a shrug, he stood. "I could have told you that, too." He stepped closer until he stood behind me. "I'm just going to look for bruises and any discoloration. If anything is broken, we should bandage it now, before you put your clothes on. That's it. It'll be quick, although not painless." He untied the strings to the back of my gown. "I don't have to remind you that your anger gets you into trouble. And I'm not here to be your knight, Firefly. We are equal partners in this journey of yours. I'm only helping you when you cannot physically help yourself. There's no shame in that." He grabbed the top hem of my gown and pulled it from my shoulders.

"No shame in being a damsel?" I scoffed.

He grabbed my shoulders and gently spun me around to face him. "None. We aren't made to survive this world on our own. We're a community. We must work together to help one another. Those villagers need you. Does that make them damsels? Should they be ashamed of needing a queen?"

I helped him get my gown off. "Villagers are made to be damsels. Queens are not. They know they can count on their queen. Nobody is going to be the queen's knight, so she must become one for herself. That is what it takes to sit on the throne."

He squatted, examining the skin on my legs. "That's assuming you aren't human."

"I'm not."

He chuckled. "You are. You're a human with magic. If you weren't a human, your parents wouldn't be either. Humans are a species. Humans reproduce and have humans. Magic is a gene—a trait. It's in your DNA and it's like skipping generations. Specific bloodlines have magic. Nobody knows what those bloodlines are."

I shook my head. "That's impossible. None of the queens had children."

"Queens are only queens for three years. After that, people forget about them. It is very possible for them to have kids after they step down from the throne." He moved to my abdomen.

I swallowed. "So, you're saying it's possible I could be a descendant of Aalia Drecose."

He poked my stomach and I winced. "This area is bruised but that's all it is." He looked at me. "And yes, it is a possibility. That is how every princess begins as a commoner. A villager if you will. Queens step down and people forget about them. They have children, and now that these queens are villagers, their children are, too. Sometimes, villagers kill the queens. Sometimes those children are raised by others and they never know their real mother was a queen of Orsadia."

"I'm not adopted. My parents are my parents."

He checked my ribs, then moved to my backside. "I'm not saying you are. But it happens."

"How do you know all of this?" I glanced back.

Luka straightened his posture. "Have you ever wondered about my parents?"

I shook my head.

"I have. I assumed my mother didn't want me. She abandoned me and nobody knew or bothered to care. That's not the entire story." He ripped his shirt and wrapped it around my backside, tying it. "It's easy to find your parents in a village with only thirty people. To find the man who looks like you." He dropped his arms as I faced him. "I found him. My parents abandoned me because they couldn't let the truth slip out."

"What truth?"

"My father was sleeping with the queen at the time. He was a scumbag. He was sleeping with my mother, and the queen at the same time. My mother got pregnant, and if he raised me as his own, the queen would know. She would have killed me for being a product of adultery. I live alone because people blame me for being the mistake. I didn't have a say in my conception and yet I'm the one at fault for being created." A humorous laugh escaped him. "So essentially, one of the queens is related to you and my father cheated on another. We're all connected to them somehow. You think that the queen doesn't have anyone, but that doesn't mean she doesn't want anyone to lean on when she can't stand anymore. She was looking for love through my father. She felt alone in that massive castle."

I lowered my eyes. "I'm sorry. I'm sorry that you had to find out what happened to you and your parents." All my life, I had my parents by my side. Luka never had his, and shame I was for scolding him for being so happy to meet mine.

He grabbed my gown and helped me get it back on. He tightened the strings and ended them with a bow. "I live alone, but this adventure with you has been the most fun I've had in a long time." He grabbed my cloak and clipped it in front of my chest. "I just want to thank you for letting me come with you on this journey, even if you hate me."

Tilting my head, I said, "I don't hate you. I just...don't trust easily. As you've seen from Alexander and Samael, I've got a distrust for men in particular. I assume the worst of them."

"I've noticed." A smile blessed his lips and soon after turned playful.

"You're nothing like them." I lifted my chin to meet his eyes. "You're a real man, Luka. I'm sorry that your parents left you, and you deserve so much more than Alexander. He lives in luxury and gets to kiss women against their will. You can look at me in my undergarments and not make a single move, and you live in a cave to make up for it. It doesn't seem fair. When I become Queen, I promise I will change things. You're going to get the fate you deserve."

He let out another laugh, although this one rang true. "Careful with making a big promise." He gestured to me to leave the tower.

We climbed out of the hole. I paused in my tracks and looked at him. "It's big. But as the highest authority in Orsadia, I can make big promises come true. I want this land to be a better place for men like you who respect women. You shouldn't be ashamed of how you were created. My brother shouldn't be ashamed of who he loves. I'm going to break this curse and be the best there was. I want to see people happy. I may have my anger—as well as my pride," I paused while sweeping my arm across my body, "but I aspire to bring smiles to their faces. Orsadia needs help and I can't ignore that. If I were to ignore the need for a happy and healthy village, what kind of queen would I be?"

The Evil Queen.

He nudged me. "You got me there," he joked. "Let's go." He began walking. "And take it easy. Your back has dark bruises from the fall."

"I figured that's why you gave me a piece of your shirt." I smiled, pulling my cloak closed. The wind rushed by today, and what kind of air it brought about was below freezing. Nobody would survive if they spent more than twelve hours in this weather.

And soon, nobody would have to worry about being cold at all.

I followed behind Luka and closed my eyes for a moment as my heart pounded against my ribcage. I blamed it on the adrenaline of the fall rushing through my veins. I'd fallen but I got back up. I just needed to hold onto that at every cost.

"Leaving Kali behind was a mistake," he added.

"Why? Still believe she's a sin?"

"I do."

"She's too nice. I don't believe the sins would ever show as much humanity as she has. And she doesn't actually fit any of the sins."

"Not everything is black and white."

I released a sigh, tired of defending my stance. "And sometimes they just are."

TWENTY-ONE

Luka and I walked near Everinthian Castle, but we didn't catch a glimpse of the Evil Queen. However, I did catch sight of red roses—a whole bush of them. Running my fingers over their soft petals, the memories flooded.

"I imagine you like the color red," Luka said.

I grabbed a rose and picked it from the bush. "Not simply just red alone, but red roses, too."

"What's special about a red rose?"

"A red rose means a lot to the princess' of Orsadia," I whispered.

The memory was still fresh in my mind as if it had happened yesterday. When I was a young girl, maybe five or six, I came across a red rose. I wasn't supposed to wander far from home, but I never listened. I'd always wanted to explore more about our land.

Mother warned me as she always did but it did no good. I wandered far and wide.

I ran through the trees, the wind hitting my face exactly right. Something caught my eye, and when I approached, a red rose stood so perfectly still in the midst of the bush. I'd never seen one before this, which is why it had captured my attention. The bold shade mesmerized every cell in my body. Blood red. I'd never been much bothered by the sight of blood before, but this became the moment I fell in love with crimson.

The sun began to set beyond the horizon, which meant it was getting too dark for me to find my way back home by myself. Mother and Father would never let me out of their sight again.

I took the rose with me as I navigated my way through the trees but to no luck, I never found my way out. As the darkness engulfed me, a calm weighed in. I could never entirely explain why or what had happened, but that was the day I realized the dark never scared me. It had instead become like a third parent. Watching. Comforting. Keeping promises.

Crows cawed, the wind whistled, wolves howled, and the trees rustled despite my compliance.

Then a small light started illuminating around me, and my eyes fell upon the rose, wondering if I'd found a magical flower. However, the glowing wasn't coming from the petals. It had been coming from me.

I'd gasped and jumped on my feet. I didn't understand what was happening, but using the light, I found my way out of the forest and back home. Mother and Father were worried and searching for me, and when they saw me, their eyes didn't deceive them.

They came running and Mother scooped me up into her warm arms before placing kisses on my head. "Lana, how dare you leave us like that? We were scared something happened to you!"

Father led us back to our humble home. "You will never run off like that again, do you hear me?"

I nodded. "I promise not to leave again but look!" I shoved my rose into their faces, a thorn on the stem nicking the tip of my thumb. "I can glow, Daddy. I glow in the dark!"

My parents didn't explain to me what that meant. They told me to drop the subject, and as much as I wanted to argue, I dropped it exactly as they asked.

It wasn't until I was a teenager that I refused to take no for an answer. When I asked them to tell me what it meant, they didn't ignore my wishes. Mother and Father sat me down and closed all of the windows, then locked the door. I didn't understand why this was a huge deal, but to them it meant keeping this a secret from everyone in the village.

"Lana, that rose revealed something inside of you that needed an extra push to come out," Father said. "What it exposed was your power. You know you can glow in the dark, and there are only incredibly special people in Orsadia who get these kinds of powers."

"Of course, I knew that, but what kind of special person would that make me?" I asked, eyes raking over their concerned expressions.

Mother nodded for my father to continue.

He reached out and grabbed my hands, enclosing them in his. "You've been chosen to be a Queen of Orsadia."

I would never forget those words as long as I lived. I didn't want to believe my father, but I knew as well as anyone that he would never lie, and my father was hardly a joker.

When those words settled in, I remembered the excitement that overcame me. I knew I wasn't different from most girls my age, but I felt like I finally had a purpose in my life. I was destined for much more than being just a wife. I could make a real change in Orsadia and that was what fueled my determination. From that day forth, I began my training.

I would train in the forest most of my days, but some days I avoided the forest for certain reasons. A boy would make fun of my skills, always getting on my nerves just right—or wrong.

When I kicked the air, he would appear out of the trees to tell me that I had barely hit anyone. He questioned why a young girl was fighting in the woods to begin with. I never told him the truth. I didn't trust strangers, and especially not some boy who only appeared when everyone else went to sleep.

He always carried around a bow and quiver of arrows, and he tried to convince me to learn to use those instead of my bare fists, but I never wanted any help from him.

Luka chuckled, bringing me out of my head. "I always knew you were lying to me. A part of me suspected you knew you were the next queen in line for the throne, after the Evil Queen of course." At the time, we had no idea she was chosen. She knew, but nobody else had a clue.

I peered over at him. "I always knew there was a reason I didn't like you. You made fun of me for training."

His smile dipped. "Well, I apologize for my behavior. I wasn't exactly mature at that age. I was a nuisance, but in my eyes, so were you."

I nudged him. "Yes, you were very much a nuisance."

"You're doing it wrong!" he yelled at me.

"Then you try showing me how to do it right, bloody useless elbow!" I yelled back at the boy.

He shrugged with a smirk. "Gladly." He set his bow and arrows on the ground as he closed the distance between us. "You need to swing at me."

When I did just that, he grabbed my fist and twisted my arm just enough to spin me around, my back facing him. I grumbled as I pulled myself from his grip.

"Your enemy will always know moves you don't. Never expect to win. Expect your enemy to be better than you and use that to your advantage." He formed a position, knees bent, fists ready.

Once I got into my stance, I took another swing at his head. He dodged it as if he'd expected that, but I needed to throw him off of his game, so I did the one thing I knew he would never expect. I grabbed the collar of his shirt and swiped him off his feet before dropping him. Unfortunately, he took me along for the ride.

His back hit the forest floor, and I fell on top. My hair came loose from the bun my mother pinned to my head.

I'd been nimble-headed to not have moved away from him before he reached for me.

"You're trying, but it's still not good enough." He laughed at my failure.

I was too frustrated with being taken down to focus on the butterflies that fluttered in my stomach from our close proximity. "Someday I'll be about to defeat you and I will take great pride in that day." I climbed off of him and fixed my clothes.

He propped himself up on his elbows. "I'll be waiting here."

Wait he did. He never left Ash Forest, and I always kept coming back for a little more danger.

"You eventually found me," Luka said. "But I still caught you off guard."

I pointed at him. "Now you know what I'm capable of. I'm not just a silly fourteen-year-old girl anymore with no training. I've had seven years to hone my skills."

A deep chuckle rumbled from his chest. "Well, yes, but I know you are not about to kill me. We've become good friends, right? Or partners in crime, however you want to look at it. We are inseparable."

"That's what you think. The reality is, when this quest is over, we're going our separate ways." I shrugged him off. "I'll be running a whole land of people and trying to make needed changes to Orsadia. You can enjoy those luxuries, but when this is over, our friendship ends there."

Something flashed in his eyes, but he blinked it away. "Whatever you say, Snow."

It didn't come off as a surprise that Luka and I had met before. Orsadia only had so many residents here, so I was bound to run into someone I once knew. However, one thought still crossed my mind.

If I had discovered my power at five or six, and I found out about my heir to the throne at thirteen, who in the village had been experiencing the same?

"An eighteen-year-old woman in the village is supposed to defeat me, and she knows who she is, but I don't know who she is," I said.

"That's how the system works. You knew you were next, and the Queen didn't know who you were." He shot me a look.

"In just a few months, I will take over Everinthian Castle and whoever is meant to defeat me will move into Drecose Castle."

He smacked his lips as if tasting wine. "And then you'll know who she is."

I shot him a glare. "That isn't my point. My point is, if I become the next queen and I do happen to beat this curse, what does that mean for the future of the queens? Will they still need to defeat me, or will I step down? Will they have a curse to break, too, or will I be the end of that? This could change everything. Will the outcome be better or worse without a curse?"

"Why should that matter? Do you want to be a moral or a wicked queen? By all means, you can leave the curse where it is and then you can be a poisonous queen like the rest of them. However, then all queens after you will follow the same path and Orsadia will never be a worthy place to live. Don't think about what breaking the curse will do to the system. Think about how breaking it will allow every queen to rule in her own style rather than by the guides of sin." He rested his back against a tree. "We can worry about the system when we cross that bridge, but for now this curse needs to be dealt with. You can spend so much time worrying about the *what ifs* of breaking it, but the reality is we don't know the outcome. We do know if we don't break this curse, Orsadia will never change and we don't want that. Breaking it's a risk you need to be willing to take if you want to see *our* future."

What did he mean by that?

I knew Luka was right, though. I had to sever the hold the sickness had on us all. We knew what our future looked like with it taking hold of every queen after me. It was not a future I'd want to settle for, no matter the cost. Whatever happened when I broke it was something we could deal with afterwards. One step at a time. We would someday get Orsadia into good shape. It wasn't impossible to input a system where the queen would change, and it would be a smooth transition. I refused to believe in the impossible.

"Luka, when I become queen and break the curse, I want you to promise me something." I twisted my body to face him.

"What is it?"

I fixed my cloak, keeping Jerry protected. "You talk about what other worlds might be out there and who else we could possibly meet. When I turn Orsadia around for the better, promise me you'll get out of here and go explore those lands. I won't be happy if you don't follow that dream at the very least."

He gifted me his best smile. "I could most certainly make that promise."

"Could?"

Luka shrugged, grin still very much alive. "Okay, I do promise. I promise that when this curse is broken, I will leave and go explore other lands. However, I want you to make me a promise."

"What is that?"

"Promise me that you'll break this curse," he said in a quieter tone.

"I promise." The words slipped from my mouth, but I didn't wholeheartedly believe them. I may not have been able to break it on my own. There'd be casualties.

And who was going to still be there when I did shatter it for good?

TWENTY-TWO

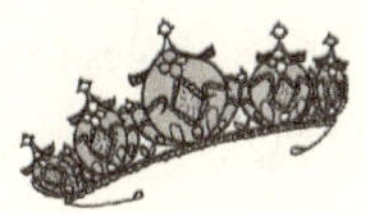

Luka had been halfway across the bridge when he turned back to face me, cocking his eyebrows. "You are aware you have to be the one to kill these sins, correct?"

"The last bridge I was on collapsed," I said as a matter-of-factly. I left Jerry back in the cave for this very reason.

"Yes, it did, and that was because you got angry and cut the ropes. Don't get angry while we're on this bridge and we shouldn't have any problems."

I grumbled as I stepped onto it. It wasn't a super long bridge, but I wasn't too fond of looking down during the walk, either. To use my bridge to get home was easy. Using a bridge I'd never used to a place unknown? Not so much.

When we made it across, we approached large buildings. The buildings looked a lot like the tower, with holes in the structure and cobwebs strewn about. They didn't invite a single soul and yet someone probably lived in one of these buildings. One building appeared to be an abandoned cathedral. The other, however, was much larger and had to be the size of a mansion. It was nearly the same size as Drecose.

"What is this place called?" I asked Luka.

He glanced at me. "Hypnotic Arythe."

"Why is it called that?"

He didn't answer me. Instead, Luka headed towards the cathedral. We entered, and despite there not being any electricity, we had a lot of natural light due to the gaping holes in its foundation.

I scanned the area for any sign of a person, but I couldn't quite call these sins humans.

As I walked up the middle aisle, I checked the pews to ensure nobody was hiding under them. When I got to the altar, I turned to face Luka. "Nobody's here. Let's head to the other building."

We headed over to the mansion.

"We should split up. Cover more ground. Don't get lost," I told him.

He may have rolled his eyes but he shot me a playful smile to coincide with it. "See you on the flipside."

Disappearing on one side, I went the other direction. The entire structure had been so utterly quiet that you could hear a pin drop.

I'd say both of us should have been aiming to not get into trouble again but that wasn't going to happen given our circumstances. Between Luka's leg wound and my bruised ribs, we were going to have to suck it up.

Aside from that, I was under the spell of protection my father placed on me. Death couldn't come for me quite yet. What was there to truly fear? Maybe it explained why the darkness never quite felt like a threat.

If I hadn't been mistaken, I'd have assumed I was in a horror novel. But horror novels didn't include royalty.

What they did include was the eerie silence paired with a full moon that cast a glow through the broken windows. Debris lay in almost every inch of floor, and what this mansion may once have looked like was no longer obvious to the naked eye.

This wasn't a horror novel.

Until the soft humming began to drift through the air, calling my name specifically.

Aalia Drecose, possibly.

I wouldn't be all that surprised if she had followed me or if I walked in on her crime scene. If she was going to show me the truth, I'd accept with open eyes.

"Aalia," I sang in the dead of the night. "Come out, come out wherever you are."

Glass shattered behind me and I spun to face the culprit. Nobody stood under the moonlight, and as soon as my skin illuminated the dark spots, I concluded *nobody* was here.

"Aalia," I whispered, "is that you?"

Claws dragging across the cement walls echoed throughout the main foyer.

Closer.

Silence.

Scratch.

I screamed as fingers wrapped around my ankle and pulled my entire leg out from under me. My head hit the tile flooring a little too hard, and I *attempted* to grip the floor, my nails digging at the surface but never catching on.

Kicking my foot at the fingers didn't do a thing.

But as my screams died down, other screams pierced the air as if they'd never left these walls.

As I fought for my life, my light dimmed. My vision began to fade and I'd been certain that my time would come to an end.

All my regrets front and center. My fears. Everyone I'd leave behind.

How could I be a selfish daughter?

Someone yelled out. The fingers disappeared. The dragging stopped.

But my head still throbbed.

"I've got you, Firefly." Luka scooped me up and carried me out like the damn damsel I was. "I don't know what the hell happened back there but you cannot be on your own in the dark."

"I've got magic," I managed to get out.

"Magic that does you no good except light your way. Maybe someday it'll help but until you understand it and have control, let's stay clear of ghosts." He snickered a little.

Guilt washed over me as I recalled my last moments of life. How close I had been... How sickly sweet it'd be to allow death to whisk me away.

Death that shouldn't have been able to touch me—but it had. Why? How? Did the spell mean nothing? Had my ego been my own downfall?

I swallowed my pride if only for a moment. "Do you know how many times I've yelled at my father? Too many to count. I've hurt those I love out of anger. I've struggled with letting people in for so many years. I've used it as a weapon to guide myself through training. It's helped me. If I try and fight her, I could lose. If I win, what happens then? I don't have the anger I need that fuels me to victory."

He shook his head, fully aware of what I'd say next. "What is more important to you? Anger or the people of this land?"

I stayed silent. Of course the people here were important, but without anger, I was worthless. I couldn't fight without it.

"Maybe you'll have to learn how to fight without your anger, but it'll be a much better skill once you can control your emotions. You will have more power."

"What if when I defeat her, I have no more anger? I need anger to drive my sword through their hearts. I can't do this on love alone. That is..." I couldn't finish my sentence. The word was there, but I couldn't dare say it.

Luka scooted closer. "That's damaging to your soul. You may begin to see what you've done to all these people, and then you won't have the strength to go on. But now I must present to you one last question to ask yourself. Are these sins worth more than those who've lived in this land their whole lives?"

As my thoughts wandered, I started back at Matt. He had been all alone. He knew I was coming for him, and he had nobody at his side. Samael was nothing but a vile prick who would stop at nothing to take my body from me. They came alone, hiding out in odd places and trying to gain my trust.

They couldn't have been breathing. Real humans had families. They had people they cared for. These sins had nobody but themselves, and I had to use that if I was going to win this war with love instead of anger.

I was angry. I was angry that the Evil Queen had hurt all these people, including my family. I was angry because nothing ever seemed to change. I was angry because I'd been chosen to be the next queen and I was never asked if I wanted that for myself. Whatever dreams I had as a child were squandered the day my father told me my destiny.

This anger had been everything I'd ever known and now it was time to let go. Orsadia needed love to thrive, and anger could no longer rule this land.

On the way home, all I could think about was how thankful I was that I didn't tell Luka what really bothered me all these years. Nobody had ever asked what I wanted. I was expected to do everything to fulfill everyone else's happiness at the expense of my own.

TWENTY-THREE

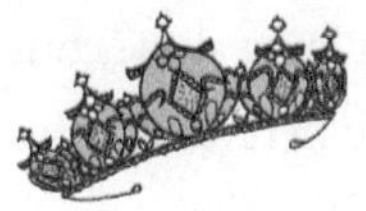

The medic bandaged up my head after ensuring I was in the clear for sleep. Bruising formed around my ankle, reminding me of what *she* had been capable of.

There was not an ounce of doubt in my mind that Aalia tried to take my life from me. For what reason, I didn't know. What I did know was I would be prepared next time. I now had a personal vendetta against the famous queen herself.

Luka was nice enough to not say much to me about how we underestimated her, but my parents and Fallon were quite the opposite.

I met someone whose anger fueled her better than love fueled me, and because of that, my family now believed I wasn't ready for this kind of journey. But if I were honest with myself, they never believed I was ready to begin with.

"You shouldn't go back out until you heal," Mother said.

Father nodded. "Your mother is right. If she could do this to you at your best, imagine what could happen to you when you're injured."

Fallon decided to input his opinion, too. "You never should have started killing. If anyone deserves to die, it'd be those bullies."

As much as I wanted to yell at everyone to be quiet, I had no energy to do so. My main worry was about Aalia Drecose and the Evil Queen.

Luka cleared his throat. "Snow and I will get our rest, thank you." How was it so easy for Luka to stay collected?

My family agreed to leave us alone, but it didn't make much of a difference. We had to hide here until I was strong enough to defeat her. "I need to train out of love."

Luka furrowed his brows. "You're injured."

"I have a wound that's bandaged. That hardly deters me from training. If I'm going to bring her to her knees, I need to train using love. She uses hatred to fight and I can never go against her if I don't do my part." I got up from the bed.

He struggled to stand with me. "I'll join you."

I spun around and put my hand out to stop him. "No. I'm done being a damsel. I'm the one who has to kill her anyway."

He released a sigh. "Your family isn't about to let you go out and train."

"I can handle my family." I left the room and walked down the corridor. Lynn came to keep an eye on me but as soon as she saw me, she knew my intentions. "I'm fine. I barely hit my head and I need to do this for the people."

She frowned. "I understand, but you, too, must put yourself first at times. If you don't, you may never finish your term."

"I'm not injured." I leaned in and gave her a tight hug. "I promise if it becomes too much, I'll come right back here."

Lynn and I both knew that was a lie, but she gave me a kiss on the cheek and let me go anyway. I'd been stubborn since birth, and that would never change.

I didn't leave the castle. Instead, I headed to the dungeons.

Everyone in the castle hardly visited down here so it was easy for me to stay in the castle and do my training without being scolded for defying their wishes.

I pulled my sword from my belt and sliced the air clean, reenacting protecting Fallon from his bullies. My love for my brother was strong, if not stronger than my hatred for his enemies.

They would call my brother awful names and make inappropriate gestures towards him. It escalated the older they got. Those kids became teenagers and those teenagers wanted to humiliate my brother for who he was. It began with pulling his pants down, and one day I went to meet up with my brother after his schooling session. I found him on the ground, beaten and bloody.

I was only seventeen at the time, yet to be a princess. Nobody in town knew who I was or was going to become. I used that to my advantage as I tracked these bullies down. I shamed their parents for allowing them to treat another human in such a way. I threatened these kids, warning them not to screw with my brother again. I hoped they would keep their mouths shut and hands to themselves, but I'd always been too hopeful.

One of the boys shouted a vile word at me, reminding me of what they were capable of. It came as a disappointment they didn't know what *I'd* been capable of. I let my anger get the best of me, and before I fully grasped my actions, I'd attacked them.

If they were going to be vile, they did not deserve to create such monsters either, so I made sure to kick their manhood as hard as I could. They threw in a few punches, and I let the truth slip then and there. I told them I would be the next princess, in just over a year. I expected fear and apologies. However, I was met with laughter. They didn't believe I was telling the truth.

I warned them they'd regret everything they ever did to my brother, and I left them there. When I was eighteen, Mira defeated the queen and moved into Everinthian Castle. Drecose was vacant for a day before I came forward and revealed myself as the next in line.

To this day, I replayed the looks on those boys' faces as my skin glowed for everyone to see, proving I was who I said. They feared me from that day forward, going out of their way to do everything Fallon wanted. It was unfortunate for them that I would never forget the way they had looked at him as if he'd been an abomination.

They never changed their ways out of love. They changed out of fear—and that kind of change was false and rotten to the core. Deep down, they were the same scum that humiliated and beat Fallon. I would never let them live that down and when I took the throne, they'd be the first ones to go in my dungeon for life. Giving them time to relay their own actions was far worse than death.

I partly didn't believe in death because it stained my hands of which I wouldn't have on my conscience. It was far too permanent. But I also didn't believe in it because it was quick. A means to an end. It wasn't a punishment.

It was *mercy.*

I groaned as I leaned against the wall. I'd been trying to train out of love and yet I had managed to transform that into anger yet again. Reprogramming my mind would be a quest all on its own, and a tough one at that.

As I swung the sword, I pictured my parents and how much they loved me. They frustrated me at times but in the end, they always wanted the best for Fallon and I. We were their entire world.

Yet, there was a possibility I wasn't their child and I'd been adopted.

I couldn't bear the thought of not knowing who my parents were. Where had I come from? Which queen was my biological mother?

The more I questioned my existence, the hotter my blood boiled at the thought of my parents lying to me. Why wouldn't they tell me? I had a right to know the truth.

I had a right to know.

Putting my sword back in my belt, I shook my head. I was far too angry to train. I needed to hear the truth from my parents before I could continue.

I ventured back up the steps and found my family in the Great Hall. This is where they spent most of their time.

"Am I not your biological daughter?" I asked them. Fallon knitted his brows together in confusion.

Mother put her book down and gave me a frown. "What are you talking about?"

"Is my mother one of the queens? Is that why I have powers and you don't? Magic is not an anomaly, Mother. It's a gene passed down from generations." I pressed my palms flat against the table that separated us.

Father put his hand over hers and gave a small nod. "It's okay. She should know."

I almost choked on my breath, stumbling over my dress.

Holy shit—I wasn't their real daughter.

Mother straightened her posture as she folded her hands on the table. "You're not adopted. You are our biological daughter," she paused, "but there is something you should know. Your grandmother was one of the queens. My mother had a bad reputation due to such a thing, and I worried that I would end up having to follow in her footsteps. I worried I would eventually take the throne. Years passed and I never got any powers. My mother appeared relieved by that. I'd never met her before she was queen, but after her term ended, she seemed so drained of life. She had been broken from the inside, and the day I admitted I didn't have any powers, she smiled. I thought maybe something was wrong, but then a woman came forward as the next heir to the throne and she exposed her powers to all of us. I knew I had dodged a horrid fate."

Horrid fate? Was that what this was to her? It was now a fate I was destined to follow.

"I eventually found your father and we got married. We had you years later and I couldn't have been happier to raise you." Yeah, having me at eighteen meant they got married young. "You were stubborn as a baby, too. You never gave up until you got your way." She let out a small laugh. "But the day you came to us, telling us you could glow, I knew what that meant. The gene had skipped a generation and you were going to be next. All I can do is hope you'll change the laws and make the best queen we've ever had. Your grandmother died before you were born, so I decided to keep it a secret in hopes you would be normal, and when that failed, it was in hopes you would not follow in her footsteps." And that explained the spell Father had put to protect me from what they knew was inevitably coming.

"Luka was right. I'm related to one of the queens." I wasn't sure how to feel about it. On one hand, it explained a lot. On the other, I felt empty, knowing I could never meet my own grandmother. "What am I? What use is glowing? I can light my way in the dark but that's all I can do. It's useless."

Mother went deep into thought. "There were a few things about my mother that I was told." Her eyes drifted towards the grain of the table as she picked her words carefully. "She would tell me what it was like to be an heir to the throne in case I did develop powers. She said that every princess is only given as much as she's able to handle."

I laughed. "Meaning what? I can't handle more than being a lantern?"

Mother stood from her chair and circled the table before halting in front of me. "Meaning that when you defeat the Evil Queen, your full powers will come in. We have yet to see what you are, and you may have been getting hints here and there. However, *you* won't know until you are queen and you have proven you are fit to control all of your abilities."

Fallon tilted his head, a curious gleam in his eye. "Like a superhero."

Mother wanted to laugh but she knew it wasn't fitting for what she said next. "Like the villain."

Those words hit me in the gut.

Like the villain.

That's what I would become according to this curse. The current queen was that of a foreseer. It could have been used for good but yet, it was a power used for wrongdoings. She would tell people the worst parts of their future, bringing them to their knees begging for a different outcome.

At this time, I had nothing but the ability to glow, and I feared what that could be part of.

There'd been a few things happening around me, but I had no clue what any of it meant. What was I? What would I become? I feared the worst of me. Would I become a demon, or would I become an angel? No, that didn't make any sense. Demons and angels were fictitious.

"Snow?" Mother asked.

I met her eyes, but neither of us said anything. She knew what I was thinking. I feared what I would become if this curse won and I lost the war. I hoped that whatever my ability stemmed from, it was nothing that could be used to harm anyone in Orsadia.

TWENTY-FOUR

"If I can't leave yet, then I'm at the very least training you," I said to Fallon as I spun to face him. A throbbing in my head made me regret that decision.

With the sword we found flat in his palms, he weighed it. "Training. Fair. Although I might be better off starting with my fists."

"Don't tell me how to train you." I snatched the sword from him, setting it beside a tree. "Fine. Fists it is." I removed my belt and sheath for the time before circling him. "Show me what you got."

He formed fists and lifted them in front of his vital organs before taking a swing at me. I ducked and grabbed his wrist, twisting it behind his back while he yelled out in pain. I let go with a laugh.

"You're actually training me. Nothing's stopping you from harming me while at it," he sputtered.

I shrugged a bit, stepping back. "I won't go too rough. But proper training is needed, and to do that, I need to ensure I *actually* train you." I bowed. "Try. Hit me again."

"Shouldn't be too hard. You piss me off all the time," he spat. He swung again near my head, but I dodged it and grabbed his arm, nearly flipping him over. "I hate you, Snow!"

I let out another laugh, louder this time. "Good. It'll fuel your adrenaline. Use that to your advantage, Fallon. It's amazing what the body can do when you're running on adrenaline."

Scowling, he spun and threw a punch to my gut and I doubled over. "That's for being a stubborn ass-wipe. And for the time you broke the vase and pinned it on me. I got into so much trouble for that."

I heaved, groaning. "You're still going on about that? It was over a decade ago."

His lips curved up in one corner. "I'm your brother, Snow. I keep a record of all your wrongs."

"Lucky for you I don't allow that to faze me. I'll still defend your life even if you get on my last nerves."

After a few more rounds of punches and slaps, he grabbed some water and downed it before washing his face. It wasn't entirely bad for a little session. Maybe soon I'd get to have more of these with him. Once those sins were dead.

"How's your murder fest?" he asked.

I released a defeat sigh. "I told you, they're not actually alive. They're just figments that the *Evil* Queen came up with. That's the difference."

"What makes you so sure she wouldn't take seven very living human beings to send your way?"

I opened my mouth to respond, but I didn't have an answer. Nothing made me entirely sure. In fact, what reason did I have to believe otherwise? She was the Evil Queen.

She had no obligation to use hallucinations to spare anyone's life, nor their morality. She had none left of her own.

But regardless, most humans didn't struggle with one sin alone. These had been too obvious, and therefore, they weren't breathing.

I'd only been in Orsadia for roughly twenty-one years but it was long enough. I'd nearly explored every inch. I knew better. That's what she did—create things from her own power to screw with our minds.

Just like the day she told me the unbearable future that I dare called mine and my father's.

Orsadia had only been around roughly a century or more, depending. The first settler discovered it and decided to inhabit the land, bringing over a few more. Within a decade, a village began, the first queen had been chosen by magic, and the castles were being built. Everinthian went up first, seeing as Drecose wasn't as important at the time, but once Drecose went up, they named it after her. They continued to add onto Drecose, but never worried much about Everinthian for whatever reason.

As we knew, she was the first vile queen to rule over. And from there, the curse carried onto every heir after that.

Now, Orsadia had grown, but not by much. Seeing as food and medicine were scarce, how could people survive long enough? The lifespan here lasted about fifty, maybe sixty years. That's why most of us never knew our grandparents. That was why my grandmother died before I was born, at about forty-four. It was the price most of us had to pay for the sins of our ancestors.

I refused to be yet another stain upon the tapestry.

I'd make changes. I'd make my grandmother proud.

"Come, Fallon. There's much to be done."

I waved him to follow, and so we set on back to the castle where I swear I heard him mumble, "I wouldn't judge you if you did admit you were killing real people to take the throne and save us all in the end."

Instead, I chalked it up to lack of sleep and a few blows to the gut. I didn't support murder, and I surely wasn't guilty of committing it.

TWENTY-FIVE

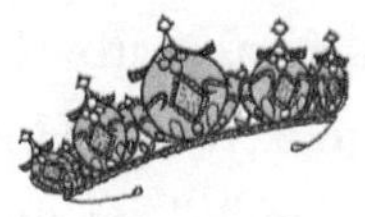

His footsteps were slow and steady, as opposed to my quick and uneven steps. "What was that about?" Luka asked as we headed towards the village.

"What was what about?" I narrowed my eyes.

He laughed. "Well, you left to go train and then you came back, and you looked so shaken up. Why was that? Did you realize you fight better with love?"

It would have been easy to tell Luka that I was related to one of the queens. It would be so simple to say I had more power than I was shown, but it was something I needed to discover for myself. Besides, I quite liked keeping a few things under wraps from him.

I was about to say something, but something caught my eye and I stopped. "Luka, what is that?" We stopped just before the bridge to Hypnotic Arythe.

He followed my line of sight and shrugged as if it didn't bother him. "Now you know why they call it Hypnotic Arythe."

As we crossed the bridge, the music grew louder. Colorful characters walked in every direction as tents stood every few feet. The cathedral that had once been in front of the bridge was nowhere to be seen, and the mansion was missing, too.

"It's..." I looked in every direction.

"It's a carnival." Luka walked further into the event. "I'm surprised you've never been here."

I shook my head. "I never had a reason to cross the bridge." I spun around, trying to see if Aalia was nearby. She'd almost killed me and yet now she was nowhere to be found. How convenient.

He grabbed my wrist and pulled me out of the way as a unicyclist passed in front of us. "Careful. Here, these people are lifestyles. They don't understand our world. Death would mean nothing to them if it means they stay in character."

"Are they not from our world? They had to come from somewhere."

He leaned close. "I don't have all the answers, but the Evil Queen holds this carnival to terrorize people. These people here will not help you." He turned me to walk in the other direction, and so we turned towards the center of the carnival.

It became apparent to me that Hypnotic Arythe was entirely in the Queen's control. Every queen, even. They had abilities to forge dreams and nightmares. People made from dust. Soon I'd be able to hold that kind of power, too.

That shook me to my core.

"We need to search for a sin. She could be watching us, planning our demise. We're here for one purpose. I'm ready to defeat her." A shiver ran up my spine.

He replied coolly, "I know, but we have to somehow scope her out from all the vibrant shows. That's not easy to do. She won't want to be found."

I furrowed my brows. "How do you find someone who doesn't want to be found? You must lure them out or think exactly like them."

Luka shrugged. "Sure, but how do we do that?"

As I scanned the area some more, I focused on one tent. "Get in her mindset. What happens to some people as they get drunk? They get violent and angry."

"You're not suggesting we get drunk, are you? That's a stupid idea."

"Just get tipsy enough to think like her. I don't doubt I could pull it off." My lips curved up to one side. "Don't join me if you're not comfortable but I will do what it takes to find her. If I can't defeat even one sin, how can I ever expect to defeat my darkest fears?" I headed towards the tent that sold beer. Without thinking, I chugged the beverage before I could process the awful taste on my tongue.

Luka leaned against the table. "You don't have the best ideas."

I coughed a bit, trying to adjust myself to the taste. "And what was your best idea?"

"Not to get drunk." He chuckled.

I knew there was no way I could drink anymore. As hard as I tried, the taste became too bitter. In fact, I ordered a snack from the menu to get the taste out of my mouth.

Luka leaned in and kept his gaze on my funnel cake. "May I have some?"

"Get your own." I pulled it away from him and shoved pieces in my mouth. The funnel cake nearly melted on my tongue, sending me into a blissful state. I had never had funnel cake as addicting as this. "Luka, buy yourself some. This cake is the absolute best I've ever tasted."

Warm. Sugary. Crunchy yet soft. Delectable by every judge.

He turned his pockets out. "Got no money at the moment."

"Too bad." I shrugged and finished the one, getting myself another. "It's like heaven, only heaven doesn't exist."

"But this cake does exist, so how can it be like something that doesn't?"

I swallowed my bite and shot him a playful smile. "You make a good point." I peered over at the tents. "She'll turn up. Let's not waste our thoughts on her for the moment. Let's try and enjoy this once-in-a-lifetime experience before it's gone!"

Arms crossed and one eyebrow lifted, he said, "To be fair, this comes every year, since Mira took the throne."

"Don't be silly, this is a carnival, not a fair!" a voice to my right and his left squeaked.

Luka sent me a wary look as he faced the man whose voice it belonged to. Short, stubby, and much too macho to have a voice pitched that high.

"Careful, if you eat too much, the carnival may never let you leave!" He twirled his finger towards the sky.

Luka grabbed my plate as if I hadn't already devoured my cake. "The food is drugged, Snow." He scowled. "We'll be trapped here if we don't leave."

"Who says you want to leave?" The man frowned.

My focus lay solely on enjoying myself to my heart's content. Luka would have to drag me out of here if he was so keen on not being “trapped”, but I was here to stay. Did a princess not deserve some fun?

Without hesitation, Luka grabbed the man's collar. "You're gluttony, aren't you?"

"And why would you assume that?"

"You're using the food to lure people and keep them here."

"Who said it was me?" He winked.

Luka yelled and threw him to the ground. "Admit it."

I hummed, a small smile plastered to my face as I watched through a filter.

The man attempted to climb to his feet but Luka pressed the sole of his boot to his chest to keep him down. "I could be envy or greed."

"Greed? In a carnival? What's to envy here? The freedom others have? Is that why you trap them?" Luka pushed his foot further into his ribs.

"Do you know what makes gluttony a sin?" his voice raised. "Because like envy, gluttony takes from others. It's selfish. It creates starvation. And much like greed, it's excess." A maniacal laugh bounced off him, and seconds later, he twisted Luka's ankle and scrambled to his feet before disappearing into the tents.

Then Luka was off running after him, leaving me to fend for myself.

TWENTY-SIX

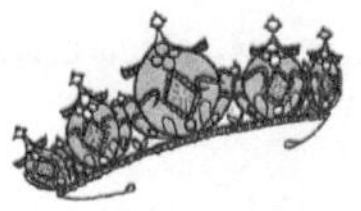

"I'll have fun on my own, Luka!" I yelled after him.

Turning on my heel, I faced the colorful tents strewn about—or so they appeared that way. They were really placed in a particular pattern so you'd visit every last one.

That was my intent tonight.

The tents formed almost a circle, and every one was sewn a vibrant color, but they never distracted the visitors from the big round tent in the center vertically striped red and white.

Characters of all sorts came jogging through. Tall and short. Skinny and overweight. Hairless and wild animal.

Laughter could be heard from every corner, from the kids and the respective employees alike. Distorted but upbeat music echoed throughout the carnival.

But that wasn't what really got me.

It had been the buttered popcorn, fried corn dogs, and powdered funnel cakes that lured me in. Nowhere in Orsadia did anyone eat this good. Even at Drecose Castle, Father insisted we rely on meat and vegetables. How wrong he'd been.

Fried foods became addicting. I'd been licking my fingers even long after the fact, and so I bought more food and tasted every bit of sweets they offered me. I always returned to the funnel cake.

I was growing attached to the pink and blue cotton candy, too.

Oil and grease stained my fingers, as well as the sticky residue from the treats.

And as I passed by the tents, I reached my fingers out to brush along the silky fabric.

"Would you like a reading?" A woman opened up her tent, in which I obliged. It could not hurt in the least. "Sit, sit, Princess, and allow me." She sat across from me and took my palm.

Smoke bellowed in the air as her room glowed a lavender hue.

"What do you see?" I leaned forward, focusing hard on the lines of my palm.

She frowned for a small second before a wide grin replaced it. "Oh my, indeed. Just as we suspected."

"We?"

"Us, dear! You suspect it, too, must I say you are right indeed." She turned my palm over as her brows knitted together. "No, no, I mustn't tell you that."

"Tell me what? What am I paying you for?"

"You're not paying me at all." She lifted her eyes to meet mine.

I slid my palm from hers. "What did we suspect?"

"Death is coming for you, Princess. You can never escape it." A cackled slithered from her throat.

I stood from the chair, knocking it back as I ran for the exit. I rubbed my eyes as they swindled me. The tents had *shifted.* A maze for me to explore. How was that possible?

Making my way through the laughter and flashing lights, red and blue illuminated a carousel directly in front of me. I hadn't seen one when I arrived but it stood before me with a horse calling my name—although its lips never moved.

I slowly approached and stepped up, screaming out as the spinning began. I reached out for the horse's leg and held on as my body swung to the left, then to the right. I attempted to pull myself up but my knees smacked against the metal floor of the carousel itself. Everything around me started to distort, bending to the whim of the ride and not my own wishes.

I yelled out and even my own voice twisted into something deeper—more grotesque.

Tightening my grip around the hoof, I moved my other hand further up the leg and began staggering them as I climbed. Once I was holding onto the pole through the middle of its neck, I forced myself onto the horse and leaned into its ear, whispering, "I win, Mira."

The carousel came to an abrupt halt, my forehead flying into the engraved metal pole. My grip loosened as I slipped off the horse and fell into the dirt just inches away. The lights shut off but the music never stopped there. It grew louder.

I climbed to my feet and rubbed the bump on my head before following where the said music came from.

It became so loud that crimson dripped from my ears and down my neck, into my cloak.

I'd barely been able to focus my gaze on the sign in front of me that read:

HALL OF MIRRORS

Before I could even process my thoughts, I hurried in the door and the music went silent.

My reflection stared at me from all angles. It wasn't often that I saw my appearance, but now that I'd been able to peer at what everyone else had been seeing appalled me. My hair had been a frizzy mess, tangles and strands scattered about. Blood left a sticky, crackling trail down the sides of my neck.

And my eyes... Oh, my pupils had been blown.

If I hadn't believed Luka before about the drugs, I certainly did now. It was impossible to miss.

Dragging my hands across the mirror, through the illusions, I made a few turns before someone tapped my shoulder.

I whipped around and came face to face with...myself. She leaned out of the mirror, fully fleshed out the same way I was. Her grin was wide and far too cunning, yet I hadn't reacted in time before she grabbed my wrists and yanked me into the ripples.

I flew to the ground with my hands out, which had been a terrible idea from the start. My wrists bent backward and I yelped as I rolled onto my butt to face the culprit. She tapped her fingers along the glass, humming. "I've waited years for an escape."

As she placed a foot through, I shouted and dove for her legs, yanking her to the floor. "You will not leave me in here!"

She kicked my nose, sending my head flying back. With a groan, I rubbed it. "You look better that way," she stated, blood beginning to trickle from her nose.

Wiping the blood from my upper lip, I stood on my feet and screamed in her face before tackling her to the ground. I pulled at her hair. I threw punches. I tightened my fingers around my neck, and when that played no impact, I threw her head into the ground, repeatedly.

Not a single mark flawed her discolored complexion.

Tilting my head, I discovered why just before she shoved me to the ground. She was me. I had to injure myself to be able to fight her.

"Not so fast," I forced out through a raspy voice. She paused, standing in front of the mirror. Glancing down at me, she snickered.

I grabbed a finger, pulling it back, crying out from the pain. She cursed me, asking what I was doing.

I was well aware.

Just when she reached for the frame of the mirror, I slid my sword from its sheath. "You cannot control me anymore. Whatever—whoever—you are." I wrapped a portion my long hair in a tight fist, slicing just above my fingers.

And like that, I'd cut off the expectations. The desperation. The envy. I'd removed from me what others had placed upon my shoulders for the last three years. I was going to fight for the good of Orsadia, but I'd do it my way. I believed in myself regardless of what others asked of me. If I continued to allow them such a firm grasp on my heart, then I'd never acquire the strength needed to fight my battles and win my war. I'd live up to the expectations *I* created, and not theirs.

I'd be different from the rest of the queens. Poison had no reign here.

Her eyes had grown the size of gold coins as she fell to her knees, hair piling around her. I hadn't cut off the whole length, but enough that Snow White no longer had the weight of the world on her shoulders. Enough that I'd be reeling from the change. It still fell past my shoulders, to my breasts. But no longer did it fall below my waist.

I stepped around her and passed through the mirror. I kept my eyes closed the rest of the way through the maze, using only my hands to guide me around the corners. I'd found my way out unscathed. Or mostly.

"Care for a show?" a man asked, offering me his hand.

Without a thought, I gave him mine and followed him into his tent.

He sat me down in front of the stage, and as I scanned the audience, everyone laughed in unison. I turned to face the man as he leaned down in front of us, showing every last one of his shark teeth. "It's all magic!" He stood and twirled, flashing his now perfectly human dental work. "And tonight I will bring every last one of you into the show!"

One by one, he brought each person up, asking, "Trick or treat?"

A few said trick, and he brought out boxes of knives and tanks of water and chains. The ones who chose treat were given carts full of delicious desserts to eat until they fattened up. Most of them did, too, having to be rolled out.

"Now your turn, Princess." He reached forward.

I stood from my seat and followed him up on stage. "Treat. I choose treat."

A chortle. "No, silly goose! You get something special. We have among us royalty." He grabbed me by the shoulders and faced me towards what was left of the audience. "Princess." He leaned into my view, his brows narrowing inward as a cunning smile formed. "Lana Edmilla."

How did he know my name? I'd worked hard to erase that part of me.

"Bring out the fire!"

A few men and women brought out rings of fire in which I tried to run, but he pulled me back, pointing towards the rings. "That is what you call a hoop." He pushed me into the chair as if I'd known where it came from.

"And I'm supposed to jump through?"

Another chortle, but this time much longer. "No. You watch the horror." He spread his fingers, waving his hand over the ring.

I leaned forward and I glanced at the ropes around my wrists. "Fallon!"

Fallon spit blood and wiped his mouth as he looked up at the boys his age. "Snow is going to pay you back for this. Just you watch."

"Oh, and who's going to tell her? You have to run to your big sister to fight your battles? Pussy!" A bully kicked his gut. "But you don't even know the meaning of the word."

I tugged at the ropes but they never gave way.

Horror was an understatement. Watching my own brother get beaten by a group of scum was torture, and I couldn't do anything about it.

The voice in my head whispered to me that this was yet another hallucination. Not real. Not my Fallon.

I believed it.

Until the tattoo peeking from under his shirt made headway. He'd never shown anyone the crow made of ink, of which he'd gotten just for me and our bond. He'd never as much as taken his shirt off in front of another person to allow them to see it.

To my dismay, this had been my brother in the center of the burning circle.

They surrounded him, giving him no escape. They outnumbered him. They were cowards to the fullest extent, and they were obtusely aware of it. I'd eventually get my hands on them and I'd wring their little necks.

"Firefly!"

My head snapped towards the one person who called me by that nickname. "Luka!"

He grabbed an arrow from his quiver and shot at the man behind me. He disintegrated into ash, and when the ropes and chair vanished along with him, I pulled out my sword and swung at the people nearest to me. "Stand back!"

People gasped as they hurried from the tent.

Luka rushed up the stage and grabbed my wrist, pulling me along for the ride.

Ride.

"I want to ride a ride."

"Are you nuts? This carnival is a scam, and you'll be sucked right in if you don't quit while you're ahead."

I yanked against his fingers and he halted, turning to face me as I ran into him, chest to chest. "Just one ride. Please." I wanted to say no and go after the man behind it, but the inkling to enjoy the pleasure of the wind on my face tickled my brain just right.

He grumbled. "No. That's final."

Glaring at the back of his head as he started dragging me, I used the heel of my boot to smash the toes in his. He cursed and let go of me, and I took my chance. He yelled after me as I darted from the tent and hurried to the tallest ride in the park.

Before he could catch up, I hopped into the seat as the man strapped me in. "Enjoy the ride." His eyes were far bigger than they should have been. He strolled to the electric box and started the ride.

Up I went, attempting to see the entire carnival from here. To find gluttony. To ensure my escape and his demise.

The seat spun, and I screamed. Seconds passed and my screams turned to laughter.

My seat spun sporadically as the pole my seat hung from spun in a clockwise pattern. I held tightly onto my bar and closed my eyes, relishing the childlike fun. Never would I have experienced this had I not come here. Everyone expected one thing of me, and that one thing did not include fun.

I expected the ride to slow down, but instead it sped up.

My head began to pound against my skull and I started to yell for it to stop. I wanted off. I needed my feet to touch the ground. I'd been desperate by now for my head to feel normal. I didn't want the nausea to bubble in my stomach, and yet I didn't get what I wished for.

The world passed by in such a blur that I couldn't spot a single soul. I couldn't make out lines, or shapes. I could barely spot colors and even that proved to be a challenge.

I blinked to try and give my eyes a rest, but after concluding that wasn't going to work, I closed my eyes and hoped for the best. No, I was done being the damsel. I had to get myself off this damned ride, even if that meant injury or worse.

Death is coming for you, Princess.

Like hell it would.

I reached for my sword, pulling it from my sheath and gripping it tight enough that it wouldn't fly from my hands, nor cut my own head off.

I felt the restraint and concurred that it'd been made up of metal and I was not able to cut through. But if I could climb out, I had a chance. Just not with my sword.

With all ten fingers wrapped around the hilt, I forced my eyes down to locate the man who put me on this damn ride and wouldn't let me off. When he was in my sight, or what I hoped was my sight, I threw the sword down.

A scream echoed up in my direction, and then I began the treacherous task of escape.

Using my strength to force my bar up was nearly impossible with the ride throwing me around like a rag doll. But I said nearly, not entirely.

I yelled out as I pushed against it, and when it snapped, I flew from the seat. I wrapped my arms through the bar and hung on, but the edge of the seat hit me in the gut as the ride switched directions.

When I spotted the ground, I took my chance and let go, flying into the dirt. I barely managed to get onto my feet as I wobbled from my warped balance. Then I leaned over the metal gate and let go of all the food I'd eaten. It became clear to me why Father didn't give us the chance to eat fried foods often enough. They went down easy but left you feeling like a corpse the second it came back up.

"Snow!" Luka hurried over, but stopped as he turned and pulled my sword from the ride operator's chest. He handed me my sword and grabbed my face, forcing me to look him in the eyes as he told me so. "We need to get you out of here."

"No," I croaked. "I have to find him. Kill him. Before he kills me. Before I lose him for good."

"You can barely walk, let alone wield a sword."

"Then show me how to shoot." I pointed towards his arrows. "Properly." I scanned the carnival as I found a ride that'd be much more forgiving. I hoped, anyway.

"You're going to kill yourself." He brushed the hair that'd fallen in my eyes away from my cheek. "I can't allow you to do that."

"Why not?" I debated using my sword to threaten his life, but I decided against it.

He leaned in, whispering, "You once told me queens have nobody to look out for them. Right now, you need someone to look out for you, and I'm him. Do you understand?"

"I am not a damsel," I spat.

His eyes softened as if he was mocking me. Was he mocking me as the next heir? That bastard. What came from his lips next had been so quiet I almost hadn't heard it myself. "Nobody said you were. But for now, you simply need to be taken care of. I'm *your* huntsman, Firefly."

I collapsed into his chest as darkness sealed me up in its cold touch.

TWENTY-SEVEN

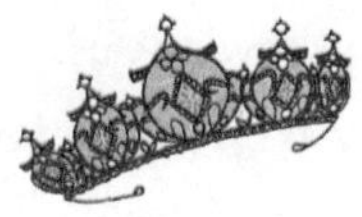

I ran over to the giant wheel lined with seats. Luka followed close behind. "What is this called?" I asked. I'd come to shortly after fainting, and even he knew I wasn't going to leave here without killing gluttony first.

Luka glanced up at the wheel looming over the entire carnival. "This is a Ferris wheel."

I grabbed his arm with a grin. "This is what I need to find him. I'll shoot from there. It doesn't hurt to try it once, right?"

He patted my hand. "Just once."

The man operating the wheel opened one of the carts and we stepped inside, taking our seats. He closed the door and pressed a button that put the wheel into motion.

We moved higher until the wheel no longer budged at the top. "Why did we stop?" I scanned the ride.

Luka sat back. "They do that every now and then to give us a view of the carnival."

I lowered my eyes to the ground and swallowed. "This is high." I shook my head to dismiss the nausea. "But we're here to look for him." I peered at all of the people below us. "I don't see him." I twisted around to reposition myself, but I caught a glimpse of the guy in the cart behind us, leaning back in his seat and watching me. "He's behind us!"

He looked back and as soon as he had, the sin stood and grabbed onto the side of the wheel. What was he doing? He placed his foot on a bar and began climbing towards us.

"Luka! He's coming this way!" I jumped out of my seat and gripped the wheel. "I need to get down."

"What the hell are you thinking? You're not going to make it in that dress!" He shouted.

I shot him a glare. "Piss off!" I placed my foot on one of the white bars that connected from the outer circle of the wheel to the center. I moved my hand down and ducked my head as I weaved through until I was outside of the Ferris.

He was moving faster than I was, and he was only inches from sending me to my maker. He reached out and almost had me, but I pulled back, letting go of the bar. I fell a few feet before catching onto the metal again.

"Snow!" Luka's head hung over the side of the cart.

"Stay there! I'm fine!" I fixed my grip and placed my boot in the V formed from two bars connecting at a point.

"Brennan, what are you doing up there?" a man yelled from the bottom of the wheel.

The guy looked at me but before he could grab me, I lost my grip and fell back. I reached out to grab anything, but nothing was within arm's length. Luka screamed my name, but I didn't hear anything over the sound of my own cries.

I had no time to process what was about to happen before I hit something—or someone. We both collapsed to the ground, and before I could register what was happening, the wheel began moving.

Luka jumped from his cart as soon as it leveled with the platform, rushing over.

He pulled me off of whoever took the blow from my fall, wrapping his arms around me to hold me from clawing my own eyes out due to all the horror I'd caused just from tonight.

The high tone of the music started to lower and cut out, until silence took over the entire carnival. Characters from every corner began to drop dead as if they were puppets and their strings had been cut loose. Lights dimmed, and with those came a clicking noise.

"Luka, what is that?"

He scanned the skies, then the tents. The tents collapsed, appearing flat as if everything inside disappeared in the blink of an eye.

The carnival was falling apart, but *Brennan* was still very much alive.

"We need to find him. Now. Before it becomes the ghost of a memory," I yelled at Luka as I gathered my skirts and ran off.

He wasted no time as he hurried off in a different direction. I searched the tents and the bodies but none of them stood out. None had his maniacal laugh, either. And as the rides began to screech and creak, they came toppling down from their massive heights, forcing me to dive out of the way.

Flipping over to face the debris, I scooted back, my back hitting a pair of legs. I tilted my head back to look up at my enemy—Brennan.

He grinned as his eyes bulged from his head. "You're not a very clever princess, are you?"

I wrapped my arms around his calves and yanked, but he'd been too heavy for me to physically take him down. I needed my sword.

Brennan leaned down and grabbed me by the hair, dragging me over to a tent that laid motionless. He swiped his hand and up it went, untouched and pristine. Taking me inside, he forced me onto the seat and grabbed the ring and lit it on fire. "You missed the best part, Snow."

I scowled, about to stand up until Fallon's face returned.

Around him laid beaten and bloodied bodies, and the final boy widened his eyes and booked it. Fallon screamed out and took off after him, tackling him. He tangled his fingers in his hair and pulled back before slamming his face into the dirt. He repeatedly slammed while I shouted at him to stop.

Blood coated the boy's face as it began to cave after his nose broke. The boy groaned while Fallon stood, his eyes narrowed in on him. "Tell me again, who's a pussy?" He squatted in front of him to show this boy who was in charge. "You are what you eat."

This side of Fallon terrified me. The cold-blooded murder. The ruthlessness. The sadistic tendency. He'd showed them the mercy I refused. They were supposed to have gone into my dungeon.

This couldn't be my brother, could it?

The boy lifted his hand as Fallon shushed him and straightened himself before crushing the boy's hand beneath his boot. "Being heterosexual doesn't make you a good person by default, and it sure as hell doesn't give you any right to torment anyone else for being different. Snow gave you a chance to change and learn from your mistakes. That was ill-advised on her part. I'll fix everyone's mistakes, because that's what I do. I'm always the mediator. Not today, Glen. Today, I'm a fighter." He lifted his boot high above the boy's head and flashed him a smile. "I'm your worst nightmare." He brought his boot down and splattered the boy's skull.

I cried out, scooting back and falling behind the bench. "No. Not Fallon. Not my little brother."

Brennan and I both turned towards the opening of the tent as Luka shifted his shoe. "Snow, I'm so sorry..."

I jumped up while Brennan was distracted and climbed onto the bench before driving my sword through his chest. I twisted until I heard a crack. Then dead he dropped—a man without a soul.

After I yanked my blade from his body, I fell to my knees as Luka approached me with caution. "We should leave. Now."

I somberly nodded, following him back to Ash Forest and away from the one place that reminded me of my loss. Tonight I'd not only taken one step closer to victory, but in turn I also fell three steps back. My baby brother was a murderer, and I feared I'd had a part to play in turning him into exactly that.

But I no longer *had* a brother.

TWENTY-EIGHT

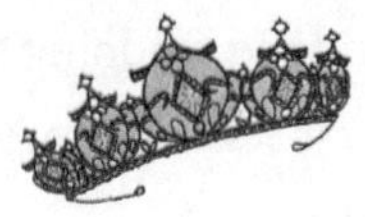

The rain began to pour on our journey to his cave, which wouldn't have been such an issue for us. But the trees couldn't create much of a roof when it came down, as if the skies had decided to dump their rainwater out all at once to start fresh again.

By the time we arrived, we'd been soaked.

At the mouth of the cave, Luka pulled some dry logs from the side and started a fire before throwing his wet shirt to the ground.

I lowered my hood and tried not to let my feminine hormones control me as I turned away from him and untied the cloak. Luka mentioned dinner, but I said, "I'm not hungry. I'd rather vomit."

"Is there anything I should know about?"

"I ate too much food."

"And?"

"And a lady said death is coming for me."

"I meant injury wise."

I touched my abdomen and winced. "I took a blow to the gut from the ride when it swung around. Broke my pinky, too."

He scooted towards me, barely inches away, which completely took me off guard. I leaned away from him. However, he said in a softer tone, "Allow me. You need someone to look at the damage."

I knew I didn't have much of a choice, but I despised the idea of being so vulnerable to him. Not even just him, but anyone in general. It showed my weaknesses and I could not trust a single soul to see what made me flinch.

Luka reached back behind me, undoing the little ties of my gown. I turned my head to make it less awkward, focusing on every little jagged edge of the cave wall.

"Pull it down to your hips. I'll close my eyes and let you undress your top and cover yourself appropriately. Just tell me when." He twisted his body the other way.

I pulled my sleeves off, then I undid my corset. I pushed my gown and chemise down to my hips before using my hands to cover my breasts. "I'm ready." Nothing prepared me for the way my heart skipped beats the second he turned to look at me.

His eyes didn't pry, nor stray from my stomach. He ran his fingers around my navel, pressing, earning a pained noise in response. "It doesn't look bad which is a good sign. Tiny bruising, but lucky for you, your corset took most of the shock. But we should still go to your castle tomorrow and see the medic."

The last place I wanted to be.

"My castle?" Where my brother was? Absolutely the hell not.

"We should talk about what we saw. I know it's eating—"

"Drop it," I said with a scowl. I did not in any shape or form want to talk about Fallon or his inhumane actions. I definitely did not want to ponder if I'd at all influenced them (to which I probably had).

He paused for a moment, but he didn't shy away from me. "Firefly, have you ever kissed anyone?"

That left me speechless. Not just speechless, but warm. No—*blazing*. Unable to form a thought. Why on earth would he ask such a question?

"Aside from Alexander, since he doesn't count," he added.

After a moment of gaining my composure, I shook my head. "I've never kissed anyone." It shouldn't have come all that much as a surprise, seeing as I had a little head-to-head fight with every boy I came in contact with. Still, at twenty-one, one might have wondered if something was wrong with me to not have had a crush or attempt to date a boy for a kiss.

Our eyes never wavered as my answer hung in the air like sugar cookies baked during the holiday season. Sweet. Tempting. Both of us begging for a treat.

His eyes were far too enchanting for a woman to say no to.

He pulled back, standing on his feet and turning away from me. "What's your favorite color?"

I hurried to pull my chemise back on, keeping my corset off as I fixed my gown and let Luka tie it. "What?"

"Your favorite color." He gestured, rolling his hand in a circular motion.

I nodded. "Oh, well, red. What about yours?"

He ripped a small ribbon of fabric from my skirt, tying my pinky to my ring finger to allow it to heal. "It's blue. I don't see much of it aside from the ocean and the sky, and the ocean only gives off its hue as a reflection of the sky. It's actually the one color found the least in nature. Did you know that?" After I shook my head, he went on, "it's the color you don't find often and I suppose that's why it's my favorite. It's rarer than all the others." I opened my mouth to say something, but he cut me off. "People, too, are rare. You are rare whether you believe so or not."

I didn't know how to thank him or what the correct response was, so I replied in the only way I knew how. "Rare doesn't win wars."

His laugh reverberated, and in that moment I had to store it safely in my memories for a rainy day. "But when it does, it leaves a lasting impression. It creates change."

I needed to change the subject before this asshole said other things that made my stomach flip, twist, and fly.

"Was your brother younger or older?"

Luka froze in his spot, but after a minute, he pushed a twig into the fire using a thicker stick. "Older. He was the more responsible one. Took everything so seriously. All the fault laid on him. I didn't realize how hard he had it until he was dead. Now I'm here having to be responsible, but I also know deep down he'd never want me to lose who I am."

The playful side of him. He was the younger brother, of course. As the once older sister, I understand the responsibility his brother held. "I'm sorry. I'd have loved to meet him."

He chuckled a tad, reminiscing over the memories. "He used to get so angry with me. Valid, but at the time I didn't understand why. I'd make friends out of the birds and he used to scold me for it saying I was too attached to our food."

A small smile formed on my face. "Much like I made friends with Jerry. So once upon a time, Luka was a friend of the birds. You never told me."

"It didn't seem important." He shrugged a little as the embers from the flames drifted along, exiting the cave in hopes of more oxygen.

I shot forward and leaned onto my hands and knees. "Nonsense. You're talking to an animal whisperer. Maybe not entirely." I tilted my head as I scrunched one side of my face. "But!" Lifting a finger, I scooted closer. "That's what I'm good at. Talking to animals. If I hadn't been chosen as the queen, that's what I'd want to do for the rest of my life." I sat back with my legs tucked underneath. "That's why Jerry has taken such a liking to me. Which reminds me, I should probably gather acorns."

"Gather acorns?"

"Jerry needs to eat."

"He's a squirrel."

I crossed my arms and gave him a stern look. "What happened to the guy who just seconds ago told me he made friends with birds?"

Luka dampened the fire. "I'm going to sleep. Don't stray too far."

I got up and looked out of the cave as the rain continued to pour from the sky. He'd put the fire out which meant if I got cold and wet, I didn't have a way to warm up, and I sure as hell couldn't take my soaked cloak with me. "Tomorrow then. Don't let me forget. I'll be up bright and early."

I turned and made myself comfortable on the floor beside Luka. "Maybe someday you can introduce me to your friends."

He didn't say a word as if he'd already fallen asleep, but as my skin lit up his features, a smile tugged at his lips.

"Goodnight, sad blue boy." With those words, my light turned off, leaving us in the pitch black.

TWENTY-NINE

No chirping sound this morning. Birds must have flown off, and crickets no longer breathing.

As I sat up and pulled the top of my gown down so I could put my corset on, I asked, "What time is it?"

Luka roasted something small over the open fire. "Nine."

I gasped. "Shit, Jerry's going to be so pissed with me. I haven't fed him!" I paused to see the animal on his stick. "Luka, where's Jerry?"

Snickering, he pointed to a squirrel sleeping behind me. "I wouldn't roast your best friend. You know that."

"Do I?"

Rushing over to Jerry, I picked him up and pulled him close to my chest. "You're starving. Let's find you acorns." I grabbed my cloak and tied it before setting off into the woods.

It hadn't entirely dried, but that was the oh-so-lovely humidity's fault.

I searched a few trees and Jerry gathered some acorns for himself before we returned back. Luka offered up some meat, but nausea still threatened me after yesterday.

When he finished his breakfast, we set back towards Drecose Castle.

As we arrived, everyone greeted us, including Fallon, whom I ignored. "Father, I need to see the doctor to assess my bruise."

Father nodded, leading me up to my room while Luka stayed behind with my mother. "May I ask how many are defeated?"

"Out of seven, three. Pride, Gluttony, and Lust. Lust was the easiest, surprisingly. He couldn't keep his eyes or hands to himself forever."

With a nod, he closed the door as we waited for the doctor. "And which injury have you received this time?"

"A bruise on my stomach. We visited Hypnotic Arythe. I saw things I wish I had not. I'll never eat another fried food as long as I live." Knowing my father would question what happened, I had to nip that in the bud. I did not want to lower anyone's hopes about me by telling them what the fortune teller told me. They'd never believe I could do it.

The doctor arrived and Father left the room to give me my privacy. After he checked my bruise and the discoloration, he ensured I was going to be fine. He still bothered to tell me to be careful even full well knowing I couldn't promise that. I was certain of what all I could handle. I wasn't even close to my limit.

Once he left, I ventured back downstairs to head back out to find another.

"I'm all fixed up. Let's go," I told Luka.

Mother tried to stop me, but that was no use.

Fallon also tried to say hi, but I gave him no attention.

"You've been cleared?" Luka asked.

I rolled my eyes, waving the back of my hand at him. "When have I been cleared? If I wait until that time comes, I'll never get back out there." In simpler terms, I'd been accident prone since birth. I couldn't help that I was an adventurous little spirit. Exploring was in my blood.

"Snow, please look at me," Fallon pleaded.

"I'm not sure when we'll be back but hopefully this time I'll *actually* be queen." I turned to my parents and released a choked-up laugh. Ignoring my own brother had been difficult, but he wasn't mine anymore. I had to remind myself of that.

"Snow!" He fell to his knees, and even in my peripheral he appeared so innocent. If only he knew that I knew what kind of monster he became.

Of the monster I created.

For that, I couldn't be around him anymore. I'd become a terrible influence.

I gestured for Luka to follow me out the door, but before I could even step foot outside, Fallon blocked me from leaving. "If you walk out that door, so help me."

"You can't be helped, Fallon."

His expression cracked before he narrowed his eyes. "We need to talk. Now." He grabbed my wrist tightly and dragged me to the kitchen, ordering the cooks out. "So you're allowed to murder people because it serves you and gives you the throne but if I defend myself, I'm the bad guy."

"Who told you?"

"Luka."

"That asshole," I hissed. "Regardless, Fallon, you didn't need to be so sadistic about it. When I kill, I make it quick. Death is meant to be mercy, an easy way out of a miserable life. And I only kill those I need to kill. The sins. I have not made any moves to kill another soul—and that's assuming the sins themselves even have souls. Which I don't believe."

His expression dropped like a sack of potatoes. "Are you defending them? You of all people know what horrid things they've done and said to me all these years. It's okay for you to defend me but when I do it, I'm in the wrong. I see what this is really about, Lana," he mocked. "It's not that you despise the damsel role as a whole, because you'd rather others be it for you. You're obsessed with being seen as the hero."

I stepped forward quickly, pointing my finger. "Take that back!"

His eyes lowered to my finger which we both knew stood in place of my sword. Had he not been family, it'd have been digging into his neck. "No."

"Who are you?"

"Your *brother.*" He straightened his shoulders, knowing he'd always be taller. "Love is unconditional, whether you agree with my actions or not. I don't regret it if that's what you're hoping to hear. They bullied me and they never felt remorse. As far as I knew, they were already dead."

Grabbing the edge of my cloak, I spun, abandoning him in the castle.

I'd created a villain.

"What the hell gives you the right to tell my brother what we saw?" I shouted at Luka as I paced by the fountain.

"I apologized. It was wrong of me. But he kept pestering me about why you ignored him and I felt bad." His eyes followed my every move.

I snickered, coming to a halt. "Felt bad? Do you think he did something right?"

"Not right, but I wouldn't necessarily call it wrong, either." He stepped forward. "Listen, Snow, I know it's a lot to process and seeing your brother kill people is difficult. I'm not downplaying your feelings because they are valid. However, his feelings are valid, too. You have to understand he's growing up and he doesn't want his big sister to step in and save him."

"So murder is the answer to you?"

One nod. "If it's the only way to stop his bullies, that's his choice. He's the one living with that now. Let him handle it."

I cupped my elbows as I folded my arms across my torso. "You didn't see the way he looked at them. It's not so much that he defended himself. It's the way he took pleasure in crushing their bones. That's what worries me. Am I responsible for that? What does it mean?" Of course it'd been my fault. It was foolish to believe otherwise.

Luka gave me a small shrug before grabbing hold of my shoulders. "We don't know for sure. You can always ask him but if you wish to do that, you have to stop trying to ostracize him. Show him that you're trying to understand. Show him you care about his well-being. If you continue to paint him in black, you'll never get the answers you're looking for. He wants to trust you with what he's feeling, but he's struggling to do just that because you keep looking down on him."

My brows knitted together. "How do you know all this?"

"You forget, Firefly, that I was once a little brother to someone like you. We look up to you as our role model. Don't make us feel ashamed for our mistakes. We're not children anymore."

It dawned on me then that I had been treating Fallon as if he'd been useless and unable to fight his own battles. It was hard to help it. Defending him had been in my blood since the day our parents found out they were pregnant. It was my entire duty as his older sister to protect him.

As his last words sunk in, it reminded me that he wasn't a child, but it also hit me in the gut because I'd never once had a chance to make mistakes.

I'd never been a child myself.

THIRTY

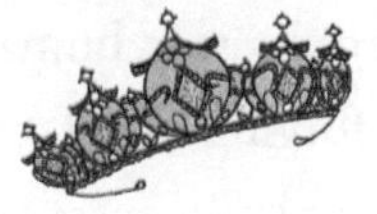

Luka slowed, but I kept going on, fingers around the hilt of my sword for peace of mind.

"Hey," he called.

I stopped, twisting my body enough to look back at him. "Yes?"

"Come here."

After blowing the strand of hair out of my face, I approached him, glancing down at the blue rose between his fingers. With a gentle touch, he snapped the stem just an inch below the bud, using his fingernails to scrape off the thorns.

"What the hell am I doing?" I cleared my throat, attempting to meet his gaze. He just wouldn't look my way.

No, his entire attention had been turned on the petals resembling the sky just after the sun disappeared beyond the horizon. "Blue," he mumbled. "Rare, but much more stunning when you catch it in nature." At last, he lifted his eyes to mine. In mere seconds, he reached up and settled the stem just behind my ear, cupping my hair around the rose. "I dare say the electric pulse of the flower captures the hazelnut of your eyes."

I had no idea what I was meant to say to that. Nobody had ever placed floral in my hair. Nobody had the guts to do so. But Luka, whatever he'd been made of was pure moxie in its finest form. Daring. Yet innocent.

That'd be what the huntsman emanated. Crafted, and carefully sewn together by empowerment, bliss, and sass.

He reminded me much of brass in human form.

I'd spent a short time forging metals. Hardly enough to know much about what smithing truly entailed, or what terms to use. However, one glance at Luka and I knew.

He exuded what I was desperate to absorb for my own benefits. Tenacious.

Him brass, and I branded of silver.

The walk from the fountain to Matt's underground cave was only an hour or so, but short in my eyes. Even shorter as neither of us said a word and I relished every second of that.

"What are we searching for?" Luka asked as he walked toward the river that matched his eyes.

"Anything that gives us intel on the sins. It's possible they're all alone but I'm starting to believe maybe they're in contact with each other. Brennan spoke of me in ways as if he knew me because someone else told him about me." I overturned rocks and scanned above us.

He glanced my way, a look of judgment made just for me. "You sure they haven't just been told by the Evil Queen?"

What I didn't tell Luka was that the Evil Queen was once a girl I conversed with. Not often, and not more than once. But when I was a teenager, she came to me to warn me. She had already known me and my future due to her ability. A small part of me hoped that she would spare me or keep what she knew about me to herself. However, that'd been wishful thinking.

"Keep looking." I shooed him off.

We searched high and low and every inch we could that didn't require taking the tunnel to the cemetery.

"Something isn't right," I said quietly.

"Hm?"

"Matt was pride, correct?"

"Yes he had a lot of pride, so much he couldn't admit that he was on the same level as the rest of us." He nodded a bit. "Why?"

"Because if Matt was pride, where does Alexander play a role? Yes, I've considered this before. A prince doesn't exist in Orsadia and he referred to himself as such. But his ego was right there with Matt's, and we are certain he's hiding something with the way he's got more skill than we thought beforehand." I approached Luka and moved a few rocks around.

His eyes never strayed from my face. "What do you think he is?"

"Aside from pride himself, he knows the Evil Queen. And not in the sense that everyone knows her, or that the sins know her. I mean..." I refused to think about Fallon. "I killed the wrong sin. And Alexander is the real pride, and he's the key to the rest of them. He's the same one who connects them all, and he tells them about me. That's how Brennan saw me. They all see me in the same eyes that Alexander sees me."

Alexander was their leader. But most importantly, he answered directly to the Evil Queen as her personal pet.

THIRTY-ONE

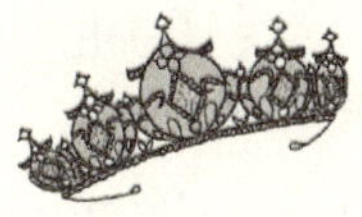

The beauty of waking up in a cave meant I didn't get blinded by light as I opened my eyes. However, it also made it possible to wake up with my head on Luka's shoulder.

I scooted away from him, fixing the strands of hair that stuck out from my head. "My cloak is a perfectly acceptable pillow."

Luka chuckled, shrugging a bit. "I tried but you insisted on using my shoulder. You said it was more comfortable." I'd never said any such thing. He was making a mockery of me.

Scoffing, I stood up and brushed the dirt from my clothes. "I doubt I said such a detestable statement. I would never choose your shoulder over my cloak."

He patted his heart. "You say that as if I'm Alexander."

I said nothing more on that topic. "We should get going. We need to find the next one and kill them. Let's check the underground caves. The last thing we need is the sin of wrath walking these parts."

Luka furrowed his brows and sat up. "You don't remember? We went last night. We settled on the fact that Alexander is working directly with the Evil Queen and he runs the show with the sins."

Now I knew Luka was messing with me. I would never forget finding vital information.

"What's the last thing you remember?" he asked.

"I remember walking through the forest." A shiver ran up my spine as I straightened my cloak.

He leaned his back against the cave wall. "You didn't seem any different last night." He started to laugh. "Eh, now you're just pulling my leg."

No, this *was* serious. "That doesn't make any sense. I don't joke." I put my hand up to stop him. "Back it up. Walk me through the night."

He began at the beginning, when we entered the caves, and ended after I fell asleep in his arms. I knew I wasn't myself because I let him hold me. What kind of queen pretended to be an infant who needed to be comforted to get some rest?

"Although, it does seem like..." Luka trailed off for a moment before coming to a conclusion. "Maybe we'll never know. However, something happened, whether in that cave or within your own mind and even if we don't actively search for the reason, it'll reveal itself. The truth always comes out eventually."

It never ceased to amaze me what he believed. I wished it would, because surprise was not a good color on me. "I suppose that's it." The horrid memory of my fifteenth birthday reared its ugly head as if warning me he'd eventually figure out the full truth. "So who is left?"

Luka gestured to me. "You know them best."

I closed my eyes to picture every last one in my mind. "Matt, who *once* represented Pride. Samael, who represented lust. Brennan, who represented...shit, what did he represent?" My memory was no good.

"Gluttony."

"Right, gluttony. That's really only two sins, still four left to discover, and one left to find. Alexander. The real pride." I opened my eyes to meet Luka's. "Let's search for them today. We have too many left, and then I'm off to defeat the queen." Knots formed in my stomach at the thought of being so far from victory.

Luka got off the ground and threw his quiver and bow over his shoulder. "I'm ready when you are."

I gave Jerry a kiss on the head before saying my goodbye. I could not risk getting him involved with our troubles.

We set out west. These last five wouldn't be so easy to track.

We passed by the fountain and eventually came upon Everinthian Castle. "I doubt they'll be here. They must be somewhere in this forest."

Luka shrugged. "Do you ever wonder what kind of people would...have sex with the Queen? Men like my father. Something must not have clicked for a man like him to choose a woman like so."

I glanced at Luka and lifted an eyebrow. "Let's not pretend you aren't mesmerized by my good looks."

He laughed. "Fair point. However, you are also a woman of substance. You have a heart of gold."

Facing the castle, I pulled my cloak closer to my body. "A heart of gold can be melted. Sometimes I think all of these queens were like me at one point, and the curse destroyed them. What if it destroys me?"

Luka shook his head, a frown lacing his lips. "Don't speak curses into your life."

I spun to face him. "What if it poisons me? What happens if I'm rotten like the rest of them?"

He released a sigh. "Why do you think you'll fail?"

"Why do I think I'll be the exception?" I pulled my hood up over my head.

"Look at me, Firefly," Luka said. When I gave him my undivided attention, he continued, "if you lose to this curse, I'll come back. I'll come back to help you defeat it once and for all."

He would give up his adventures to help me. It was a weakness, and weaknesses got people killed. "Don't. Don't end your adventures to put me first. If I'm evil, the last thing I need is to be put above others' dreams."

"You can't just ask me to let you destroy our own land. I can't enjoy my journey if you're destroying yours."

I narrowed my eyes. "Luka, you will obey me when I tell you to forget about me. When I'm queen, this quest is over, and we go our separate ways. I'm not your problem after that. Is that clear?"

He nodded a little reluctantly. "Yes, it's clear."

A red coat caught the corner of my eye. I turned to face the person wearing it and my eyes didn't seem to deceive me as Alexander came from the queen's castle.

"So it's true," I whispered. Before Luka could answer, I did. "I should have put the pieces together earlier. He said he came from a castle and I never questioned which. Orsadia only has two castles." I scowled. "This is our chance." I glared at the figure disappearing into the forest. Without thinking twice, I followed him. "Hey! Assxander!"

He stopped in his tracks and turned to face me. "Princess Snow White."

"You work for her. She sent you to marry me to stop me from becoming Queen. You're the lead sin. Her bitch."

He shook his head, scoffing. "There's much more to it that you're missing."

"Tell me, what am I missing?" I lifted my chin.

He closed the gap between us. "I'm not permitted to tell you, but you have to trust that what *we're* doing is for the best."

Everyone seemed to warn me about something else but wouldn't let me in on what it was. "It's about the curse, correct?"

Alexander walked the other way, ignoring my question.

"Talk to me, damnit!" I grabbed his shoulder, pulling him back.

He twisted himself, slapping my hand. "There are things in this world I can't talk about!" He backed away until he put enough space between us, then he made a run for it.

I let him go.

Luka came through the trees, sure to take his sweet time so I wouldn't look like the damsel who needed a *bodyguard*. "What was that about?"

"People are keeping secrets from me. After everything I've learned, they have the audacity to keep these mysteries to themselves." Gripping the handle of my sword, I tightened my fingers around the embossed metal.

Luka grabbed my hand to keep me from doing something I'd regret. "Let go of that anger. These secrets will eventually be revealed. They can't be kept forever because we both know that isn't how the universe works."

I closed my eyes and drew a sigh. "But what if these secrets are revealed when it's too late?"

"Too late for what?"

"Too late to break the curse," I whispered.

He pressed his lips into a thin line before shaking his head. "No, we have to believe things will work out. If they don't then what are we doing here?"

My grandmother was a queen. If I followed her footsteps, I'd eventually get to follow my own dreams when I was no longer queen. I only had to defeat her and survive three years.

"What are your dreams?"

I glanced at Luka, confusion knitted into my brows. How did he read my mind? "Excuse me?"

He tilted his head to the right, squinting. "I didn't say anything."

I thought maybe I'd been hearing things, but the voice came through clearer and I knew from the tone that a woman was calling to me.

She asked again, *"What are your dreams?"*

Turning around, I searched for a woman, but nobody was nearby. Where was this voice coming from?

"Snow, just close your eyes and listen for a moment. Think. What are your dreams?" the voice appeared right in my ear, and now I knew I was losing my mind.

"Are you okay?" Luka asked me.

Looking back at him, I nodded. "I'm doing fine." Yet, I couldn't seem to believe my own lies. I wasn't doing fine. A voice was invading my head and it hadn't come from me. Was Aalia trying to speak to me?

The voice disappeared and didn't return. Where it had come from, I couldn't say. However, there was one question that kept coming back. What were my dreams? If I hadn't been chosen to be a queen, what would I be doing now? My options were endless. I could be a maid. I could have been a medic if I chose that. Neither of these options appealed to me, however. There was one dream that beckoned me.

"Animal trainer."

"What?" Luka asked.

I took a deep breath. "I wanted to be an animal trainer." When I was a young girl, I would find so many animals in the forest during the summer months. They all fascinated me, and I wanted to work with animals. Being an animal trainer wasn't a practical job in the village, but when I glowed in the dark, I knew I wasn't a practical human being.

"I never knew that. You wanted to train animals? And here I am, a huntsman. Maybe we aren't a match made in heaven," Luka joked.

My eyes met with the forest floor. "It doesn't make much of a difference now. I'll be a queen and that is my destiny. Come, Luka. We must find these sins." I gestured for him to follow, and he did.

We spent the rest of our day searching high and low for sins that seemed the hardest to catch. Sloth should have been the easiest and yet sloth was hiding somewhere we couldn't locate. Envy was another that seemed to be hidden well.

I hardly focused as we walked this quest today. My mind wandered on the truth that I had revealed my dream to Luka. It disgusted me that I would ever let such a thing slip. What kind of queen would I be if I told people that I never wanted to be their queen?

Luka knew now.

Stopping in my tracks, I spun and faced him. "Promise me you won't tell a single soul about what I said today."

He crossed his arms. "Why? Is it such a bad thing people know you want to train animals?"

"Yes. If you tell a single soul, I will have to banish you. Promise me that you will never tell anyone."

He nodded, sighing. "I promise that this will stay between us." And yet as he said earlier—*secrets couldn't be kept forever because we both knew that wasn't how the universe worked.*

One arrow. Two. Then a third. The only arrow that remotely hit the tree was that third.

I hurried over to retrieve them, shoving them back into Luka's quiver slung over my shoulder.

A crow cawed in the distance, hidden amongst the thick foliage and bright leaves barely hanging on by a thread. The moon hardly lit through the canopy, which had the birds squawk more frequently. To my left, a twig snapped.

I whipped out an arrow, placing it perfectly within the string. Then I aimed. As I let go, an animal cried out. No, not any animal. A deer.

As I rushed over, I kneeled beside the doe. "You poor thing." I laid my hand over its wound. "I did not mean any harm." I swallowed the dryness forming in my throat.

The doe exhaled with a whimper. So, I stood and removed my sword from its sheath, lifting it over my head. "For your sake." In one swing, the head had been clean cut. Quick. As painless as possible. Never in a millennium did I want to do such a horrid thing to an innocent creature, but it had been my duty to put the doe out of its misery.

I removed the arrow from his chest, glancing back at the cave. I could bring it for breakfast. Part of me felt guilty doing that. As if I was taking advantage after a heartfelt apology.

Yet another part of me said that it was dead now, and to make good use of it was to eat. That way it hadn't been for sport.

We both knew it hadn't been.

No, the arrow I shot was out of defense. Black was the forest tonight, surrounded by the sins of the damned. Every living organism succumbed to the power. The question remained: who was that power?

Me.

I'd been the most powerful creature that walked through. With magic I had yet to master.

Fitting for a princess, I supposed.

Just not quite fitting for me.

When my thoughts settled, a decision had been made. I would not be eating the doe out of respect. Rather, I'd bury her. Allow her flesh and bones to flourish into something more magnificent. Even in death, she'd give back to the very home that raised her.

After spending half the night on a walk to the cemetery, I used the shovel to bury her carcass outside the gates, before trekking back to the cave. By the time I'd arrived at the cave, a sliver of light peeked from beyond the horizon.

Luka slept on his side, arm under his head for cushion. Peaceful. Like this, I almost didn't recognize the man. I almost didn't want to punch him in the arm when he said something stupid.

After witnessing a shiver ripple through his body, I removed my cloak and draped it over him before I planted myself on the ground. I got a fire going and leaned back, glancing at him one last time.

His eyes were glued to mine as he grumbled, "Good morning, Firefly."

As the name left his lips, my skin illuminated on cue, responding solely to his command.

THIRTY-TWO

Music echoed into the sky. Everyone danced in circles, and laughter floated into the air as the wind carried it all the way through the village. Birthdays were a huge deal here, and my fifteenth had been no different.

Nobody else around us knew the truth—that I was the next heir to the throne.

The commotion became too much at one point and I headed off in one direction, attempting to leave behind the chaos that was my day. If I had a say in the matter, we wouldn't be celebrating anything today. I'd much rather be in the woods, training to take down the Evil Queen.

I ventured off into Ash Forest where I belonged. Where home called to me. Crows cawed and the wind whipped through my hair, daring to loosen the strands from their hold.

Mother and Father warned me of Ash Forest and yet my fears never surfaced. Something about the danger of Ash Forest lured me in with whispers of my name.

Lana...

Lanaaaaa...

Walking further, I stopped at the sound of a twig snapping in the distance. I searched through the trees to search for a face and yet not a single one came into view. Whoever they were, they had no intention of being found.

As I came upon a woman, I paused. "Who are you? Nobody else comes into this forest but I."

She shook her head. "I do not wish to say."

I let out a gasp. "I know you. You're the new princess." I curtsied out of respect. "I apologize for my rude words."

Her head snapped back and her blue eyes pierced holes through my soul. "Don't you dare treat me that way. I'm not worthy of your respect."

"Why is that?" I folded my legs under me as I planted myself on the ground. This would someday be the queen I'd be required to defeat.

Her head dropped and her brown hair created a curtain around her. "There are things you do not know, nor wish to know. I've been cursed with knowing these things."

"Things?"

"Tell me, is there something you're keeping secret from your entire village?" she asked.

I swallowed. "No."

She snickered. "You're not the one who is destined to replace me someday?"

How did she have any idea who I was? Of course. She said she knew things I didn't know. But I did know I was next in line.

"You should go back to your party," she said.

I dropped my arms at my sides. "No. If you know so much about me, you know that I'm also rebellious when it comes to rules. I wouldn't be out in Ash Forest if I followed rules."

"Go back to your party, Snow*."*

"My name is Lana."

She stomped her way to me and grabbed my chin. "You don't know the horrors I've seen."

"Have you witnessed your brother being called names because of who he likes? I've witnessed the ugliest side of humanity. I think I have a clue." I pushed her arm away from me.

The princess stepped back. "That is not all that happens. Someday, the anger will consume you until you don't know who you are anymore. I envy *those who've got the choice to be themselves. They don't understand the curse that plagues this land, the curse that plagues each of us from within." She dropped to her knees.*

I crawled over to her. "What are you seeing that we can't see?"

She lifted her eyes to meet mine. "What you can't see, Snow White, is that when you believe everything has worked in your favor, it will be ripped from underneath you like a rug. Your loved ones will suffer. Your rage will devour you. Your father will not make it out of this war alive."

I hadn't believed her when she said those words, but everyone in the village knew the princess had the power of sight. She could predict things—awful things.

When she told me about my own father's demise, that day became the worst day of my life. I vowed to shut my father out. I changed my name because if I was Lana, the girl my father loved so dearly, I would never survive his tragic end. I had to cope with the news that I had little time left with the man who raised me to be who I was.

Deep down, I hoped I could change the future and save his life.

A hand grabbed my shoulder and pulled me back, holding me in place. I looked over at Luka who seemed to be focused on something—or someone. When I followed his line of sight, I saw a man who was throwing rocks into the Evil Queen's garden. A telling sign indeed.

Luka stepped out of the trees, clearing his throat. "What has the queen done that'd be so awful?"

The man looked back at us. "What does it matter? The queen is awful to everyone who crosses her path."

I couldn't continue to hide in the shadows like a coward. I stepped out, placing my hand on my sword. "Certainly, she is. However, Luka asked a question and we're still waiting for an answer. You must know who I am, and I more than anyone want to defeat the Evil Queen and take her throne. So, we ask again with more dominance: what has the queen done that'd be so awful?"

He grumbled and dropped his rocks. "She took everything from me. I once had it all and she took everything I had in my name."

I glanced at Luka before facing the man. "And your solution is to throw rocks at her flowers? Hardly seems beneficial to you. Those rocks are merely pebbles." I waved my hand over them.

He rubbed his face, swallowing his shame. "What I do is my business. It may not be logical, but it is my choice either way."

Luka chuckled. "Fair enough. I'm Luka, the huntsman. This is Princess Snow White."

"Cain."

What were two sins we were asked to kill? Envy and sloth. This man was throwing rocks at flowers without real goals or purpose. I knew sloth would never do something as pointless as such. Although, envy might.

I stepped forward and studied his features. "Cain, does the queen know you're out here?"

Snickering, he shook his head. "She could care less about me."

"The phrase is: she *couldn't* care less about me," Luka corrected.

Cain dismissed his input. "Tomato, tomato." He has pronounced both versions of *tomato* in a different way. "I want revenge on the queen. I need reprisal. I want to take her for everything she owns."

Luka's laugh barely carried over the foliage. "And I suspect you want our help?"

"It couldn't hurt." He shrugged.

I grabbed Luka by the arm and pulled him aside. "If we agree to help him, this could help me with defeating her. If I know more about her, I have more leverage. If we can get into the castle, I may be able to map the layout." It was certainly a long shot, given that princesses couldn't enter Everinthian before their coronation, so to speak.

"He may very well be a sin. Are you aware of that?"

"I'm aware."

"You propose we help a sin get revenge on the queen, and then what? We kill him?"

"Precisely." I smirked. "Two crows with one sword."

We faced Cain and agreed to help him with his cause. Cain didn't waste another second on standing around. He snuck us into her garden, but we had no time to stop and smell the roses.

He got us close to the castle and pointed to the top. "We must get in that window. That is the only room that is empty at all times."

"How do you know this?" I asked.

Cain rubbed his neck. "Because we used to go on dates."

I made a face. "You dated her? Absolutely despicable." I caught an eye from Luka, quickly apologizing for my insults. His father made the same mistake, and my grandmother was one of the queens. I wasn't worthy of judging, given I was the next heir to the throne.

Cain diverted the subject. "If we get inside that window, there will be a door to the right. Follow that and we will eventually be led to her valuables. I want all of her gold."

This could very well be envy. He was envious of what she had. Maybe Cain did date her and if that were true, he also dated her and envied her stuff. When she broke it off, he wanted vengeance. He was willing to do whatever it took to get her possessions.

Luka pointed up to the window. "How do you suppose we reach that? I don't see a rope anywhere nearby."

Cain ran off for a moment and returned with a rope. "I have one." It seemed a little suspicious that he could attain it in a matter of minutes. Were Luka and I walking into a trap?

When Luka met my eyes, we both thought the same thing. We had to keep our eyes open and guard high.

It'd likely be a trap.

"Cain, you're forgetting one crucial bit of information. I can't get into the castle. Magic Law doesn't allow for that," I explained.

Shaking his head, he nodded towards the window. "Doesn't hurt to try. If you can't make it, then Luka can."

I lifted a finger to argue but Luka cut me off, insisting he play his part. He'd stupidly put his life on the line and head into the castle, even if it meant I couldn't save him. Why? What had been the point of it?

And if it had been a trap, in which case I was relying on it, he'd be dead in minutes if he was lucky.

Cain threw the rope up to the window, missing a few times. When it finally caught on something, he tugged on it to make sure it would hold. "I'll go first." He grabbed the rope with both hands and placed his feet on the wall, beginning his way to the top.

"We can bail out now if you wish, Luka." I looked over at him.

He was too focused on Cain to give me any attention. He wasn't stepping out. Between my bruises and other injuries, I couldn't forfeit now. Accepting defeat would be a humiliation all on its own.

Luka went up next after Cain made it up a few feet. He wasn't taking any chances of getting cut off when he was almost to the top, so he made sure to stay close behind Cain.

When they were a little farther up the side of the castle, I started walking up the rope myself. I took it slow until I got the hang of my movements. When we got to the top, Luka reached out and told me to grab onto his hand. I refused, climbing into the window on my own strength. I didn't refuse because I wasn't a damsel. I'd refused because he already had an injured leg that ached with every lift he made, and I was not about to make that any worse than it was.

And I'd made it into the castle. That hadn't been right. I shouldn't have been able to pass the protective barrier.

I scanned the room. "Where did Cain go?"

"He went to grab the gold. Let's go," Luka said.

As I looked back at the rope, I noticed it was tied around a hook in the wall. "Stop. Someone inside the castle helped Cain get us up here."

"We can take them."

When I turned my head towards him to tell him we were a woman and half a man, guards burst into the room. "Luka!" I yelled, pulling out my sword.

Luka grabbed his bow but before he could get an arrow on the string, the guards seized him.

I held my sword in front of me and swung. "Stay back!" Multiple guards pulled out their swords, and it didn't take long for them to knock mine from my grasp. A guard grabbed my hands, pinning them behind me. He knocked me onto my knees as someone entered the room. I could never forget her face. "Mira Sunder."

Luka choked, wiggling in their grasp. "You two know each other? You could have told me you were acquainted with the Evil Queen before dragging me into this war!"

"Quiet!" the Evil Queen snapped at Luka before turning her attention back on me.

There had been a day when I pitied her, but that day had long passed. This would only end in more bloodshed, and I prayed it was not my father's, nor my own.

A sharp noise echoed as she pulled out her sword, burying the tip of the blade in the hair around my neck. "Snow White, we meet again."

THIRTY-THREE

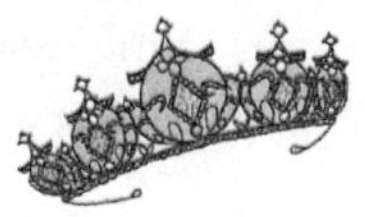

The Evil Queen had left us for a while. It was no secret now that I had met her before all of this. I'd interacted with her once and I knew Luka was disappointed in me for lying. However, I never asked him to come on this journey. That had all been on him.

I gulped down my nausea, but it hadn't helped with my dry mouth. "It's not what you think, Luka."

"What do I think?" His head snapped toward me.

"You think I was friends with her, or maybe I had done something awful to her. However, neither of those are true. I ran into her on my fifteenth birthday. She said something to me, something awful. I've hated her since. I knew I would get the chance to take her down someday, so I trained as hard as I ever have." It'd been no use. He would believe what he chose to, and I hadn't trained hard enough.

Luka turned his head away from me, not saying another word. It was hardly a huge deal that I didn't tell him I hated the Evil Queen *personally*.

She entered the room as if she'd heard my thoughts, eyes falling on me. "How's your father?"

"Don't talk about him. You have no right to mention him." I struggled against my chains.

She shrugged and approached Luka. "This your boyfriend? Suppose you shall have some fun before your timely demise." She faced me. "Why haven't you taken to Alexander? What's so wrong with my brother?"

Brother... He was her *brother.* Yanking at the chains again, I said, "He has no respect for women. He kissed me without my permission. He's hardly anything interesting."

My face stung as she slapped the daylights out of me. "Don't you talk about him that way."

I spit onto the stones. "You'd rather defend his immoral actions than dare defend a woman's right to her body? You sicken me, Mira."

She bent down and grabbed my chin. "Do you not defend your brother, Snow White?"

I scoffed. "Don't you dare compare his sexuality with what Alexander did. The two are not the same."

She straightened her posture. "I was referring to his murderous spree, but I suppose that falls on me for implying otherwise. I've been trying to help you. I was hoping Alexander would woo you and you'd forget about trying to defeat me. There are things you do not know, Snow. I wish I could tell you but if I say a word about this, my end will be far from pleasant."

"Allow me to go out on a limb here—the curse is real? I'm usually right. However, the curse has its tight grasp on you. Why can you not defeat this? Is it hard to break such a curse?" I watched her with curiosity.

Unfortunately, her expression never faltered. "I've found the cure, but you need to trust me."

I laughed. "Why, because you want to be the one to break it?"

A sigh escaped her lips. "No, because I want it to be broken for good. I was in your shoes, Snow. I have been there. I know you have this urge to be the one who breaks the curse, sending the wickedness to the underworld for good. I know what that's like, but as soon as that evil takes hold, it becomes much harder to control yourself. It becomes harder to resist the darkness. I crave watching innocent men and women bleed to death, but I don't wish to be this way. I don't do this because I can't trust you to defeat the curse. I do this because I can't trust the curse to not pull you into a world of immoral desires. I must be the one who breaks this curse. If I don't, there is no telling how long it will be before the next queen can muster up the strength to fight it."

I fought to keep my eyes open as something had flooded my veins. Someone had drugged me.

She stepped back. "I must do this for both of us and everyone in Orsadia. I'm sorry."

...and my world had been engulfed by darkness.

As I peeled my eyelids open, my vision blurred until my sight adjusted. "Wh—" I could barely utter a word. My saliva thickened until it was all I could taste.

I turned my head to study my surroundings, but it had just been I in this room. Luka was nowhere to be found.

A needle was placed in front of me. "This should keep you subdued long enough for me to carry out the plan," Mira said.

"Lu—" I closed my eyes, attempting to move my wrists. Whatever she slipped into my body was strong enough to control a large animal. Every part of my body weighed at least ten pounds, and that was more than enough to keep a woman like me from fighting back.

"Is the final dose ready?" Alexander asked.

Mira said, "Almost." A finger touched my cheek, but I didn't react. I wanted to sleep off the rest of this drug, but I had to try and wear it off somehow. People needed a new queen. Pronto.

In one word, she added, "Ready."

I opened my eyes to meet a red coat—one I despised with a burning passion. Alexander kneeled and grabbed my jaw. "I wish I didn't have to do this. If we had just worked it out, we could have avoided everything." He lifted another needle and inserted it into my neck. My throat closed up and I squeaked as I tried to get air to pass through. A blazing fire began in my lungs as I struggled to take a breath at all, but whatever they had put in my system had told my throat oxygen was our enemy.

As the tightening continued, so did my small squeaks. This would be my end. I couldn't stop the inevitable.

With one last failed attempt at trying to suck in air, I dropped my head back. My eyes shut, and the world slipped away quicker than it had come into existence.

THIRTY-FOUR

Something pinched me. A rush of air entered my lungs and the world swooped in to hold me tight. No, that wasn't the world. Someone had me in their arms.

A hand landed on my cheek, giving it small taps. "Firefly, wake up. Come on, you're not dead yet."

I followed orders and met a pair of green eyes. A wave of relief hit me, and I scrambled to grab whatever weapon I had. Luka wrapped his arms around me, pulling me against his chest. "Shh, it's all going to be okay. I promise it will be okay, but we need to make a move fast. Your heartbeat stopped. You're lucky I'm experienced with this kind of thing to know how to flush it out."

So she *did* kill me.

It could have been easy to just let myself relax in his arms and accept the comfort after everything I'd just experienced. However, there were still sins and an Evil Queen for me to take down.

I grabbed Luka's arms and struggled to pull them off, and when I did, Luka grabbed my face to stop me in my tracks. "Don't do anything stupid. You still have drugs in your system."

His words hardly registered in my mind as I focused on the color of his eyes. They'd been such a deep shade of green that I never noticed how much emotion they hid within. The greatest emotion he conveyed at this moment was concern for *me*. How lovely to have someone care this much about my existence.

If only it wasn't because I was the one who'd save us all...

For a split second, a thought occurred to me as I lowered my eyes. We were just inches apart and it would take less than a second to ease my guess on whether or not he was a good kisser. I could kiss him and forget everything that seemed to be going wrong for me. His warmth could lock me inside a box of euphoria for an unfathomably long time.

"What's on your mind?" His question snapped me from my thoughts.

I shook my head, dismissing such silly ideas. Luka and I were *partners* for this quest, and it would never be anything more. After this was over, we'd go our separate ways.

"Nothing is on my mind except for her. I need to get out of this dungeon and find a way to take her down." I stood but my legs gave way.

Luka caught me as if he knew it'd been coming. "Careful. You have drugs in your body. It's going to be a bit before you're able to fight."

I grabbed his arms, squeezing my eyes shut. Nature decided to pay me a visit, my moods about to be all over the map. "No, Luka. I must fight now. I must." I managed to get my balance in check as he let go of me. I shook both of my feet, one at a time, until I proved to my brain that my feet were mine to control. This drug was not going to take anything else away.

As I walked up the steps, I noticed a few guards at the top of the stairs. They were laying on the job but as I got closer, I knew Luka had dealt with them before he came to get me.

A familiar face came into view and I stopped, scowling. "You set us up."

Cain put his hands up. "In all fairness, I never said I wasn't *still* dating the queen. I just said she took everything from me, and I wanted revenge."

"On your girlfriend! You set us up. I died down there, and there is nothing else like experiencing death that strengthens Snow White." I stumbled toward him as Alexander exited a room and caught sight of us both.

"What do you want? To kill me again?" I eyed Alexander.

He shook his head. "I want to apologize."

That was a lie in itself. "Cain, Alexander still has what you don't."

"Excuse me?" Cain asked. Alexander shot me a warning.

I'd use this.

"You may be dating the queen, but Alexander will always come before you. He's her brother. She'll defend him no matter what he does." It wasn't even a lie.

Cain snickered. "I doubt that. He can't hold her at night."

"And yet if it were you or him, she would always choose him," I finished nonchalantly.

Antagonizing caused Cain to focus his hatred on Alexander, giving me a moment to pull the sword from Alexander's sheath. I ran over before either could process my game, swinging my blade at Cain's neck. His head flew to the ground with a thud, blood splattering across everything nearby.

Alexander watched me with wide eyes, blood tainting his skin. I knew what thoughts ran through his head, but I didn't address them. Cain was envy in the flesh.

"Kill me again and you will wish I'd taken the suffering from you." I pointed the blade at Alexander before handing him his weapon back. I called to Luka in the stairwell. "I know who you are." Pride. He'd get his moment. Eventually. And it may have been why I had been allowed to enter the castle. “Give me my sword.”

With honor, he fetched it for me just as I hadn’t used his to take his own life. Into my belt it went.

It didn't take long for Luka to make it to us. He glanced at Cain's body, not a single question dripping from his tongue. Instead, we left the castle in silence. Death couldn't hold me now. Maybe I would be the one who broke the curse for good.

"What did you do?" Luka asked.

"What any woman would do to take the crown. I appreciate you saving my life, Luka. Thank you." I stopped to face him. "However, I've made it this far and if I give up, everything we have done up until this point becomes useless. I refuse to let my quest be just a failure. The drugs may be in my system, but we can focus on detoxing my body while we search for the last sins. Is that understood?"

Luka nodded without hesitation. "Yes, understood."

"Good. We will continue our search from here. I expect no more questions and no more commands. I will do what needs to be done for the people of Orsadia. I may come off as selfish or stubborn but it's for a good cause. I care about this land. I want to see people healthy. Thriving. I want to make sure people do not go hungry and children do not get bullied for being themselves. Women will be treated with respect and humans will feel the true compassion they deserve. That is what I intend to do for Orsadia, and nothing will get in my way. The Evil Queen may try to stop me, but we've shown her that it's not that easy. It never was." I turned on my heel and walked along Keenain River, in the direction of the bridge.

The leaves fell ever so gently from the trees, saying goodbye to fight the harsh winter on their own. It was the circle of life and I did not question it. Nature was beautiful the way it had been made. However, I disagreed with that notion when it came to the circle of life that was my uterus. The hormones were a whole other argument on its own. In the end, it just proved that women could handle blood and we were fit to be queens. We just had to break a curse and soon Orsadia would respect women for who they truly were.

"Envy is just jealousy. How could that be so deadly, aside from Cain's sin?" I asked Luka as I glanced at him.

With a shake of his head, he replied, "They're not the same. Common misconception. Jealousy is relatively harmless. Envy is selfish to the core, which if it lingers long enough, leads to far more dire situations. Envy is like jealousy in wanting what others have. But it is the thought that you *don't* want others to have it, too."

THIRTY-FIVE

Having been personally killed by the Evil Queen felt a bit like an honor in the same sense that it stung. Luka became increasingly aware of how much I hid from him, as well as he discovered how weak I truly was.

I was not invincible.

Not indestructible.

Simply just alive.

And that spell father put on me? Gone. Obliterated.

Leaving me alive like every other human in Orsadia. That was a damn curse upon itself.

My walk down to the ocean had been an hour or so judging by the location of the sun, and when I did arrive, it hadn't taken long for my hair to frizz. The closer I got to the saltwater, the more a bird's nest built on my hair. However, that was the trick to my flawless complexion.

Humidity had been both a curse as well as a blessing.

Sand lined the shore for about a mile, possibly more. Cliffs stood just beyond that, leaving only one entrance to the beach itself. A seagull called every now and then, and it was awfully peaceful mixed with the roaring of the ocean waves. Seafoam would greet us with a gentle hello before retreating. Much like a swing.

Some things never changed.

I supposed that was comforting in its own way. Even if this curse was broken, where I stood now would bring me solitude. Serenity.

Waves rolled gently along the shore, begging for my forgiveness from the moment they'd tried to drown me. How convenient of them now to apologize after the fact.

"Now you choose to bend at my every whim. Don't think I forgot how desperately you wanted me taken out of this world." I scoffed, rolling a strand of hair between my fingers. "I never forget."

I dismissed the grudge with a wave of a hand. "That's not why I've come, however. The Evil Queen took my life from me a few days prior. She stopped my heart. She made a fool of me. In return, I wish to make a fool of her times ten. However, I'm not certain how I should go about that. Do tell me your secrets and I'll swear to it they'll never be revealed to another soul."

The ocean stayed quiet.

"Alexander is her brother. Were you aware of that little bit of information? It should have been so obvious when she said he was a prince. My father called him such a thing, without realizing he tried to marry me off to the Evil Queen's brother. Fallon is sort of a prince, although I suppose he wouldn't entirely be until I take the throne myself and have him in my castle. I doubt I'd do that. He's got a sadistic side to him now and I'd rather not entertain that any further." I stepped closer, running my fingers through the seafoam. "What do you say?"

The waves receded before rushing upon my boots. Something small clanked against my toe and I reached down to pick it up, rubbing my fingers over it.

"A compass." I flipped it over and studied its engraving. "Mira Sunder's compass." The corner of my lips tilted upward as I thanked the ocean for its help.

I wasn't entirely sure what I could do with it but that was the start. A compass was a key. Evidence. It had her name on it and if I used it wisely, I could ruin her from the inside out. That was my goal, too. How fitting for the Evil Queen.

How fitting for Mira Sunder—a girl whose entire ability relied on reflections and tragedy.

The only issue I ran into was: what would I do with this compass? I'd need to search the library but it wouldn't give any information on her personal objects, and even if it did, it'd only be in the library that stood inside Everinthian Castle.

I couldn't ask Alexander about it, seeing as he despised my guts by pretending he wanted to help.

I had to find someone who knew personal things about her and would be more than willing to give that information up without asking for a fortune in return. A sin, possibly. Aalia, if she knew enough. If her ghost had been roaming this land, she had access to Mira's castle.

I doubted I'd find any more sins close enough to her, however, and I also doubted they'd be anywhere near her castle.

So, I had to ask myself where did I turn? What did a girl do when all she had was a sword and a nightlight?

Sneak into her castle? Risky, and I'd rather not walk into any more traps. No, this had to be done solely from the outside of those walls.

I could enlist the help of Luka, but there was no guarantee he knew anything and if I had gone to him, he'd surely find it a little barbaric to follow through with my intentions. Intentions that were, though pure, also entirely guided by vengeance. I preferred to avoid men like Luka with their scolding statements and scouring gaze.

All I needed was enough information from this compass to humiliate her that way she had me. It sounded so easy, but it certainly wouldn't be.

THIRTY-SIX

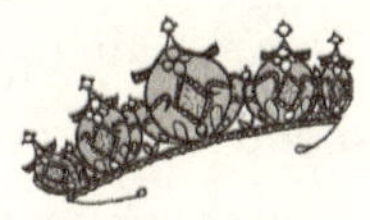

Jerry stood on my shoulder, watching the sun rise alongside me. "Nature is beautiful when you forget about the evils that plague our world."

The rise had been slow-going, but the orange and pink hues lasted for miles. It had been autumn's most sacred hello.

Luka took a seat beside us. "Still friends with dinner?"

I gasped and covered Jerry's ears to protect him from the insults. "Do not call him that. He is a person." I grabbed Jerry and hugged him with my hand. "He is a sweetheart."

"You will kill people who represent sins, but you can't kill a squirrel for food."

A kick to his foot was all he needed. "Another word about this and I will make sure you never return to Orsadia when you leave. Jerry is my friend, and he loves to cuddle."

Luka's eyebrows shot up. "I can cuddle, too." In what sense had the huntsman himself been so eager to cuddle? Had he really been so deprived of human contact, or was it something deeper that I refused to acknowledge?

"It's not the same." A shake of my head gave him a frown.

Getting up, I ventured into the forest. With four sins left, I was close to the end of my quest. It was time to head back to Drecose Castle and check in on my father.

Luka followed me the whole way back, and when I saw my father at the door, *love* claimed me. I ran and hugged him, forever grateful he was still alive. The Evil Queen hadn't gotten to him just yet and that was what I had to hold onto until I became her ruination.

"Lana, what's gotten into you as of recently?" He pulled away from our hug.

I swallowed my fear. "Nothing, Father. I just missed you."

His smile lit up my entire morning. "I always miss you."

I pulled out Jerry from under my brown cloak. "Father, can you watch Jerry for a moment? I need to wash up while I have a chance."

"Of course." He took Jerry from me.

After thanking him, I headed up the steps to my room. Lynn was there to greet me, then she undid the strings in the back and helped me get out of my gown. "Miss Edmilla, are you prepared to finish this war?"

"I always am, Lynn. Thank you for your concern but I need to make this decision on behalf of Orsadia." I faced her.

A frown disfavored her face. "You're ready to kill the queen?"

Those words nauseated me where I stood. "Pardon? Kill the queen? She may have killed me, but I have no intentions of doing the same to her."

Lynn grabbed a new gown and hung it near the mirror in the corner. "If you're going to defeat her, you must kill her."

"Lynn, no. Every princess in the past has defeated the queen without resulting to murder. I may be killing sins, but these sins are created by the queen. They are merely a figment of her imagination. The queen is a living person, and I will take her place but not at the shedding of her blood." I pulled off my undergarments as Lynn ran the hot water.

She finished setting up my bath as she shook her head. "Snow, it must be done. That is your quest. If she doesn't die, the throne will never be yours. Do you wish to be queen under such circumstances?"

I glanced back at her. "I will never kill her. No queens have to die. We defeat them in battle and they step down while we step up, and they return to the village or wherever they go." Although, Aalia had been an exception, and maybe many others, too, but I wouldn't be part of the problem. I simply wished to humiliate her—to warn her never to threaten me or steal my breath again. "She has threatened Father's life and I will not result to such lengths."

She released a sigh. "What if she succeeds in such horrible acts?"

"Do not speak curses into our lives. I will protect Father. He'll be okay. I will make sure he is always okay. I do this to protect him." I stepped into the tub and laid back, letting the hot water wash away my worries. "Lynn, please leave me be."

"Yes, Miss Edmilla." Lynn left the room.

I'd heard her correctly. I had planned to defeat the Evil Queen. I trained to fight her, but never to kill her. I made a vow to not let hatred and anger skew my vision. I would become a queen out of love because if I didn't, what power did I hold over this curse? I could not be like the ones before me. I refused such disgrace.

As I looked over at the window, I watched the first snowfall of winter precede itself. In past seasons, snow never came so early, and yet this winter it was doing just that.

A knock sounded on my door, and I sat up as water splashed onto the stone floor. I covered my chest. "Who's there?"

"It's just me, Snow. I was coming to warn you that we may need to head out soon. Our time to find the last four is running thin," Luka said through the door.

I could at the very least say I tried to enjoy a bath but that was not on the agenda today. Interrupted, I was.

Getting out of the tub, I dried myself and pulled a robe over my shoulders. I tied the string and opened the door. "Where is Lynn? I require her help putting my gown on."

He lowered his head in my view, nodding a bit. "I'll get her." He disappeared down the corridor.

I glanced back at my bed, but before I could walk to it, Lynn entered the room. She helped me with my gown. I pulled on my cloak while she fixed my hair.

I headed down the stairs and grabbed Jerry from my father. "We will be back when this war is actually over." I nodded.

My father grabbed my shoulders. "Be careful."

I wrapped my arms around him, giving him a hug before the last half of my war. "I will be, Father. I love you." I swallowed.

"I love you, too, Snow." He pulled away and planted a kiss on my head. My heart ached at the fact that for the first time ever, he'd called me by the name I'd begged him to use for six years. Maybe our relationship could be repaired after I tried so hard to shatter it. He leaned in and whispered, “and your hair looks lovely”, before letting me walk out of the castle doors for the last time as a *princess.*

"They say I'm required to kill Mira. I refuse to." I peered at Luka.

He didn't look back at me as he spoke his poisonous words. "Well, whatever it comes down to, correct?"

I stopped dead in my tracks. "Piss off."

He whipped around to face me. "What?"

I covered Jerry's ears. "Piss. Off.. Everyone keeps telling me I'm obligated to kill her if I take the throne and that's a lot to ask of someone. They are not asking me to do dishes. They are asking me to take a human life."

"She is hardly human."

"I spent my life wishing to become an animal trainer. When I was fourteen, my parents told me my fate was sealed. I dropped all of my dreams for everyone else. I chose to follow a path that did not interest me. I have dedicated years to training for a future I did not wish for. Now I am being asked to sacrifice all of my morals for a throne. I am being asked to erase the progress I made of learning to use love as a weapon instead of hatred. I cannot kill the Queen. I will not murder her in cold blood because that is not what a queen should do to another," I said.

Luka didn't say a word. I didn't need to be told by him of all people that I was going to be wicked—a curse I could not escape. What I needed was reassurance and support. Is that not why he came on this journey with me in the first place?

I redirected my attention to my only advocate "Jerry, where do you believe sloth would be hiding?" I set him on the floor, and he ran off. "This way!" I hurried after the squirrel.

Jerry stopped at a nest of nuts. "What the hell? I told you to take me to a sin. Do you not listen to me?" He grabbed a nut and nibbled on it. I grabbed him, hiding him in my cloak to keep him warm. "We should head back to your cave. This snow isn't letting up anytime soon."

Luka nodded without a word.

When we arrived at the cave, we started a fire and decided to take a small nap to pass some of the time. If the sin were true to sloth, he or she would not be moving much in this weather. We had time to look when the snow slowed.

"Luka, we're screwed." I pointed to the snow piling. It had already almost grown by a foot and the snowflakes still continued down from the sky. They were multiplying by the minute.

With a shake of his head, he asked, "Is this snowstorm going to let up anytime soon?"

The snow never came this early, nor did the first snowfall become a snowstorm. "Hard to say. I didn't imagine it would be this heavy. We'll wait until it stops."

He leaned his head against the wall. "You're prepared to spend a longer amount of time with me in my cave?"

"Do I have a choice?" I gave him dagger eyes. I scooted closer to the fire and put my hands nearby while Jerry slept in my cloak. "I doubt sloth is going far."

Luka's laugh bounced off the walls of the cave. "I doubt so..." His smile fell and he cleared his throat. "I apologize for my behavior earlier. It was misguided and I shouldn't have spoken out like that. You deserve to be happy as much as anyone else here and I wish I could help with that. I do propose an idea, however."

I locked eyes with him, weary of his words.

"I was thinking that maybe you could still be a queen and an animal trainer at once. Who says a woman is limited to one destiny? Can you not achieve everything you wish for?" He put another stick in the fire.

I diverted my eyes. "How do I break a curse and train animals?"

He scooted around the fire until he settled beside me. "You just do it. You're Snow White. You can do anything you put your mind to."

Snickering, I said, "I still have to kill the queen according to everyone."

He nodded. "That's what the verdict says...but what if you don't? Rebel. That is what you do, and it seems to work in your favor sometimes. Maybe this is one of those instances where you have the opportunity to make a life-or-death decision and you get to choose. Nobody else gets to decide what you need to do for *you*, Firefly."

"But almost every queen has lived past their reign. What if killing Mira is the only way to end this curse? What if I'm allowing this curse to continue because I'm trying to make the *better* choice? What is the better choice here, Luka?" I whispered the last question.

Luka couldn't answer. We both knew this decision was not easy but the only truth remaining was that it was my *own*. Nobody else could make it for me.

"Which animals should I train?"

He let out a tiny chuckle. "Jerry. He already took a liking to you. He could be your first animal, and you could train him to do a certain little goal. Maybe you train him to collect nuts for him and other squirrels. It's all up to you."

I scoffed. "That's what they all say. It sucks being a queen, because I have to make all the decisions. It's a lot of pressure and it's tough to make all the decisions alone. Maybe my father was right about me marrying someone, but at the same time, I can't love"—I paused and closed my eyes—"what I meant to say was I'm not in love. I'm only in the castle for three years and in that amount of time, it won't be worth trying to fall in love."

"You don't try to fall in love, Snow. You just do. It happens without your consent, and I understand consent is a big deal in many situations but with love, you can't control it. You shouldn't marry just to get help on making decisions for Orsadia. You should marry when you love someone and want to spend forever with them. They would always have your back. Love is a beautiful thing when used right."

I furrowed my brows. "When is love used in the wrong way?"

It wasn't as if I'd gone my whole life without love. I had two loving parents. I experienced love every single day, and yet I still barely understood its power.

Luka took a moment to gather his answer before settling on what I was certain was a jab at a wounded secret of mine. "When you deny your love for someone who needs it, despite knowing that it could make both of your lives better if you just went for it."

THIRTY-SEVEN

I crawled out of the cave, thankful the snow had finally stopped. It came up my calves, almost to my knees.

"What are you doing?" Luka asked.

I glanced back at him. "Seeing if we can leave to find sloth."

He sat back. "We can't. I've tried but it's still well below freezing. The fire is thawing out my toes." He had his boots near the fire.

Groaning, I sat back against the wall. "What do you suppose we do to pass time? I bet my murderous brother is cozy in his bed and I'm here with you. I know I'd much rather be in his position."

Luka's eyes were glued to the ground as the fire crackled. "I'm sure that is true. My brother would have loved to be in my position, with you."

Those words froze me to my core. Luka had mentioned his brother died after he got a lock of his own hair, and that Luka was the younger one, but I never pressed further. Now, maybe I could hear the story. "What was he like besides being responsible?"

He turned to look at me. "Thomas was Thomas. We weren't entirely related, but he was *my* brother. He came across as any normal guy did. When he was younger, he was always afraid of the forest. I found him when I found my parents, and we became best friends. He was the only friend I had, really.

"When we got together to talk or do fun things, Thomas always refused to go into the forest. That is why we would play games in the village. One morning I came to the village to meet up with him, and he came running. He had received a lock of hair at his doorstep. I knew the superstition and I disbelieved it at the time. We knew the queen was attempting to scare us. However, my parents came running to me for help when he turned up dead. I was so angry because he didn't deserve to go the way he did."

"Were you blood brothers? I know you mentioned that your father was cheating with the queen and when you came along, he left you on your own to hide that he was cheating on her. Was your brother the exception?" I asked.

He let out a sigh. "My parents already hated themselves for getting rid of me. They blamed themselves but they kept Thomas. They refused to send their first son away to the forest, but if we'd be obviously raised as brothers, people would know. Thomas and I looked nothing alike. Thomas looked nothing like my father, nor mother. He was a spitting image of the *queen.* She made my parents raise him so nobody would ever know about their affair. When I came along, I got a few years before my features set in, thus leading to what ultimately happened. I lost all of them eventually."

I thought maybe the queen had discovered that his father cheated on her. Given, she wasn't queen at the time his brother died, but she could have conversed with the current queen. I didn't want to mention this to Luka because if I had, it would piss him off.

"I should have never treated my family like they didn't matter," I said. "I know you lost yours without any choice and I choose to treat mine with disrespect. I should be grateful I have them."

Luka swallowed a laugh. "You have family issues at times. I don't dispute that, and I certainly don't preach about you being an angel for them. Sure, you should always make up with them at the end of the day, but I can't ask for perfection. We will never be such a thing."

A shiver ran up my spine as I pulled my cloak closer. "I admit I've always had a bit of an issue with authority since I knew what my fate was. Maybe I'll make a horrible queen, but I can't do so by treating my family like their opinion doesn't matter. They have supported me the whole way and I thought maybe they were attempting to stop me, but I was wrong. Mother was worried about me because of who my grandmother was. I'm the granddaughter to an evil queen and if I don't break this curse, what will that mean for Orsadia? What will that mean for my father?" I whispered the last question.

Luka kept his eyes fixed on me, my troubles becoming his all the same.

I met his gaze and swallowed the impure thoughts. "I apologize for the subject. We were talking about Thomas and I destroyed his memory with my worries. It was uncalled for."

He shook his head and repositioned his legs. "Don't apologize, Firefly. There will come times in this world when things happen, but we must focus on now. We cannot focus on the future or our past. Our past cannot be changed. Our future cannot be predicted. What we can do is make the best decisions for the present to guarantee we get a better ending."

I dropped my head into my knees as tears rolled down my cheeks. I hadn't intended to cry. I never intended to expose my most vulnerable side to Luka and yet I couldn't stop what clawed its way from the inside out. The doubts and fears pounded against the walls I built around me. The dam broke and now I couldn't reverse the shattered glass.

Luka moved around the fire and pulled me into his arms. I hit his chest and pushed him away from me. "Don't. I don't deserve to be comforted. I'm the monster of this world. I'm the one they fear. My vessel is the playground for the demons, and I'm terrified I cannot stop what has happened to every queen before me." I choked on a sob. "I am four sins away from defeating Mira and yet I am a lifetime away from figuring out the curse. I can't stop the curse before I complete my quest, Luka, and if I take that throne, I will never be a good queen. I'll hurt innocent people."

He grabbed my shoulders to keep me from fighting him off. "You will do what is asked of you because you have determination. How can you say you will hurt innocent people when this curse is what controls you? When you control yourself, you care about people. If this curse controls you, it suppresses the best parts and uses your darkness to rule Orsadia. That's not your fault. You didn't choose this life."

"My hands are responsible for taking lives. We cannot escape that truth," I said in a quiet voice.

He pulled an old, dirty blanket from his corner and wrapped it around me. "That is why we fight."

I shook my head. "No." I wiped my tears. "You said you were here to help me defeat the Evil Queen. I have to break the curse on my own."

Luka chuckled, although it held no animosity. "Well, you also didn't want me on your quest and yet, I'm here. Things change. If you need my help with the curse, I'll help you."

"Why would you help me break the curse now? We aren't friends. When this is said and done, we'll head separate directions." I pulled my hood on to keep myself warm.

He leaned against the wall and grabbed my wrist, pulling me onto his shoulder to keep us both full of life. "Orsadia is my home, too, and I want to see the day my brother's death means something more."

Jerry lay asleep in my skirt as I curled against Luka. He rested his head on top of mine. My sobs quieted down as sleep drifted my way, pulling me under.

Yet, I heard Luka whisper one last thing before I succumbed to dreams, "And just maybe, I've grown tired of denying that I've fallen in love with you."

"Wake up..." a female whispered.

I sat up, careful not to wake Luka. "Who said that?"

Nobody responded to me, and as I focused more on the sound of her voice, I recognized it as Aalia's. She was trying to contact me and yet she couldn't. She needed me to search for her bones and break the curse *she* started.

I left Jerry with Luka as I grabbed the skull and headed out into the forest. The trees had fallen bare as stars glistened above. Despite how dark it was this time of night, the foot of snow that layered every nook and cranny lit up my path. "I'm trying to find you, Aalia, but you need to lead the way. I cannot do this alone."

That had been the first time those words left my lips. I was not one to admit I needed help and Luka could argue the same. I defied odds and rebelled against laws, yet I was here begging Aalia to pull me from the waves before they swallowed me while she disappeared into the abyss.

"Aalia Drecose."

Despite my best efforts, she never responded. I turned on my heel to head back because I was in no state to search all of Orsadia for bones. Just as I took a step back to the cave, my path before me lit up. No—I was glowing.

I looked toward the sky. "Is this how you're communicating? I'm listening." I turned around and headed farther into the forest.

The voice had not reappeared, and I was not given any direction. I wasn't certain which direction I needed to go.

Stopping in my tracks, a realization hit me. Samael had mentioned that Aalia was hanged and burned by the villagers. If that were true, she would not have bones to find, and that could explain how her coffin had been empty. However, her skull was intact—as intact as it could be with a crack in the cranium and a missing jaw. None of it was coming together and now I had a mystery to solve about her death. Samael could not have told me the whole truth if her skull was in my arms at this moment.

"Find me..." the voice whispered in the trees.

I ran toward the sound, but I lost track of which tree it came from. The way this forest grew created a space for sound to bounce off of the trees without any particular indication of the source. It was an impossible mystery to solve.

"Aalia, where are you?" I screamed into the sky.

The whispers floated away like a feather, and then she was gone. I'd lost her. Had something trapped her? Why could she not communicate with me to the fullest extent? Whatever the reason was, I needed Luka's help.

"Firefly, what are you doing out here? It's freezing," I heard from behind me.

I spun around and faced him. "Aalia was trying to contact me from the dead. She needs me to find her, but I don't have any idea where to look. Samael said she was burned by the villagers when her term was over but if that were true, her skull would have been scorched—or worse—ashes. Someone is telling a lie and she was killed somewhere. She wouldn't be contacting me for no reason. I must find her." I hurried away, but Luka caught my arm and pulled me back. "If I don't find her, I can't understand the curse and break it."

He rubbed his eyes and sighed. "It is freezing out here. We can search tomorrow."

"She needs the dark to communicate with me."

He grumbled. "You will freeze and die before you find her. I promise we will search when we can, but this is the worst time." He placed both hands on the sides of my face, rubbing his thumbs over my ears to warm them up. "Come back and sleep. We will search when the weather permits."

All other thoughts scattered as one surfaced. *"And just maybe, I've grown tired of denying that I've fallen in love with you."*

Luka had admitted the way he felt, and I had no idea how to process it. Now we stood inches apart and it would be so simple for him to lean in and fill me with his warmth. However, I wasn't sure of my own feelings. I had to focus on my quest and not on the possibility of romance.

So I gave in, nodding. "Okay, we'll return back to the cave, but tomorrow we search."

THIRTY-EIGHT

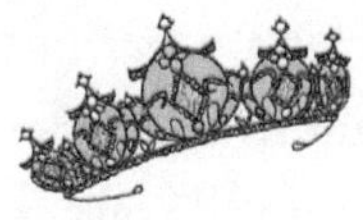

As I spun around, I fell into the snow and screamed at the ground, "She isn't out here! It's too damn light outside!"

We even came to the cemetery, to get closer to the thin barrier between the living and the dead, but despite all my best efforts, I couldn't summon Aalia Drecose. What a useless queen. An untrained princess. A smear on the Edmilla family name.

Luka rushed over and pulled me from the snow where I lay between a few gravestones. "Stop this complaining. Queens are better than this. They don't act like children."

"Yet, the queen acted like a child when she sent your brother to his demise." I ripped my shoulder from his grasp.

Luka stopped moving and his eyes fell on mine. "What?"

I'd been a moment too late to realize what I had said. "Luka, I'm sorry. That was uncalled for."

He stepped closer. "Snow, *what* are you talking about?"

"Luka, we do not want to go down the road of my dark thoughts. I swear I meant nothing evil by it." I turned away but he stepped in my path. He refused to let me walk away without giving him an answer.

"You made it clear the Evil Queen chose that woman to die next. She was given a lock of her hair as a warning. Your brother experienced the same fate, and I just think maybe your father's transgressions came back to bite him in the ass."

As much as I wished to unsee it, Luka's eyes filled with rage. I'd been the one who set off the bomb and I couldn't reverse the effects.

He turned around and hit a tree, but the tree fought back, and Luka had to shake the pain from his hand. When it subsided, he leaned his head against the trunk. "You're saying the queen my father cheated with killed Thomas, and now you're following the same fate."

"When you put it like that, you make it seem as if *I* killed him. Luka, you know I would never want to kill anyone for sport. I am trying to break this curse. I was in the freezing cold in the middle of the night because I do not want to do to someone else's brother what she did to yours." I approached him once I knew the anger couldn't threaten me. "I was prepared to freeze to death if it meant I wouldn't have to be like the rest of the queens."

He twisted his head until his eyes landed on me. "Nothing changes, Snow. Nothing here ever changes." His tone lacked all threats. All that'd been left was a soft begging. He'd given up all hope. His fist balled up and I knew he was attempting to punch the tree again, so I did something stupid and slipped between him and the tree. He did not need to break his hand over this. None of it was ever his fault.

I placed my hands against his shoulders to keep him grounded. "Thomas was a good brother to you and what happened wasn't fair. None of this is your fault. Your fault was the one who made the mistakes, and he's to blame."

He swallowed. "If I had just taken him away from my parents, he wouldn't have paid for their sins."

"We can't change the past. We can only make the right choices to guarantee a happy ending." I lowered my hands.

Luka closed his eyes for a moment, gathering his sanity. When he opened them, his gaze stayed glued to me as if I were about to turn on him. However, he rested his forearm across the trunk of the tree, right above my head.

Giving him a small nod, I parted my lips as he leaned closer. Inches shortened between us, and eventually his hot breath was all that called to me. I closed my eyes as his kiss brushed against mine in the slightest.

"This is like a romantic movie," someone said.

As Luka pulled away from me, the frigid wind bit my cheeks and nose as my eyes shot open.

We faced whoever it was that interrupted what would have been a *mistake.*

She waved her hand. "No, keep going. Pretend I don't exist."

"But you do," Luka said.

She shook her head, stepping back behind a tombstone. "I don't. Go on. Kiss her."

Luka glanced at me, and we both knew the moment was ruined. I was thankful that she had been there. Part of me wanted to kiss him, but I also knew that it would never work, and there was no use in getting involved with Luka when the crown was at my fingertips. Soon, he would explore the world and I'd stay *right here.*

Shaking his head, he asked, "What's your name?"

She shrugged. "I'm Aelin. I like to watch others because it's like a scene in my mind. It's almost as if...you're not really there but you are. I get romance and horror and all of the above."

Pulling my cloak tighter, I asked, "What do you mean by horror?"

Aelin shrugged. "I've been watching you. You kill people. Luka admitted he loves you. Now what's left is a kiss."

I stepped forward, raising my voice. "You've been watching us?"

"Well, of course. You two are so interesting. What else would I be doing if not watching two go from insults to lovers? That is exactly what you are." She pointed out.

Luka grabbed my arm. "Firefly, leave her be."

“Adorable nickname, by the way.” Aelin gave us a smile. "I apologize for invading your privacy, but your life is so much more interesting than mine. Oh, I should probably introduce myself." She put her hand out. "I'm Aelin, also known as a sin. Sloth, at your service. I know you've been searching for me and you need to kill me. I thought maybe now was a good time to let you, to move the plot forward. Aalia is not about to ask for your help and Mira wants to finish her war with you."

What a crock of shit.

THIRTY-NINE

Whispers floated all around me, weaving through the tombstones to remind us left living of the dead who'd lost their lives too soon.

Luka reeled his shoulders back as he faced Aelin. "Why are you here?"

"In the cemetery? Because it's the quietest place to be," she said as she turned in a circle to gesture at all of the bodies six feet under. "Nobody bothers you here. You are free to be as lazy as one pleases."

While furrowing my brows, I stepped forward with my fingers around the hilt of my sword. "Why haven't I seen you before? I come here often. You say you're sloth and you're ready to let us kill you, yet there are holes in your words."

"As I told you, I was watching you. I was hiding. I dare say I'm good at that. You had no idea. I guess I have these guys as my role models." Her eyes fell to the graves. "The plot needs to move. I'd also hate to see you fail."

A laugh got caught in my throat as I gave Luka a concerned look. "You're working for Mira. In what world would you hate to see her enemy fail?"

She put on a frown for show. "In this world, Snow. I do care about you. You're the one I'm supposed to despise but that takes far more energy than I can give. I've grown to admire you. I'll never be the girl who wields a sword or finds love of her own. I don't go on adventures or quests. I'm just a forgettable sin who sleeps among the dead."

The whispers around us grew louder. How on earth could I be the only one who heard them? Sure, I was an heir. But that should not have meant so much in the grand scheme of things. All I could do was glow in the dark and see a few ghosts.

Aalia, possibly. Regardless, I did not take lightly to the reality that I was the one of three being bothered by those who've long passed. I simply just needed to pretend I was fine with it.

"Does it ever become too much?" Aelin's voice grew quieter.

"Pardon?"

"The weight. The task. The expectations. Does it ever become too much for you to handle? I'm aware you're nothing like me—useless in the grand scheme of things. I imagine as the next queen, it's gotta take its toll. You hide it well."

A little string of anger had been strung. "Hide what? There's nothing to hide from anyone."

Her apology was written all over her expression as the wind drifted through her hair. Very real. Not a figment. Not a ghost. Certainly not a sin. Instead, she was just a woman who wanted some kind of purpose, or she was a woman who wanted to off herself but had no way of knowing how to go about that. Thus, she enlisted help. *My help.*

She was posing as sloth so I'd take her life for her. I was not that kind of person, nor queen.

By the way she spoke of herself, and her interest in my life, she envied me and all I had going for me. She wished for the same in her own, but for whatever reason, she could not bring herself to make those changes. She no longer wanted to be alive at all. She envied me. She envied the corpses.

And it'd never be that easy to catch a sin. Whoever she was, she wasn't who she pretended to be. She'd been nothing more than a woman whose depression left her feeling hollow.

Despite what I told her, some days things did get tough. It became too much. Too overwhelming. There were days in which expectations crushed me and I desperately begged the universe not to let me go on. But those were moments of weaknesses.

Even as badly as I might have wanted to peacefully go in my sleep, it wasn't my purpose.

I'd certainly never admit to anyone that it was more than I could handle. I'd never admit to fleeting suicidal thoughts, and strictly because they'd assume I needed help and it would only make me feel worse if I allowed myself to be the damsel once again.

Truthfully—I didn't want anyone to see me differently. I did not want everyone to look at me as the princess who lost her sanity before she took the throne. I'd lose everyone and then I'd be utterly alone.

So I stayed quiet. I said nothing.

My toll was my own business. They'd never know. Because if they knew, that was a humiliation so great even I couldn't recover.

In my own twisted way, I, too, envied the corpses.

"We're here to find some answers," I told Aelin with a click of my tongue.

Luka pointed to me and gave Aelin a look. "She's here to find answers. I care little about the cemetery and ghosts that haunt it."

"You admit ghosts haunt it," I said in an a-ha tone.

"What I admit is you are so fascinated with the afterlife. You might blame all of it on the royal side of things but I can see behind your eyes, Firefly. I know that even if you weren't—"

"The chosen one," Aelin interjected.

Luka shot her a glance. "Right, the chosen one—you'd still go after the ghosts in the graveyard."

"Does that scare you? Frustrate you? Repulse you?"

"Your fascination only causes my curiosity to skyrocket." He stepped forward, twirling a strand of my hair around his finger. "There must be a reason."

"Death is coming for me," I whispered. "It must have been a clue, correct? But how would she know before I do? Nobody truly knows. Unless she was actually the fortune teller." A gasp slipped my lips. "Luka, she knows what my magic will do."

"Who?" He leaned in, and not to kiss me but to ensure Aelin didn't hear my words.

"The fortune teller. Mira Sunder—the Evil Queen.She knew the extent of my abilities. She saw what I am." I couldn't be *certain*, but I assumed I was a medium. I had to be. It explained why I was connected to the dead, and possibly why I glowed. I was a beacon of light for the ghosts lost in the darkness.

I was the mediator between those beyond the grave and those who still breathed.

FORTY

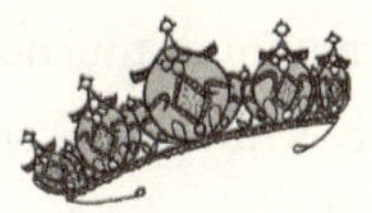

"A trouvaille this place is." Aelin let out a small sigh. "To stumble upon a cemetery. It only makes sense that sloth would end up in the most perfect of locations."

"You'd say that. To make us believe you." I headed for Aalia's headstone.

Her footsteps echoed as she followed. Fog swept in, covering the ground up to our ankles and making us the villains when we accidentally stepped on a headstone that laid flat in the dirt.

"You don't believe me?"

"It's nothing personal. I've met the Evil Queen before. She'd never make it that easy."

Aelin scoffed for the first time. "Sloth is lazy. You truly believe sloth wouldn't be that easy?"

"Yes!" I turned and grabbed her by the shoulders. "Now leave me be. Stay with Luka. I've got to go solve a mystery and I'd appreciate all the silence this world can muster."

She nodded a bit as I let go of her. "I'll be right here." But I didn't take that as a comforting promise.

I trailed off towards the back of the cemetery and as I did, the fog thickened. Even if the cemetery hadn't been entirely that big, I still couldn't spot Luka or Aelin who stood less than a quarter of a mile away.

Trailing my fingers over the gravestones, the humidity dampened the air a smidgen. The cemetery had been next to the ocean so it did not at all surprise me that the clouds touched the grounds of Orsadia. It never came as a surprise. Knowing Everinthian Castle was a few miles north of the graveyard meant I'd need to get used to it.

If the souls of the corpses didn't make me run in the opposite direction, neither would a little bit of humid clouds.

My boot hit something hard and I heard a, "Watch it, Princess."

I turned to apologize to the decaying corpse. "Entirely my fault. The fog blocks my view."

He grumbled before turning back to his grave.

Nothing appeared out of place. No gravestone slandered, no plot dug up, and not even a set of bones littering the dirt. Whoever kept up with these took pride in their work.

Ah, yes. Aelin. I was certain she'd been the woman who kept a close eye.

The taste of iron disgraced my tongue.

Blood.

"That's how it got me," Aalia whispered as her voice echoed all around me. "That's how they got me."

"Who? Who got you? How did you die?" I spun in circles to pinpoint her exact location but came up empty.

I was met with silence.

However, she didn't leave my question unanswered.

Among the taste of iron, a pit of dread weighed in my stomach. Hopelessness. The end of my life. The sinking feeling that I'd never find my way to happiness again.

Like a weight in water, I sunk to the bottom lined with rocks. No will to live. No purpose in life. Had this been how I felt all along? No, that had been unlikely. It was off. Much like what I'd felt with being overwhelmed, this imitated that. Trapped was one word to describe it.

Alone.

No escape.

I'd given up.

And just as that feeling grew, blood spilled from my mouth.

I'd been poisoned.

As my breath caught and blood spurted from me like milk from an utter, I fell onto my knees before I curled into a fetal position.

Had anyone ever loved me? I came to the conclusion that I'd never felt such a thing as true love. Not from Fallon, nor Mother or Father. I'd never understood what it was like to have someone care so immensely they'd die for you.

What I had understood was the existential dread. The birds going off in the wee hours of the morning. That first step outside into the crisp winter air that made you contemplate every choice you've made.

It was taking your last bite of food for what you knew would be for weeks. It represented displeasing the queen and fearing for your own life as she took it personally, spending her energy on plucking you from the crowds and laughing while you begged for her mercy.

What I felt was no different than the moment Mira told me my father was going to lose his life soon. While that was something many experienced from a queen, it became far more suffocating when I realized there was not a single thing I could do to save him.

I feared that even killing the Evil Queen herself wouldn't stop the inevitable. They referred to that as helpless, and oh how such a horrid impression left a taste of rot on my tongue. Nausea bubbled in my stomach as last night's dinner threatened its way back up.

When it dawned on me, I realized what I experienced wasn't my own, but rather Aalia's.

Her position was not discovered, but the words came through the fog clear as day, "That was exactly how I felt before she snuffed out my last heartbeat."

FORTY-ONE

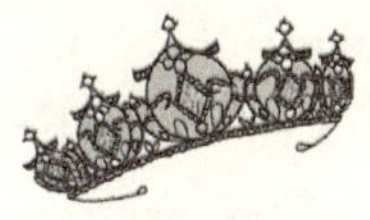

"How is Alexander doing?" Aelin asked.

I met her gaze—her eyes filled with genuine concern. She knew about Mira's brother. Not another living soul here knew about him, and I assumed she had kept him secret for good reason.

To some, Prince Alexander was a dead giveaway, seeing as everyone knew I only had Fallon as a brother. To those who were certain he wasn't related to Mira thought maybe he was her creation, or that he traveled from another unknown land.

"We were so close growing up. He helped teach me what I know today about sneaking around undetected. His father was always so strict." Her eyes wandered.

It'd never occurred to me that if she *were* a sin, the sins had childhoods of their own. How?

Then I was left questioning if she was sloth after all.

When she came closer, she grabbed my sword and wrapped my fingers around the handle. "You're confused. Debating it. I've been alive long enough, Snow. It's okay to kill me. Just do it. But I wish to ask one thing before you do."

With a swallow, I replied, “What is that?”

“Tell Alexander I'll miss his blue eyes the most.”

I looked at Luka, but neither of us knew what to say. Sloth was just giving herself to us. Although now that I thought about it, it made all the sense.

She wasn't supposed to be hard to kill because of strength or rebellion. No, sloth had always been about as lazy as the cat that perused the village. She had been hard to find because she was a master at quiet. That was what she used against me.

It was clear to me now that the girl standing before me was sloth.

"Maybe it is my fault you didn't kiss. I did ruin the moment. I was hoping for one kiss before you killed me, but I guess I can only hope. My thoughts just come out of my mouth and I can never stop them." She laughed a little too sadly. "Let's not waste any more time on this. I'm ready." She straightened her posture.

A girl who was giving up everything for me. Aelin was selfless, and killing her would only be that much more difficult. I had to do it quickly without thinking before I gave up my throne for a girl who begged me to take her life.

I pulled out my sword and looked at Luka. He gestured for me to go on.

I plunged the sword through her abdomen—the blood exiting from two different places—her wound, and her lips.

It spilled with so much ease that one may have assumed the blood was not hers and it belonged to another who'd long passed.

Thick and dark—the liquid moved back into the earth as her body collapsed to the forest floor. She choked on her blood until her form laid lifeless, left with nothing but the nightmares of life after death. Aelin was all but a memory, and yet a blood stain on *my* hands.

Looking at Luka, I furrowed my brows. "Why was that so hard?”

"She didn't deserve to die simply for existing. I'm starting to believe the Evil Queen enlisted seven people to play her sins who otherwise should have lived long lives. You're not killing figments of her imagination. You're taking the lives of actual human beings."

My heart cracked upon the realization.

I put my sword away. "They say the calm comes just before the storm."

He released a desolate sigh. "They do say that, indeed." He grabbed Aelin's body and dragged her body from the graveyard before throwing her over the cliff. Her body hit the water full force and the waves devoured her the way they had me.

"What do we do now? Three sins still remain." Something dark pounded against my chest as I said those words. All the sins were *people*, and soon my next fight would be with Mira Sunder, the Evil Queen.

"Now we prepare for your final battle to win the war."

The homestretch.

He faced me. "She will expect you to be a certain way. You must prove her wrong. You need to master the skill of using a bow and arrow. You need to master using your bare fists. She is expecting Snow White to be limited and that is why you need to prove you are anything *but*."

I nodded a little, mesmerized by the way his hair moved. "How must I defeat her? We've established I won't kill her and yet I have not planned how else to bring her to her knees. I've come up with this idea that I'll take her down, but I assumed I would have discovered my plan by now. Yet, I stand here with none in mind."

His laughter was the medicine I needed to heal the ache in my heart from Aelin's demise. "That's not something I can give advice on. You'll know when the time comes. This is your war, and I won't tell you how to fight it. You do what you need to do to save Orsadia from the darkness surrounding us."

"The darkness surrounding us in the form of a curse. The darkness that has a firm grasp on the queens. The darkness that has yet to be defeated after two dozen have ruled," I said.

He nodded along to my words.

"Let's prepare me for my final battle." I turned and walked from the cliff as we headed back to his cave.

Once we'd arrived, I put Jerry next to the fire Luka built to keep warm, and he curled up like a fetus.

Luka followed me out and handed me his bow and quiver. "Show me what you're capable of."

I grabbed his bow and slipped an arrow on the string, positioning myself. I aimed my arrow at a tree. I took into account my body's angle and the trajectory of the arrow. I let go and the arrow hit its target.

Luka choked on a laugh. "Firefly, you're getting better."

I gave him a smirk. "I've been practicing while you sleep. I thought it would be useful, don't you agree?"

He grabbed the arrow, yanking it from the tree. "I do agree. That is why I suggested you learn to use a bow and arrow."

"And yet I may just be better than you." I grabbed my sword and swung it. "I can use both weapons with ease. What can you do, huntsman?"

Luka grabbed my sword. "I can use a sword." He swung it but it didn't fall smoothly. I'd proved myself to be the better of us both. "It's harder than it looks."

I grabbed it from him, weighing it in my hand. "You must feel the weight of the sword. It takes time and practice. If you don't feel it, you will never be able to have power over the blade." I swung in through the air. "It's a weapon and nothing more. *You* command it. It bends to your will."

"What was your grandmother's name?" Luka asked.

I stopped swinging and cleared my throat. "Anne Regali. I never met her. She died before I was born. Mother told me my grandmother was nothing but a hollow shell of herself when her reign was over. She feared my mother would be just like her, becoming a queen and filling her heart with darkness. When my mother never got magic, my grandmother was relieved. She thought maybe it was over and her family was safe. She died before I came into this world and nobody saw it coming when I got my ability. Mother knew the truth. The gene skipped her and passed onto me."

He leaned against a tree. "Your grandmother was one of the queens. That's tough news to bear but it comes full circle. Magic cannot be created from nothing. There has to be a seed for it to grow."

"If magic needs a seed, how did Aalia come without a gift?" I asked.

Another question without any answers. I just needed to know exactly where to look.

Luka didn't know. However, Samael mentioned that Everinthian Castle had the history of all queens who had lived there. I could defeat Mira and begin my research on magic and its source. It had to come from somewhere.

We continued our training throughout the day. I was going to prepare myself for every possible move I could use on Mira.

Maybe it had everything to do with the fountain that once held said magic, and *who* created that fountain.

FORTY-TWO

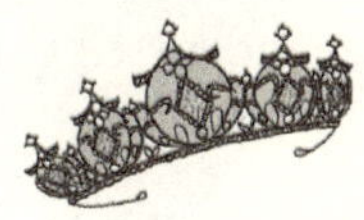

Luka roasted a bird over the fire as Jerry hid in my cloak for warmth. The snow was beginning to melt away by now, but it was far too cold to do much. Once the temperature dropped, what was left would become a sheet of ice. Fire would keep us warm until spring.

"We can't sit here forever. We must do something. *I* can't sit here all day. I refuse," I said.

He gave me a look—one that judged me for being so restless. I had a war to win, and three sins left. Little time to find them. The Evil Queen was waiting for me. "You need fuel. If you don't eat, you'll get weak. What good are your skills if you aren't at full strength? Have you seen the snow?" He gestured.

I glanced over at the snow that covered the ground. "I have, but it's melting. The snowstorm is over, and the sun is shining. Snow is no threat. What is my name again?"

"Firefly?" Luka joked.

I shot him a glare. "It's Snow White. If I were afraid of snow, I would not have named myself after it."

He cleared his throat. "Why did you choose Snow White? It seems unusual for someone to name themselves after a form of liquid."

With a small smirk, I shrugged. "Snow is an ice crystal. I've been told I'm cold when it comes to people. I treated Alexander coldly. Maybe I like to believe I'm an ice crystal. Would you oppose a woman holding herself up? Men treat me like nothing more than a piece of meat so naturally, I must remind myself that I'm more than that. If I don't, who will?"

"Why do you need to remind yourself? You've been confident in everything since the day I met you when we were young teens."

I swallowed the lump that formed in my throat. "I'm still a human. Deep down, insecurities gnaw at my insides until nothing is left, and without a reminder that I'm more than what people treat me as, I will never learn to love myself the way I should. I may have not gotten a lot of boy crushes growing up, but that doesn't exclude me from the moods women have during that time of the month. I'm a female and despite popular belief that I'm invincible, I'm not. I've been put on a pedestal that I didn't create for myself. I've been chosen as the next queen and people expect so much of me. I hold my head up high to show them that I'm fit to *be* their queen but when the sun sets, that armor comes off. Underneath the exterior, I have hopes and dreams of my own. I have feelings, and I think people forget that because I present myself so confidently, they don't see *me* behind it all. They don't see Lana. They see Snow White."

Luka finished with the bird and handed me half of the meat. "That's a big weight to carry on your shoulders. Curses really are just that."

Chills ran up my spine, goosebumps formed along my skin, hairs raised on my forearms. I tore off some meat from the bone and savored the flavor. "I added White after it to make it sound more cohesive. That I didn't want people to hear my name and think of the brown sludge or the yellow puddles in which animals piss."

He ended our conversation with a nod.

We both finished our meat in silence and Jerry had fallen asleep by the last bite.

I leaned back against the wall and pulled my cloak tighter around me. "I must set out on my final war soon, and when I do, you can't come with. No exceptions, Luka. Is that understood?"

"Understood, Firefly." He scooted by the wall and closed his eyes.

A thin sheet of iced-over snow crunched under my boots, leaving behind an indication of my path. It had begun melting days ago, but what was left had been untouched by every creature of Orsadia. It further proved how terrified people were of Ash Forest.

I couldn't confirm nor deny if their fear was rooted in the Evil Queen or the wailing banshee, but I wouldn't put it past them.

"We're almost there," Luka said.

I glanced back at him. "We're going to scope out her castle first, but I have a feeling she may not be home. If that's true, we search the tower, then Hypnotic Arythe. She's forbidden from Drecose Castle for law purposes."

He agreed with my plan, and as we neared the fountain, I took a moment to stop and admire the layer of ice that protected the water below.

Luka kept his gaze focused on me. "Anything interesting?"

I put my hand up to silence him. "Something about this fountain... Alexander said it once had magic and I had always questioned how he knew that. Knowing now that he's Mira's brother, he had access to the history of the queens. My history books do not talk about the queens, nor the fountain ever possessing magic, which means this fountain must have been connected to one of the queens. What if this fountain created the curse?"

"It could be possible." He scanned the trees.

Facing him, I shook my head. "It *must* be possible. This fountain plays a part in the curse because it is somehow only mentioned in Everinthian Castle where the history of every evil queen resides." I circled the fountain, searching for anything out of place. "Aalia's magic has a source and if my theory proves correct, this would be said source." I brushed my fingers along the cemented edge. Which in turn meant the fountain was the same place to reverse the curse if I could simply figure out how to bring magic back to its waters.

Luka waited for me to finish, but I found nothing. Not a single clue laid nearby.

"Let's go." I walked away, hurrying to get to the castle and defeat Mira. The quicker I defeated her, the quicker I could break this curse for good—and my time was running out. Winter had approached quickly, but it didn't mean there hadn't been a deadline looming over my head. The new year was just around the corner and if I didn't succeed in my war before then, I'd never be able to wear the crown.

We approached her castle, but it appeared empty. When I climbed up to the same window we had the first time, nobody waited at the top to imprison us. I left the room and scanned the halls, but silence engulfed me. The castle had been far too quiet.

"She's not here." I stopped and turned around, running into Luka. "Sorry," I mumbled.

He grabbed my shoulders to stabilize me. "Careful."

"Thanks for the tip." I snickered.

He scanned the area. "Is she trapping us, or is she elsewhere?"

"Knowing she failed to kill me the first time, she wouldn't attempt to attack here. Insanity is using the same methods and expecting different results and Mira doesn't strike me as the type. She's seen the future. She knows." I cleared my throat. "She's gone. She's gone to prepare herself for our battle. Which doesn't make any sense if I haven't killed all seven sins. Should we find her?"

His nodding was not without hesitation. "You're sure you'll be able to win this?"

I furrowed my brows. "I must win. If I don't, what happens to Orsadia? That's not a chance I'm willing to take." I rubbed away the dubieties.

Luka frowned. "You all right?"

"Not particularly. The front of my skull aches no thanks to you." I rubbed the area between my eyebrows and nose with my palm. "Although, truth is I can't say why."

He placed two fingers on each temple and rubbed in circular motion. "I apologize for coming off like an ass as of lately. I don't mean to make you feel as though you're not worthy to fight her."

I relaxed my muscles a bit. "You never made me feel that way. It takes a lot to make Snow White feel as though she's not adequate."

He chuckled. "And you're positive of that?"

I released a sigh. "Positive. In fact, you're the only person who's stuck by me this whole quest. Nobody else has stood by my side. Any male I'm not related to wants to rip my gown off. Males I am related to don't believe I can do this and stay the same Snow they've always known. You're the one person who has not made me feel inadequate. I appreciate that."

His smile became infectious. "I'm glad I could be at your service." He pulled away and bowed to mock me. "It all happened because you became a damsel of your own flaws."

"Piss off." I crossed my arms.

"Wish I could but I am here until the end." He waved me away.

An aching pain in my legs surged throughout the nerves and I leaned myself against the wall to take some of the weight off.

The look Luka gave me was one of concern. Was I all right? I wish I could say yes, but the truth was, I couldn't go to war like that. Luka had made a point about being at my best, and I knew he'd been right about it.

"I just need a moment to rest is all."

Beside me, he leaned against the wall. "Our bodies can only withstand so much. No shame in resting."

I glared daggers. No, for his sake I shot him arrows. "Did I say I was ashamed? Are you trying to implant this idea that I should feel shame? Am I just a woman who supposedly feels guilt all the time?"

"I've gotten to know you over these past couple of months and trust me when I say that you do tend to feel ashamed for things you shouldn't. It's normal."

My eyes fell closed as I rubbed my face with a groan. "You are absolutely a nuisance." I opened my eyes to see the distance left between us. In the time I'd shut him out, he had pushed himself off the wall and now he stood mere inches away in front of me.

A chuckle passed his throat as he pressed his forearm against the wall beside my head. "I am, but that makes you *the* solution."

I hadn't made a move to put any more distance between us, and Luka had taken notice. Within seconds, he had closed the gap further by leaning towards me.

He stopped for a moment, his voice like gravel as he asked, "Am I your problem, Firefly?"

I said in a quiet voice, "That's inevitable."

Seconds later, Luka's lips brushed against mine. For a moment, I thought Mira would find us and interrupt us the way Aelin had.

But not a single soul ever came.

The kiss began as something slow, inviting, and loving. We both took the time to get to know one another and move as if we'd been lost lovers from over a century ago. As more seconds passed us by, the craving grew—sending us both spiraling towards a side neither of us thought would come of our endeavors.

Together we both ignored all the warnings that we shouldn't have been doing this at all. Instead of following rules, we poured ourselves out and expressed our most repressed impulses.

I could have said no. I could have told Luka this was wrong on many levels, and yet I didn't *want* to. All I accepted was the chance for me to give myself at least one thing I had wished for. I deserved at least that.

He grabbed my chin as he pulled away just enough to inhale oxygen. His hot breath fanned across my lips as he struggled to catch it. After I seized my own, I closed the last of the gap and pulled his breath back into my lungs.

With one kiss, Luka trailed his lips across my cheek until they met my ear.

I grabbed his hand with mine, intertwining our fingers together. "Should we be doing this?" I tilted my head towards his.

He captured my kiss again and left a trail along my jaw, but as soon as his lips brushed down the side of my neck, I released his fingers.

Pulling away, our eyes locked on each other. "I didn't mean to go there."

After I took in a sharp breath, I shook my head. "This is wrong. We can't do this."

"Why? Why would we deny ourselves this *luxury*?"

Despite the racing of my heart, I had to let go. "Because Orsadia must come first. I cannot give into these desires and expect the curse to break itself. I have a duty to fulfill and you are not part of that plan."

He lowered his voice a few notches the way that weakened my knees—damn him. "Can I be part of it?" He leaned closer.

I pushed him away just enough for me to slip from his grasp. "No. I must not lose sight of what I've come to accomplish so far. I'm sorry, Luka, but it has to be this way. We cannot pursue more than what happened."

The frown on his face became embedded in my mind for eternity. "Snow..."

"No." I stomped my foot lightly on the ground. "This is where our journey ends. We split up. I'll finish my war on my own to protect you and I from something that could destroy us both." I turned on my heel and began stumbling in the other direction.

"Firefly," Luka called out. I kept moving despite his attempts. He threw out three words that shattered my heart. "Don't abandon me." As battered—broken—I may have been letting go of what could have saved my soul, I never stopped walking in the opposite direction of where promises called my name.

FORTY-THREE

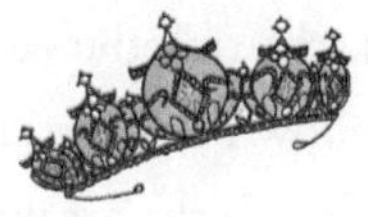

The tower was empty the moment I arrived. Mira had gone to one place, and it was the one place she could go that wasn't on *this* piece of land. Hypnotic Arythe.

That's where I headed next. Crossing the bridge alone wasn't as easy as I'd hoped it would be but going to Luka for help was not an option. I had told him to leave me be after our mistake, and I was not about to run back to him for help. I was on my own from here on out.

After I made it across the bridge, I lifted my eyes and grumbled. "First you were a mansion and a cathedral. Then you became a carnival. Now, you're this?" I threw my hands up.

Surrounding the entire area were old, dirty dolls left for decay. I had no idea what they represented or who they came from, but dozens of them littered the area.

Dolls were a kid's favorite toy, and yet they could also be an adult's worst nightmare. My teddy bear had been my most precious, too, but he came from a world in which I went by Lana. I'd never return to those memories.

Mira had made it clear to me that my father wouldn't make it through this, and I'd wondered since then why she would say such a thing. Was it to cause misery? Was she so disappointed in herself that she didn't have room to care about anyone else?

"You must face the truth..." A whisper floated by.

Aalia was attempting to speak to me again and yet if I tried hard to go find her, I would lose the trail the same way I always did. This time, I was not going to follow her voice. Instead, I would focus on finding Mira and bringing her to the ground first.

"Face the truth..."

The truth was the last thing I wanted to face. I'd forever run away because Lana Edmilla was dead to me, even if my father struggled with it.

I returned home from Ash Forest, trying my best to forget what Mira had told me. She threatened my father, and I couldn't sit around and do nothing with that bit of information. I knew I'd defeat her someday and she knew, too.

Father and Mother asked me where I ran off to, but I never gave them a sufficient answer. Instead, I enjoyed the rest of my party until night fell and everyone turned in.

I couldn't sleep. The only thoughts that poisoned me were those of my father dying—a reality I was terrified to face. What could I do about it? Killing Mira was not an option. I would throw the entire balance of Orsadia off and everyone would blame me. If I was to be their queen someday, I could not result to such lengths of violence to achieve what I wanted.

Training was an option, and one I would take gladly. If I didn't get this anger out of my system, how would I ever deal with it in a timely manner? I could not let it explode and hurt those around me.

What I did the following day was something my parents did not approve of, nor accept. However, I did it anyway. I told everyone that

I would no longer go by Lana and instead my name was now Snow White. Mother thought maybe it was just a phase but when I didn't budge on my name, she knew something had happened.

I never told my parents what Mira told me. I did not want to worry them. Everyone knew that every queen had a power no one else did, and it turned out Mira's was about seeing the future. If she saw my father's death, I could not tell Mother that she didn't have long left with the love of her life. I didn't want to come to terms with it myself.

After I made the name change, I ventured into the forest for training. I had used every last bit of strength in me against a tree that never once threatened those I loved.

When my training came to an end, I wanted to cry. I refused to let myself do such a thing, though. If I sobbed, was I fit to be a queen? Certainly not so.

So I didn't weep. I trained and changed my name to protect my father, and every time he called me Lana, my anger grew by a mile. He refused to leave the past behind as if he knew what his fate held for him and he accepted it. I didn't accept any ounce of it, but he made sure to remind me that he was never going to survive to see me take the throne.

"Mira, where are you?" I asked. I got no response. Either she'd been in hiding or she wasn't here. If that were the case, where had she gone? She wouldn't forfeit this war. She needed to kill me, and I needed to defeat her. What was set in stone must be played out.

I'd been traveling for a while since I left Luka behind and all that was left of me was exhaustion. The moon had risen high in the winter sky and I fought hard against drowsiness.

Unfortunately, I wasn't indestructible.

I dropped to my knees and laid back on the ground. If I could give myself just enough sleep to recharge my strength, I could climb back to the top and be ready for what she was about to throw my way.

Jerry was no longer with me. He'd been left at Luka's cave, so he wasn't a target for Mira, but I hadn't anticipated leaving Luka behind when I did. After that kiss, there was no doubt I should continue this journey alone. If I hadn't, there was a high chance I would have kissed him again and fallen victim to a fate called love. Love was complicated and messy. It was not something a cursed queen was supposed to have.

Love put others in danger, and if I'd become putty for him, he'd be another target for Mira just as my father was.

I refused to let my destiny become the destruction of Luka's future.

As I awoke from my deep slumber, I adjusted my eyes to the darkness. I'd only been out a few hours by the looks of it. The sun had not yet risen.

Mira hadn't touched me in my most vulnerable state which told me she wasn't anywhere nearby. Where had she disappeared to, and why?

Standing up, I scanned the area. The dolls still hung from the trees and hid in the nooks and crannies of the dirt. I had no idea what dolls had to do with any of this, but I assumed this was my chance to find out. Everything here had a purpose and if I didn't connect the dots, I'd never get another chance.

Where did I begin?

Once I asked that question, whispers began. "Aalia? Is that you?" I asked.

I'd assumed it was her but the harder I listened, the quicker I realized that the whispers were not from one woman. They came from many different children and now I faced the horror before me.

Had there been children's souls trapped inside these dolls? No, that couldn't be. Mira had no power to do that. But someone did, and *someone had.*

I thought for a moment maybe I could break the dolls open to release their spirits but most of the dolls had been broken, and yet they still trapped children inside.

"What the hell happened here?"

How could so many children be inside this many toys? Something I didn't know about happened in Orsadia and that thought terrified me.

Once I became queen and owned all the history books of those before me, I would know exactly who did this and why. I wanted to help free the children, yet I wasn't sure how I could do that yet.

It was cruel to trap them in the first place. What kind of queen would choose such a horrible fate for the innocent people of our land? A foul queen.

I hadn't realized until I discovered my fate just how complicated my future would be. Every queen before me had a major secret to hide that no one knew about. I feared I was going to end up in the same situation and then what would be left of me then? I'd be yet another one who fell into the same curse.

If I was going into a history book, it would be for the purpose of saving Orsadia. It was not going to be because I was yet another queen who had destroyed the one home I've known and loved for twenty-one years.

Walking forward, I passed the dolls but what I came to next was much to my surprise. The cathedral was back in its place, but it had been impossible to spot through the tall, dark trees.

Mira had to have been in here, and if she wasn't, I would wait for her. It seemed like the most fitting place for a battle. Our only other options were a castle, forest, or village. Neither of those options were feasible. The less casualties, the better.

"Mira, come out wherever you are," I antagonized. My voice barely echoed with the gaping hole in the corner of the building. However, this cathedral was small enough for her to hear me. The last time I had stepped foot in here was back when Aalia was after me. She'd been able to catch me off guard and it brought back an awful memory.

Maybe I didn't want to fight Mira here after all.

I left the building and made my way through more trees, now approaching the mansion. Surely Mira was hiding in this large structure.

As I walked inside, I called out her name, but she never came out. The mansion was large enough for me to explore until Mira did arrive, and so I began on my next adventure.

In most rooms, nothing could be found aside from furniture and cobwebs. This mansion had been abandoned for so long, or it could have been yet another illusion created by this piece of land.

At some point, I would need to read more about Hypnotic Arythe to see why it was the way it was.

I entered one room and while it had cobwebs in every corner, it also contained a few letters spread out on a desk. I walked over and picked them up, reading them one by one. The handwriting was hardly legible at this point—faded, but I could make out just enough to understand they were love letters.

Glancing at the name they'd been signed by, I swallowed. "Anne Regali." I held the letter against my chest. As much as I despised the queens, I couldn't ignore that each and every queen had once been like me. They fought against a curse and lost. I'd be a monster to not acknowledge the humanity they once owned. My grandmother was no exception, and whoever she had loved had never written back.

Not a single letter was addressed to her. They had all been addressed to another man, *from* her. I could not imagine an unrequited love. As much as I wanted to be with Luka to pretend I wasn't responsible for breaking this curse, I had to do it for the people of Orsadia. However, we both still cared for one another.

But my grandmother had been in love with someone by the name of Harry who never returned the feelings. It must have had been heartbreaking to know she never had a chance. If this Harry never loved her, then who had? Someone had to have loved her enough to create my mother or I would not be here.

"Don't worry, grandmother. I will uphold our name and make sure this curse is back in hell where it belongs. I will make you proud. I promise you—if it's the last thing I ever promise," I whispered.

And surely it would be the last one I ever made.

FORTY-FOUR

"Anne Regali was your grandmother? It doesn't at all surprise me," Mira said as she entered the room. "My mother was a queen, too, so everyone figured I'd follow in her footsteps. However, with your family, it skipped a generation. Your mother thought she escaped the curse, but it turns out, her daughter got caught in the crossfire."

I whipped around to face her. "You know how this will end. You see the future, Mira. I'm sure in that future I'm going to be the new queen."

She leaned against the wall. "You don't know what I see, Snow. I have explained to you one unfortunate outcome. Your father won't make it through this. I can't change the future if that's what you're hoping for. I am only responsible for seeing what it looks like. No, I have not seen the outcome of this war so I can't tell you who wins. I'm warning you that if you win, things will get uglier. I *can't* let you defeat me."

"You still want to be the one who breaks the curse."

Mira pushed herself off the wall and approached in slow strides. "I could care less about who breaks the curse. I am not that self-centered. What I want is the same as you. I want to break this curse for every queen after me. I want to see Orsadia get a chance at a better life."

I snickered. "I must die for this curse to be broken? You must commit an act of murder to break a curse? I doubt evil defeats evil, Mira. That's just a scam. Someone is lying to you. More fire does not put out the fire. Those flames burn stronger. This curse will be limitless if you kill me."

She stalked closer, her boots making her just an inch taller. Normally, Mira was shorter than me by a few inches. "You don't know what is needed to break this curse. I have lived through it as a commoner and a queen. I have discovered what is needed. If I take out the heir to the throne, who will be next? No one. I *step* down and then Orsadia gets a break from a queen. When the next one steps up, it'll be a clean slate."

"That's not how that's going to work! There may not be a queen for three years but what happens when the queen after me steps up? She has no queen to defeat. She just walks into the castle? You are telling me she does not earn her place that the rest of us fought for. We all were chosen, and this curse has a system we follow. We'll break the curse, but the system is there to prove that every chosen queen deserves her position."

"I am doing what is necessary. I would rather a queen be chosen and walk into the castle with a chance of not being good, than have a queen fight her way in and always be doomed to a life of sin. With an unearned position, a queen has a chance at righteousness."

Shifting my body weight, I asked, "I must die to break a curse?"

"It's unfortunate but a sacrifice must be made." She let out a sigh.

"To break the curse, you must feed into your evil desires one last time." It wasn't right. None of it was moral, and Mira must have known this wasn't to break a curse. This was to feed into the wickedness and let the curse grow until it was unstoppable. That was why I had to take victory over her.

Shaking her head, she stepped closer. "This is how it has to end. Break the routine. Break the cycle."

I swallowed. "You're asking me to lay down my life for a future that is not certain. You haven't been able to confirm this would even save future queens. You're asking me to give up everything in this world. My family would lose me. I would lose all hopes and dreams." *Luka* would never see me again.

"You would be saving an entire kingdom, Snow. Do you wish to save everyone? You would be the hero!" She stepped so close I could feel her wretched breathing. "You would get to be remembered as the princess who gave up the throne and her own life to save a whole land from a curse."

Clever, to use my wishes as a weapon.

She had no remorse for what she was doing. Murder was second nature to Mira now, and if I willingly let her have it, Orsadia would be forever tainted. There would never be another chance to break this.

"I'm sorry, Mira. I can't agree to this. You can call me selfish or evil for putting myself first, but I won't back down." I pulled out my sword. "I am destined to defeat you. I did not come this far to give it all up."

She stepped back and pulled out a dagger. "I didn't want to result to this, Snow, but I can't stop the future. I'm sorry." She cleared her throat. Two figures emerged through the door, and I choked.

Alexander forced my father onto his knees, his hands gripping my father's shoulders. Father's hands were restrained behind his back and his mouth had been gagged. Inside, I knew the ending and yet I was going to do everything in my power to avoid that.

"Don't do this. My father has nothing to do with this. Murder is not the answer." Despite my best efforts, my hands were shaking.

“I never told you *who* would kill him, and that had been more for my own safety.” She closed the gap between her and my father and gripped his hair, yanking his head back. "I don't have much of a choice. As far as we're all concerned, I am still the curse's puppet. I want to end the curse for this reason." She pressed the blade against his neck.

My voice trembled as I pleaded, "Mira, *please.* Please do not do this." My heart pounded in my chest as I attempted to erase the moments I yelled at Father. I'd been the worst daughter and I couldn’t let that be my memory in his mind. I had a lifetime to make up for my actions.

"I wish I could, Snow. I wish I could," she whispered, slicing from the right to the left side of his neck.

Everything moved in slow motion as the blood spilled from his body in an attempt to escape the horror. Alexander dropped him, allowing my father to soak in his own pool of blood.

I dropped to the floor, screaming into the void. The pain clawed away at my chest while tears poured down my cheeks.

As hard as I tried, the agony flowed from me like water from a bucket. Every part of me ached. I didn't see an end to this war. Instead, all I saw was the look in my father's eyes as his last breath passed his lips.

Mira and Alexander disappeared but I couldn't say when.

I crawled to Father and pulled him into my arms. "No, please. Father, you can't leave me like this. If you leave me, who will continue to remind me of who I really am? Who will call me Lana?" I hugged him. "You can't leave me." I sobbed into his hair.

Begging didn't bring him back to me.

Too many thoughts invaded my mind about what I was going to do without him in my life. Who would I turn to? Nobody was there to get rid of the nightmares when I saw no end. If I woke up in the middle of the night, Father was not going to be at my side.

How could I return home knowing I got Father killed? I was a disgrace to the Edmillas and my grandmother. If I had maybe given up everything, including my life, my father could have kept his.

Yet, Mira made it clear he would have died either way.

"Father, I love you." I tightened my hug and turned my face the other way. Nothing in my mind made sense. It was too early. I wasn't ready to lose him. I may never have been, but he hadn't even survived long enough to see me become queen. He would never watch me change Orsadia, and that thought tore apart my heart.

Difficult was an understatement. Holding my dead father would forever be every nightmare from this point forward. How did it seem fair that I got to keep my life and he didn't? He would make more people happy than I ever could. Father had always been so helpful in the village. He had taught me to always help others.

"Lana, can you come here for a moment?" Father waved me over. I wish he would stop calling me Lana. I went by Snow White now.

I ran over, waiting for him to teach me today.

He pulled up the bucket from the well. "Will you be kind enough to fetch some water for the crops? The Williams' are a bit short-staffed this morning. Their son has fallen ill."

"Will he be all right?" I grabbed the bucket.

He nodded. "He just needs a bit of rest to get himself back on his feet."

I dropped the bucket and turned the crank to lower it into the water. When I had filled it, I reeled it back up. I poured the water into their water pail and tilted it to rain all over the crops. Something about quenching the thirst calmed my every fiber. Maybe it was the way the water flowed from the holes, or the way it resembled rain. It brought hope when there seemed to be none.

When we finished with the crops, Father led me to help out some more villagers. He had always taught me that we were no better than anyone else. Everyone had equal value, and the same color of blood pumped beneath our skin.

"Someday, you will make a wonderful queen," he said.

"How do you know?"

His smile brightened as he spoke my name. "Lana, I know things about you that no one else knows. You are a kind human being. You have a heart of gold and if you don't let anyone take that from you, I know that heart of gold will spread like a cure until everyone has a piece of gold in their heart. You are going to do so many amazing things because you're destined for that life."

I tilted my head out of curiosity. "I'm destined to be amazing?"

He chuckled in response. "Certainly. You will change the world. You will be the one who changes everything.*"*

He had always made it clear that I was chosen for a reason and I could be used for so much more. To keep his memory strong, I would do just that. No matter what it took, I was going to make a change. I would save Orsadia from further destruction.

Mira asked me to give up my life, but something told me that was not the answer. I was required to defeat her but if I let her live, what was I proving? She had taken my father's life and expected me to lay down my own. She was shedding blood for her own gain and hiding it in the name of sacrifice. Disgust barely described it and I would certainly put an end to her reign.

I stood from the floor and glanced at the blood that now stained my gown and cloak. "Maybe you were correct, Father. Everyone told me that I was required to kill Mira and I denied such an evil. What difference would it make if I defeated her? The curse would do what it always does—control every queen. Every queen before me has followed this path of defeating the previous. What if murder is the answer? Maybe, just maybe, Mira is trying to kill me because while a part of her craves that blood, the other part must save her own life. She knows it's her or me. *I choose me.*"

I grabbed a blanket from the bed and laid it over his body. "I'll come back for you, Father. When Mira is dead, I will come back to give you the burial you deserve. I won't let anyone forget your memory." I closed my eyes.

Taking a moment of silence for his death, I bowed my head and folded my hands together. I had loved my father more than anything and I shamed myself for never letting him know it enough.

When my moment was over, I left the mansion and made my way through the trees and trapped souls of children. My goal was to kill Mira and avenge my father's death, then break the curse. Not a single queen before me had been killed *in* the war between the current and the upcoming, and now it was my chance to turn those tables and pave a new road for queens following.

From the words of my father, I said with utter importance, "You will be the one who changes everything, Lana."

FORTY-FIVE

The tower before me loomed over the land, and knowing if it could tell me all it has seen, it'd be no shier than that of a lion.

"Snow! Oh, Snow White, up here!" Kali shouted from the top, waving a hand in the air to attract my attention. It worked as I made my way up and she greeted me with a tight hug and many smiles. "I've been waiting. Where is Luka?"

"He had things to do," I answered quickly. "Please, tell me how you've been faring."

With a shrug, she showed me a bag of gold coins. "I've been doing just fine. Stole these if you must know. But in all fairness, I do need the money. I need the coins to survive and do I not deserve that? I'd also love to have a gorgeous gown tailored just for me. Do tell, Snow, which color would make my eyes pop? I wish to look ever so pretty as you do."

Grabbing the bag from her, I tilted my head. "Where did you get all these?" Stealing wasn't one of the seven sins but it was still a crime.

"The man didn't have use for it any longer. He found a lock of hair on his step and I figured somebody could use the money to at the very least stay alive. It's only fair." She pried the bag from my grip and placed it over in the corner. "I heard about your father. My condolences."

"I'd rather not speak on that. I'm in search of a few more sins. I just can't bring myself to murder Alexander yet, Mira's brother, even if he is pride himself. It's not in my blood. How could that be fair? And I'm required to kill her in which case I know now I have no choice. But to kill her own brother? Would it be fair for me to require the next heir to murder my brother before battling me? As a sister, I could never impose that upon Fallon, and I'm certain Mira wouldn't do the same. Part of me knows who he is but another part of me also knows it doesn't make any sense for Mira's own brother to represent a sin if she loves him dearly."

Kali fixed her cloak as her eyes fell to mine. "Sometimes we must do unspeakable things, even to those we care for. Break the routine. Break the cycle."

Those words struck a chord. They were the exact words Mira said to me when she insisted I die for the curse. But Kali had no idea I recognized them, and I had to keep that under wraps for several minutes, for now I knew she worked for Mira. She was one of the sins I'd been searching for.

Greed.

That explained why she admired all the luxurious fabrics I wore now.

I glanced at Kali and gave her a nod. "In other words, I need to kill him, no questions asked. As well as kill all who stand in my way—all the sins that Mira placed for my quest." Kali agreed, turning towards the hole in the tower's wall that overlooked Everinthian Castle. I backed up and slowly pulled my sword from my belt. "Point understood. I'll do anything it takes to get there." I lifted the sword.

She let out a sigh. "I'm certain that's true." She dropped to her knees. "Do it, Snow. Kill me."

Her words took me off guard. She knew what my plan was? Of course she did. She wanted to take my position. We wanted the same future but only one of us was destined to have it.

She wasn't a second chosen. She was deceit in the flesh.

Without another thought, I brought the sword down into her back before I had time to think over my consequences. It sliced through every layer of her skin, including her organs. She choked on her own blood and collapsed forward. Her head and her right arm hung over the edge of the hole as I backed into the wall opposite of her, sliding down. I brought my forearm over my nose and mouth as sobs wracked my body.

In that moment, I'd come to regret my magic and its ability. I'd come to wish for an entirely different ending where I didn't have to steal lives. I didn't want to be the queen anymore.

FORTY-SIX

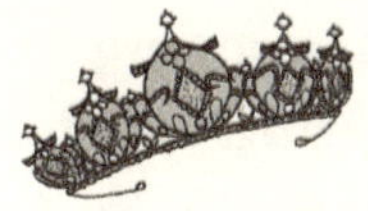

As I approached Everinthian Castle, what was once love now festered as hatred. I could not deny the reality that Mira had murdered my father in front of me to prove a point.

Getting into the castle had been a breeze. Mira expected me. I found her in the Great Hall, sitting on her throne, waiting for me to arrive. "Nice of you to show up to your own battle."

"You killed my father. I wouldn't miss this for the world." I halted before her.

She stood, patting her black pants. "Don't look so glum, Snow. You knew it would happen. I told you the truth when you were fifteen. You had time to prepare."

I lifted my chin with a scoff. "Let's cut the bullshit. I'm here to kill you and you want to kill me." I pulled out my sword.

She walked to the wall and grabbed her sword. "Whatever you wish." She stepped down from the platform. "But I did warn you."

Swinging my sword, I spun around and aimed for her neck, but she blocked me with her own blade. Mira pushed my sword forward with hers and swung down at my skirt, tearing into it greatly.

I pushed my sword towards her, but she dodged the blow, falling to the floor but catching herself. She glanced at me and gritted her teeth before jumping back onto her feet. She sliced my arm, but I blocked her from further slicing my side.

Our swords clanged together multiple times before I got a nick in her leg. Unlike me, she didn't have a skirt to protect her.

Mira swung hard, knocking my sword from my hand.

I ducked when she swung again, running toward my sword and sliding across the floor. I grasped the handle and scrambled back onto my feet. I kept my sword pointed at her as I circled her. "You can't win this and break the curse."

Her maniacal laugh reverberated. "And you can? You are going to tell me that murdering you will make the curse worse but murdering me will not? You cannot be that naïve."

I yelled as I swung my sword downward on her. She twisted hers sideways, blocking me from cutting into her flesh. The clanging of the metal echoed around us. If I could catch her off guard, I would.

Mira moved away before mine came down on her. She wrapped her arm around my neck, pulling me back in her chest, squeezing the air out of me. "I tried the first time and failed. Do they not say the second time is the best?"

I fought against her strength and as I struggled for any amount of oxygen, I flexed my fingers, my sword clattering to the ground. Maybe I could let go now and my problems would disappear. I would not have to worry about anyone else here. I'd cease to exist.

"Don't give up," Aalia whispered.

I bent my arm and shoved my elbow into Mira's abdomen. She grunted and let go, giving me a chance to escape her grasp. I almost tripped as I ran forward, giving myself the space to catch my breath before Mira came for me again.

She shoved her sword forward, barely missing me. I ducked and ran toward her, wrapping my arms around her legs and knocking her onto the ground. Her blade flew across the room, hitting the wall.

"It seems we both have no weapons," I said.

She jumped to her feet and swung her fist toward my face, missing by a few inches. I wrapped my arms around her waist, throwing her to the ground as I sat on top, squeezing the life from her lungs. "You took away my father. I never even considered taking Alexander away from you as soon as I knew who he was to you."

She clawed at my sleeves while kicking her legs.

"You keep telling me that this is what you had to do but this is a lie the curse has taught you. You are the problem, Mira. I'm simply a means to an end." I squeezed tighter.

The wind got knocked out of me when her knee hit my back, and my grip loosened as I doubled over. She threw me off and gasped for air before pinning me down. "You don't get it," she spat. She leaned down and pressed her forearm against my throat. I understood perfectly well.

With my hands pinned and her body too far forward, I had no way of fighting her off.

My vision began to blur and distort and just as that happened, Mira fell off me.

I sucked in a gulp of air and whipped my head to look at Mira, the shock evident in her eyes. She hadn't fallen off me. Someone had *pushed* her.

She scooted back and scanned the room but whatever she was looking for couldn't be found. This gave me a chance to get back on my feet but even when I was up, she didn't move a muscle. What was she afraid of? Just moments ago, she was determined to take my life.

Whatever had her freaked out gave me a chance to grab my sword. I cornered her and pointed the tip at her neck. "Who hurt you, Mira?"

She didn't answer me. Instead, she swallowed her fear, eyes darting to the blade.

Something had her spooked, but she wasn't willing to reveal what. Either way, she wasn't getting out of this one.

"You're not going anywhere," I told her.

She swallowed. "I'm well aware of that. I don't plan to go anywhere until I'm dead. Don't you see, Snow? I'm fighting for this cause like my life depends on it because it does. You say they're for the wrong reasons but just like you, I want this curse to be over. I don't want to see myself taking the lives of the innocent. The unfortunate truth is I knew the curse existed long before you knew you were chosen. My mother *was* an evil queen herself and as hard as she tried to break it, she never could. I vowed to break it when my turn came. I watched my own mother fall to pieces because of the *sin* that lived inside her. She could not undo what was coming."

"And you cannot undo yours. I ask, why are you adamant about living with the painful truth? Why must I give up my life?" I pushed into the soft of her skin.

"I am willing to *live* with my regrets, so you never have to. I am willing to do what is best for Orsadia because that was what my mother taught me. It destroyed her and watching her break from the inside was the day I died. You try to kill me, Snow, but I'm already a decaying corpse. Slaughtering an evil queen will not make any difference. It will *haunt* you. It will be the start of your path to destruction. You have not seemed to wonder why there is so much death and that has me questioning if you were born this way or somewhere along the way, you learned the truth."

I narrowed my eyes. "What truth?"

Mira closed her eyes. "The truth of what you are. Have you not questioned any of this?"

Laughing, I shook my head. "I question everything. This is no exception. What am I, Mira? You claim to know me so well."

She let out a sigh. "There are things in this world that you have always questioned. If you kill me, those questions will be answered, but at what price? You lose your own soul to the curse. If you die, those questions will be answered and at least we have a chance of ending this curse. If there is no queen in this castle for three years, they can take those three years to search high and low about this curse. *We* can end it before the next queen takes over, but if you kill me, you have no one to stop the curse but yourself and there is no guarantee that you will want to stop it when that foulness poisons your soul and festers like an infected wound." She opened her eyes, meeting mine.

"But why must I die? You are asking me to give up my life, Mira. Can you not understand what kind of choice that is?" I moved closer, nicking the vulnerable of her neck.

Mira flexed her fingers. "I know what I'm asking of you, but do you have a reason to live? Your father is dead. Luka is gone. Your family will blame you for everything. You have no one left to fight for."

I lowered my sword to her abdomen. "What do you mean Luka is gone?"

Taking a deep breath, she said, "I gave him a boat. He's gone. He left Orsadia to go explore the world. That was what he wanted."

Why would Mira care to send Luka away at all? She must have known that Luka and I cared about one another and if he was gone, I had no reason to keep going. She wanted to rip everything from me. Who was next? Mother? Fallon? That alone was the reason why I didn't believe she told the truth. Why tear me down at all, then pretend it was for my benefit?

"You sent Luka away like he asked for. I cannot condemn that. You killed my father, but it was not my fault. You said it would always happen and it was your blade that sliced his throat. My family may blame me, but I know that one day, they will accept me back because that's what we do. Love is unconditional, Mira. I have a reason to fight because I want to see the day my family forgives me. I wish to be there when Luka returns and gushes about his adventure. If I give up on them, what good am I? Love is a two-way street, and I will be there for them when they need me the most. That is *why* I live."

"I'm trying to protect you! You don't know what I've done—what bedevils me!" Mira yelled.

I pushed the sword into her abdomen a tad. "You protect me by killing my own father. You turn me into a monster and call this protection? I never asked you to be my knight in shining armor. I am *not* a damsel."

My weapon flew to the side as Alexander kicked it from my grasp and tackled me to the floor. Horrid images took place in my mind as I recalled the forced kiss and how much further he could take it if he truly wanted to. Like this, I was powerless.

I had to do the one thing I never wanted to do.

Elbowing him in the gut, he rolled off with a groan as I scrambled back up and found my blade near Mira.

I stepped away from her and turned to face Alexander. "Men like you will no longer hold any power." And as promised, I would hold to it that Alexander was punished for the way he treated me. Everyone would be taught bodily autonomy.

Mira made no moves, nor Alexander as I charged at him. Neither of them screamed for me to stop as I shoved the blade through his chest and twisted with a crack of his ribs. Why hadn't they fought back? Why did they allow me to kill him?

Ripping it from his body, he slumped forward, placing his hand against his wound and falling onto it. A smile formed as his eyes shut. Something was very wrong here, the stench of perjury rotting within these walls. Mira hadn't once begged me to spare Alexander, and that made me question if this had been her plan all along.

He'd been pride, and she had set her own brother up for murder.

"You would subject your flesh and blood to such a cruel fate," I whispered.

"A sacrifice had to be made, Snow." Her voice had been quiet—soft like a feather that meant no harm. "All I ask of you is that you give up your life, too."

Facing her, I closed the distance between us with my chin held high, pretending I was not bothered by such abhorrent memories. "I make no promises, Mira."

I plunged the sword into her stomach.

The blood traveled up her throat and poured from her mouth. As I pulled the sword out, her body made a thud as it hit the floor of the castle—*my* castle. Everinthian was now my home and I was the *Queen* of Orsadia. The people would no longer fear us. This curse had no power over me.

Turning to take in all of the tragedy, a sigh left my lips. "I never wanted it to end this way. Truly. But it's become clear to me, Mira, that you'd told me the demise of my own father to put terror in my soul, then to force me to train, and for what? To ask me to sacrifice myself? Why?"

A familiar voice answered, "In hopes that you would team up with me, instead of train all on your own. I wanted us to be able to break the curse together before it destroyed us both. Your father was simply a casualty, and I cannot change what's foretold. Foreseers only have the power of sight. I killed him, relying on the idea that you'd accept death without a fight."

As I spun to face Mira's body, I stepped back. "What the hell?"

Mira's spirit stood next to her vessel, staring at what was left of herself. "I wanted to warn you, Snow. I tried hard to warn you. The seven sins were never easy to spot, and so I had to use the only people available to ensure this curse wouldn't make it to the next heir. Alexander—pride. Me—envy. You. You were wrath. If you'd just lay down your life, the seven sins would be conquered and this curse would be no more. But my magic never allowed me to kill them myself, at least not before your sacrifice. You *foolish* woman. I pity you."

I choked on my words and looked at my hands. "How is this real?"

Mother's words replayed in my head, reminding me that when I became queen, my full power would come. Now, it was here. I walked to the window and looked out over the land. My eyes grew wider by the second as each spirit began to appear before my eyes. They littered all of Orsadia, and now I could see every life lost in our forsaken land.

"I'm a medium," I whispered.

Mira's spirit appeared at my side. Not an ounce of sympathy laced her voice as she said, "No, Lana. The last necromancer who ruled Orsadia almost brought Orsadia to shambles and I feared the same would happen again." She swept her arm across the view. "I failed—you won. You were always supposed to die *with* me."

Despite what she said, I couldn't shake the thought from my mind.

I was a necromancer.

Luka

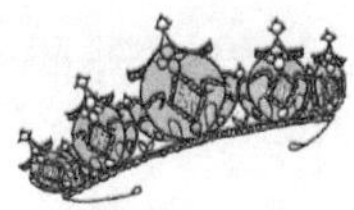

Much to my aggravation, the sun still set. Birds had mostly hidden themselves from the harsh realities of winter that I'd now been forced to face.

The rejection. Loss.

Snow had been unlike any other. Resilient—yet afraid. Afraid to let me in, not that I blamed her entirely. If I'd been in her shoes, I would have been cautious, too. That much wealth... That much power... Most people who came to her, pretending to care, were using her for what she could offer. It was the downside of being a chosen heir.

Every trip to the village, I heard their whispers about her. For years, the second she announced being a princess, the residents had only been kind to her out of fear. We all kept our distance to ensure we were safe from the reign of terror every queen was responsible for.

But I never had the heart to tell her people didn't like her. She had enough hope to fuel her to do better for this land, to defeat this curse. I'd be a cruel man to rip that from her.

She lit up the darkness, and I hadn't just been referring to the glowing skin she had. Maybe she wasn't that hope for others, but for me, she was. I'd seen past the rough exterior so to speak. I'd got a glimpse of the begging for anyone to crack into it, to give her a chance to get attached. The moment in the forest when she picked up the bear from my cave, I saw the soft side. It hadn't lasted long, but I caught it. Then again, when I found her in the waves. My stroll became an adventure that sprouted into something deeper. And for that, she changed my life in all the best and the worst ways.

It'd been most evident the first time I found her in the woods when we were teenagers. She never wanted help, but she needed it. If anyone knew a thing or two about survival, it'd been me.

I almost didn't believe my eyes when she came to my cave after six years. She definitely didn't remember me, and I could see it in the knitting of her brows and the creases on her forehead. Still as breathtaking.

Snow had no idea how deeply rooted this love had been. Her grip on me didn't waver for even a second. Not when she told me we couldn't get wrapped up in a relationship, nor when she told me to leave her.

In fact, that need for her escalated deep in my bones. I ached to feel her hair between my fingers, to soak up the warmth she embodied. Pain was all I knew now that she'd sent me away. How did I pretend I could thrive without her at my side?

Footsteps sounded behind me, and I turned swiftly, my heart racing and hoping I'd find her asking me to come back. However, I found Mira before me.

"Hoping for someone else?" Her eyes darted to the sky before returning to me. "She's not going to come running, and we both know that. She's stubborn if I were asked to describe her in one word."

Scowling, I shoved my hands into my pockets. "What is it that you want? You're supposed to be there, fighting her. That's what she's doing." I faced the ocean.

I slightly twisted my head down in her direction as she stopped at my left side. "You've wanted to get out of Orsadia for a while. Your parents disowned you, and your brother died. Forgive me, Luka, but what's left? Before Snow teamed up with you, what kept you around?"

I wasn't sure what it was. Maybe the splintering dream that I'd run into her all over again and get a chance to help.

It happened, and then she shoved me away.

Just like that, it was over.

"Why are you here?" I asked again.

She puffed. "I have something you might like. If you want it, it's yours." Glancing back in the direction of her castle, she paused. "I have a boat. You could go explore what might be out there. You've wanted that for over a decade now." She waved her arm over the horizon.

"Take your boat and leave Snow behind? In what world would I do that? She may have forced me to leave her alone, but I'm not going to abandon her. I made a promise to only leave once she took the throne and broke the curse."

Mira snorted. "Don't be naïve. She'd be much happier the moment you followed your dreams. Admit it. You may love her, but your goals never meshed well. Are you willing to drop all of that to satisfy her?"

"Yes," I said without hesitation.

"Would that satisfy her?"

This time, I had no response. Knowing Snow, she'd never forgive herself, or me if I didn't do what I wanted.

"Snow has a duty here. You can't stick around for that, and you know it in your heart." She released a sigh. "I want this curse broken as much as you both do. My entire life has centered around being a queen. I followed in my mother's footsteps. I've exhausted myself with researching every last solution. I've found one which requires Snow's cooperation. But you don't need to be there, Luka. Your job is done. You're free to go explore. She made that clear, didn't she? She'd want this for you. The rest, we can handle. We will, and you can rest assured that the curse will be broken."

As the waves collided with the base of the cliff, I pondered her words. I tasted them on my tongue. I savored their flavor, and when I met Mira's gaze, I didn't detect even an ounce of a lie. She wanted the best for Snow and for Orsadia, too. Everything she told me was pure, and that's when I concluded I could safely leave Snow here with her. They'd break this curse together.

It's what Snow would have wanted.

So, for her, I'd explore the world and return when this was over. I'd have adventures to share, and stories to tell. We'd have a chance at something when our dreams were no longer the forefront of our lives.

Still, with a sour and bitter bite, I regrettably said, "I'll take your boat."

Here's a sneak peek at

One Poisonous Queen

by *Monica Shantel*

ONE

Soulless eyes. Blackened hair. *Ghostly* appearance. And that damned scar that Mira left behind on my once flawless complexion.

As I gazed at myself in the mirror, I touched the dark spots that formed on the base of my neck, where she had choked me multiple times before injecting me with a drug to close off my windpipe.

"Seems fitting, is it not?" the Evil Queen asked from behind.

I turned to face the spirit that sat on *my* throne.

She sighed. "Snow, we've been over this. I'm not going anywhere until this curse is broken. Aalia agrees with me." She snapped her fingers and pointed in the direction of where Aalia stood in the shadowed corner.

Aalia's white hair was a beautiful contrast against her dark skin. It seemed so...*fitting.*

I approached the window and scanned the village. "I've said a million times before that I'm in no position to break this curse. What

I am interested in is an apple."

"You hate apples," Mira said.

"Precisely, but an apple is Zoe's favorite snack and that is exactly what I need to kill her before she takes this life out of my hands. I don't expect you to help me, but I do expect you to keep your mouth shut. Understood?" I turned to face Aalia and Mira.

Neither of them responded and I lifted my chin while uncurling my fingers like a flower. "Understood?"

On cue, both of them said, "Yes, understood."

Facing the land once again, I gripped the windowsill. "What's one more corpse for a necromancer? It'll be my playground to control."

"That sounds great and all, Snow, but we should focus on the task at hand." Mira gestured to the book on the table over by the wall. "Hypnotic Arythe."

"Must I remind you I go by Lana?" I whipped around to face her.

Regardless of the power wielded, her demeanor never cowered in my presence. "Lana. Snow White. You've gone back and forth. Forgive me for not keeping up with whatever your fleeting feelings decide on for the day."

I could have smacked the smugness from her expression. It'd be so easy, given how much contact I had with the dead.

So I said nothing at all.

"What do you plan to do with it?" Aalia piped in.

Approaching the table in slow strides, I placed my palms flat on the top, leaning over the pages. "I can only touch it in a way that my power allows." A sigh escaped my lips. "Such a shame for Orsadia. My magic is certainly great. I want something memorable. Alluring. Something that even Zoe could never resist. A carnival is out of the question," I spat as Mira opened her mouth to suggest it.

With a groan, she leaned her head over the arm of my throne. "It was certainly exquisite. It lured you in."

"When I was searching for the sins. It had never been earlier than that." I shot her a murderous gaze.

Her eyes lightened as she met mine. "I was never in this for myself. This whole royalty duty I'd been given. My father taught me long before you'd been born about what my legacy would entail. He prepared me from the moment I could walk, along with my mother of course. I had been set up for failure. But you, Snow, were not supposed to be the failure. When I set up those seven sins, I knew you'd never be able to kill living human beings. I expected you to come running here the second you found out your quest, giving me the chance to take your life myself. I assumed you'd have asked me to take your life so you'd never have to commit such horrendous, immoral acts. I hired them. Each and every single one. Offered them gold. Riches. Homes. Food. They took the offer. And they fit their sins perfectly. But you defied me. You convinced yourself to murder them in cold blood." She slumped. "For me, it was never about keeping my magic. I simply wanted the curse to be over. You were supposed to die. Then I would have killed every sin, and then Alexander and myself. However, here we are..."

And against Magic Law, I'd been granted the right by Mira Sunder to enter Everinthian the night she killed me before I took the throne.

"You sent Luka away," I snapped. "Knowing it'd leave me with nothing to fight for. Just so I'd lay down my life for you."

"I had to ask myself: you or tons of innocent people? I chose the people. I don't regret the decisions I made. I only pity you for never making the right one."

With a snicker, I brushed away her insults. "Don't bother with the pity, dear. I don't request it."

“What you did request was my brother’s absence. I imagine watching the light disappear from his eyes was the most satisfying event of the century,” she said in a bitter tone. “I knew that from the start, just how deep your hatred ran. Using him, I tried everything I could to get you to do what I needed. You didn't care for his hand in marriage, and so he had to *try* to kill you, just so you'd kill him. That was the plan. However, he lied about his past because we needed to see how deeply rooted the darkness was in you. Fortunately, not deep. Much to our dismay, you were never willing to sacrifice your life for the people of Orsadia. Selfishness is your vice."

Before she got another word in, I clutched my black skirt and slipped from the Great Hall down the stairs, and out the main entrance. Strolling down to the garden, I stopped to say hello to the hemlock on my right and black hellebore on my left. They flourished just as more bodies dropped. A creation I had been insanely proud to have grown. Greenery thrived, filling every crevice of the garden. With spring sweltering the earth beneath our feet, I delighted in the desiccation to come.

The sun warmed every surface, every petal, every leaf. I brushed my knuckles under a few buds, stopping just before I came in contact with deadly nightshade.

"You're doing exceedingly well," I said with envy slithering between my teeth.

Something caught my eye, and I lifted my gaze. Approaching the blue roses, I caressed the curls at their tips, inhaling the subtle scent.

In a land far away, I despised Mira for what she did. I blamed her, and I wanted her to suffer in agony for centuries.

However, that land had been out of my sight for a while. Luka had to leave for me to carry out my plans. Without his incessant advice, I could make like the plants among me, contaminating every living creature left.

Watch them wither. Crumble to ash.

I took pride in being the very hand that incinerated the ones who defied Magic Law.

They certainly didn't call me the Poisonous Queen without any reason.

Also by Monica Shantel

THE FEATHERS AND FLAMES TRILOGY
Beauty of a Crimson Soul
Beauty of a Burning Flame
Beauty of a Persistent Love

THE TO BELIEVE DUOLOGY
To Believe in Peter Pan
To Believe in the Demon King

STANDALONES
Blissful
37 Nights
The Goddess in the Shadows
Tainted

ACKNOWLEDGEMENTS

I want to thank Ashly for always supporting me, helping me with ideas, and being the best friend anyone could ever ask for. Thank you to my mom for raising me to dream big, and standing by those dreams. Thank you to Jasmine from Salient Books for providing a community and a lovely place for me to thrive and be myself entirely.

Thank you to my betas for allowing this book to find a home and become the best version of itself.

About the Author

Monica Shantel has always had an interest in artistic and creative hobbies of sorts, including but not limited to: drawing, crafting, graphic design, and painting. Although all she has is a high school diploma under her belt, she is not new to the writing community. At the age of twelve, she began building stories to escape reality and find hope in life once again. Her debut novel is Beauty of a Crimson Soul. Along the same genre, she writes dark tales of mythical romance which only add more to the growing fantasy worlds inside her head.